Return to The Acreage

Donna Every

Return to The Acreage

This book is a work of fiction. Names, characters, places and incidents are either products of the author's imagination or are used fictitiously.

Cover photography by
Julie Chalbaud
Models: Arron Fernandes and
Rona Williams

ISBN: 9781074433062

Author Note

This is the fourth book in the Acreage series. This one and the next two– are about the descendants of Richard and Deborah from *The Price of Freedom* I can't say that I had planned to continue the series, but readers kept asking me what happened to Deborah, Richard, Thomas and Sarah after they moved to England. I decided not to go into details of their lives in England but to write about their descendants instead. In case you don't remember who everyone is, as it has been six years since *The Price of Freedom* was published, I've included a family tree.

James Fairfax, the hero of this book, is the first son of Richard and Deborah. At the end of *Free at Last,* Deborah announced that she was pregnant, and she and Richard decided to stay in Barbados until after the child was born. Twenty-six years later, James returns to Barbados and The Acreage. Although most of the book is set in Barbados, Richard and Deborah make an appearance, and you will also be introduced to James' siblings, Charles and Alexandra, who will have their own books.

I hope that you enjoy *Return to The Acreage* as much as you enjoyed the first books in the series. If you are a new reader, you might want to start by reading the first three books in *The Acreage Series* so that you have an appreciation of the whole story.

Sincerely
Donna Every

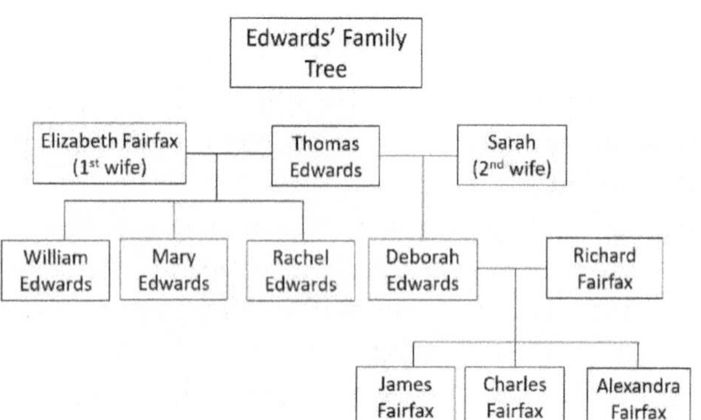

Edwards' Family Tree
Elizabeth Fairfax (1st wife)
Thomas Edwards
Sarah (2nd wife)
William Edwards
Mary Edwards
Rachel Edwards
Deborah Edwards
Richard Fairfax
James Fairfax
Charles Fairfax
Alexandra Fairfax

Chapter 1

January 15, 1726
Fairfax Cottage
Bristol, England

"Harriett?" James peered into the kitchen expecting to see his wife at the stove, but the kitchen was empty and spotless.

"Harriett! Where are you?" He crossed the room and pulled open the back door, but the yard was deserted. Closing the door, he realised that the house had an empty feel to it. Where could she be? She always let him know if she was going out.

He glanced into the living room as he passed it, not really expecting to see her there, and paused at the hall table in case he had overlooked a note that she had left. The table was bare. Not even the customary vase of flowers that she put there every day was in its place. He could not remember ever not having flowers on that table even if they were dried flowers during the winter months. What was going on? Where was Harriett?

"Harriett? Harriett?" His voice, laced with fear, went before him as he raced upstairs. Throwing open each door, he glanced around the room quickly, knowing already that she was not inside each one. His panic mounted as he tore open their bedroom door, the last room in the house. He skidded to an abrupt halt on the threshold. The sheets on the bed were undisturbed and there was a slight film of dust on the bedside tables. That was a strange sight to him, for Harriett kept their cozy house in spotless condition.

Looking around the room, he realised that all her things were gone. There was no hairbrush on the vanity, no creams or hair ornaments. Nothing! It was as if she was never there. Pain began to pulse in his heart. Harriett had left him. Why? What did he do?

A loud knocking on the door startled him. Was that her? Did she only go out and forget her key? He turned to race down the stairs. In his haste his foot missed the first step and he tried in vain to grab the handrail. Fear filled him as he felt himself falling. Over and over he tumbled down the unforgiving stairs until he sprawled onto the floor. The knocking was more urgent now, but he could not move. He could not get to the door. Was it Harriett or someone coming to tell him that something had happened to her? Panic gripped him as he tried to heave himself from the floor without success. He was paralysed! The pounding went on relentlessly.

James' eyes flew open and he stared in confusion at the open doorway of his bedroom which he had staggered through the previous night just before he had dropped into his bed in exhaustion. That was the only way he could get to sleep – by working himself to the point of exhaustion. It had been Harriett's birthday and just when he had thought that the pain of her loss was abating, it had silently been waiting for a day such as this to spring upon him like a lion on its unsuspecting prey.

The noise of someone pounding on his front door sounded again. That was what had jerked him out of his dream. He was lying in his bed, not at the bottom of the stairs. Slowly, reluctantly, he reached his hand back across the bed, hoping to feel a warm body next to his, but his hand only clenched on the cold, empty sheet. Harriett was gone, just as in the dream, but she had not run away. Sickness had stolen her. What had started out seemingly as only a sore throat and a low temperature had turned out to be Diphtheria which had quickly taken his wife after barely a year of marriage. She had insisted that she would be fine and not to bother the doctor and he had listened to her, not realising how serious it was until it was too late. He would forever blame himself for that. Pain tore into him, forcing tears from the corners of his eyes and her name from his lips.

"James!"

His father's voice from the stairwell startled him. He had obviously not remembered to lock the front door the night before. He dragged himself up to sit on the side of the bed, rubbing his face.

His father appeared in the doorway and quickly took in his appearance, dressed in his creased and dirty work clothes from the day before with his boots still on his feet. His jaw that was covered in a two-day old stubble and his red-rimmed eyes told their own story.

"James, you cannot go on like this." His father's voice was full of shared pain. "Harriett has been gone for nearly two years and I know it still pains you, but you have to try and move on. Your mother and I were talking, and we think it would do you good to take a trip to Barbados. The change may be what you need and perhaps you can even go and see The Acreage.

James met his gaze with a steady one of his own. He knew that they were right. Staying in the house where memories of Harriett haunted him was not helping. Silently, he nodded his agreement. He would go to Barbados.

ຯ ☙

March 25, 1726
Off the island of Barbados

"Barbados in sight!"

The lookout waved excitedly from his perch at the top of the mast. James Fairfax's heart gave a leap of anticipation in response. His journey was almost at an end and soon he would set his feet on the land that he had left over twenty-six years ago with his parents Richard and Deborah. He drew in a deep breath of salty air at the sight of the tiny piece of land that could now be seen above the horizon. A slight smile hovered on his face that strongly resembled his father's, although the waves in the long brown hair that was struggling against the restraint of a thong were from his mother.

He bent and leaned forward, resting his forearms on the top rail as if his stance could somehow hasten the ship towards the island. As one who thrived on being active, being cooped up on a ship was akin to torture for him, and he couldn't wait to be free of the floating prison that he had endured for five weeks. He could well understand why, although they owned ships, his father seldom felt inclined to sail long distances on any of them since the family left Barbados and moved to England when he was one year old. It was God's mercy that he did not suffer from sea sickness or the trip would have been much worse.

He and his brother, Charles, now partly owned and helped to run the business which his father and his mother's father had started together when they moved to England. It had expanded over the years and now had three new ships that serviced the Caribbean and America. He preferred the challenge of finding profitable cargo to transport rather than travelling on the ships himself. His brother, on the other hand, loved sailing and planned to visit the Carolinas soon to meet the family there.

The thought of setting foot on the soil on which he had been born and lived for the first year of his life filled him with a longing that surprised him. He had been numb for such a long time – two years to be precise – that any emotion felt almost foreign to him. Any emotion, that is, except sadness which had been his close companion for those two years. Sadness was really a poor euphemism to describe the wrenching ache that had taken up residence in his chest. His familiar companion nudged him again, forcing him to give up the pretence that he had forgotten what day it was.

It was March 25. Two years to the date that Harriett had died. They had both been young when they married; he, twenty-four and she, twenty, and they had each only celebrated one birthday as a married couple. He steeled himself for the pain that would come as he allowed himself to remember, but he was surprised to find that it had lessened, somewhat like a wound that had scabbed over and was now able to withstand a gentle probing. The guilt, however, was still very much like a fresh a wound. He wondered if it would ever heal.

It was ironic that it would be on this day that they would reach Barbados. It was almost as if it had been orchestrated to signal a new season in his life. He knew that he couldn't go on living a half existence. At least his head knew it. It was his heart that was a little slow in catching up. He was causing concern to his family and that was the last thing he wanted. His parents had almost audibly sighed with relief when he agreed to visit Barbados.

From his youth, he, his younger brother and his sister, Alexandra, had heard stories of the island that had been home to his mother and his grandparents Thomas and Sarah. They were not all happy tales. As they grew older, he and his siblings were told how their father had left Carolina in America to visit his grandfather's plantation, The Acreage, in Barbados and had fallen in love with his mother who had been a slave on the plantation at the time.

He couldn't even conceive of his mother as a slave. She was one of the most independent and outspoken women he knew, and to think that she had been owned by his grandfather (her own father) was beyond his comprehension. Worse yet, what William, his uncle, had done to her while she was a slave, even though they shared the same father! It was hard to reconcile the depraved creature he had been then to the man he had become. Even more amazing was that his mother could forgive him and even come to love him. Truly God was a transformer of lives.

His grandfather, Thomas, had died when he was sixteen and Sarah was now sixty-seven and still a very beautiful woman who looked years younger, although a few wrinkles now graced her forehead and around her eyes. No one would even suspect that her blood ran in his veins except for the slight wave in his thick brown hair and skin that tanned nicely in the sun.

He would be considered black on the island, and for sure in Carolina where his father's family hailed from. Not that he cared, nor was he ashamed of the blood that ran in his veins from his black ancestors. He did not go out of his way to hide it, nor was it a topic that he spoke of at every opportunity. More importantly, he had told Harriett of his ancestry and she certainly hadn't cared. If anything, he was ashamed of his white heritage and the race that had enslaved his mother and grandmother and still contributed to the suffering of so many others.

He and his brother had been spared nothing of their family's story when they were old enough to hear it, and it was only to preserve Alexandra's innocence that she was sheltered from the more distasteful parts of it. Not that she was any fragile miss, for she had truly inherited their mother's independence and fierceness. It would take a special man to embrace her as she was. He smiled as he thought of her now with her thick reddish-brown hair and green eyes so like their mother's. Like him, his brother favoured their father, being tall and dark haired although he showed even less trace of his African ancestry than James did and certainly passed for white.

His heart quickened with excitement as he began to discern trees and buildings as the ship drew nearer to the shore. The island probably bore little resemblance to what it looked like when his family left, but he was eager to discover the places that he had heard about and pictured in his mind – The Acreage, Needham's Point where his parents had lived and where he had been born, Holetown and Bridge Town. He wondered who owned The Acreage now and if the shop that his mother and grandmother had owned in Bridge Town was still there. Barbados was foreign to him, yet something was calling him to it as if he needed to return. He remembered the morning his father had woken him up just two months ago and suggested that he should go to Barbados. He had agreed, hoping that some time on the island would heal and restore him.

His mother and grandmother had started a school before they left the island, teaching a few free men, women and their children how to read and write. Also, any slaves who wanted to learn and could sneak out from their masters or mistresses would come one night a week for just an hour. While teaching slaves to read and write was not illegal it was certainly not encouraged, so they kept the night school secret.

His mother, being the last to leave the island, had groomed another woman to take over the school and had kept in contact with her by way of letters. She would also send supplies to her by one of the trusted captains of their ships. When she heard that James had decided to go to Barbados, she encouraged him to spend some time helping with the school while he was there. Although he was not gifted as a teacher, he had volunteered to bring some supplies and promised to try his hand at some basic teaching while he was on the island. He desperately needed something to give purpose and meaning to his life once again. He hoped to find it in Barbados.

ꙮ

James had been given the name of The Royal Inn Boarding House by one of the captains that sailed their ships to Barbados. It was located on the outskirts of Bridge Town and, because it was near to the sea, it would enjoy the cooling breezes and be quiet compared to any of the ones in town.

The carriage he had hired pulled up in front of a whitewashed building with blue shutters identified by an elegant sign with the words "The Royal Inn Boarding House". While he wouldn't quite call it royal, as it had seen better days, it looked fairly clean and tidy from the outside, so he hoped that inside would not disappoint. Not that he was overly fastidious, but if he ended up staying a while he would at least like a clean and comfortable bed.

He climbed down from the carriage and instructed the driver to hand him his trunks from where they were stored at the back. They each hefted one to their shoulder and deposited them just inside the front door. James paid the driver who seemed keen to be on his way, probably to find more customers, preferably those who were travelling farther distances than The Royal Inn. His eyes scanned the room which had chairs arranged in small groups around colourful, if rather faded, rugs before landing on a stout woman seated behind a large desk across the room. She looked to be in her late forties or early fifties with greasy-looking brown hair liberally streaked with grey and pulled back into a no-nonsense bun, leaving bare her rather plain white face.

"Welcome, sir," she greeted him as she stood up. He watched her make a thorough assessment of his clothing after which her eyes landed on his trunks and a smile appeared on her face. He could practically hear her mentally calculating the money she could earn from him if his trunks were any indication of how long he intended to stay.

"Thank you…"

"Sally Perch," she offered. "Widow Sally Perch. Welcome to The Royal Inn. I am the proprietress."

"Pleased to meet you." He approached the desk, extending his hand to shake hers. "I am James Fairfax. I would like a room for about a month, possibly longer, if you have it."

"We certainly do, sir, and we can accommodate you for as long as you like. From your accent I would say that you have just arrived off the boat from England."

"You would be correct," James confirmed with a polite smile.

"Are you here to carry out business or to visit the island?" She was quite shameless in her quest for information.

"To visit." James did not elaborate.

"Good, good. I would be happy to accommodate you for as long as you need," she assured him again.

Business was slow and she had had to hire out one of her two girls a few months ago to earn some money for her until things picked up again. While the boarding houses in town seemed to be doing well, hers, being a little on the outside of town, was suffering as it catered more to people visiting the island for longer spells. With the money from this gentleman who, from the look of his clothes, seemed to have no lack of funds, she would be able to take back Jemima who generally did the cooking and the washing for her guests. At present, she had one couple staying there and they would be leaving soon.

"I will need the money for the first month upfront, you understand."

"That will not be a problem. How much is it?" The sum she named was not extravagant and he agreed to return it to her upon settling in his room as he had no desire to show her the size of his purse. In any case, he would have to retrieve the money from the hidden compartment at the bottom of his trunk which was under the slates, chalks and the few rare books he had brought for the students. If he decided to stay longer than his money could support, he could write and ask his father to send more by one of the ships' captains.

"Breakfast and dinner are included in the price. I do not serve lunch, but there are many places around town where you can get a meal. The dining room is through that doorway." She gestured to a door that he had noticed in his initial scan of the room.

"I will get my boy to take your trunks up to my best room." With that, she put her head through a nearby window and shouted to someone towards the back of the property to come.

The "boy" was a stocky black man of an indeterminate age, but he had long passed the age of being called a boy. James assumed that he was a slave.

"Morning, sir," he was greeted and returned the greeting.

"Take this gentleman's trunks up to the room at the far end of the hallway," she instructed, handing him a key from a drawer in the desk.

"I can take one and save him a trip," James offered, easily lifting one of the trunks to his shoulder and following the man up the stairs. They passed several doors in the hallway until they reached the one at the very end which the man opened and deposited the trunk before handing over the key.

"Thank you," James told him, giving him a couple of coins from his pocket.

The negro looked a little surprised at James' expression of gratitude and quickly pocketed the coins with his own thanks.

"My name is Rufus. If you need anyt'ing, anyt'ing at all, I will get it for you. If you want a nice mulatto girl to keep you comp'ny, I can get one for you," he added with a sly smile.

"That won't be necessary," James assured him. "I have everything I need."

"If you change your mind, just let me know." He left him with another knowing smile.

James shook his head as the door closed behind the slave, if he was in fact a slave, for he seemed quite bold. He had not even been in Barbados a day yet and already he had been offered a woman. Nothing had changed on the island from what he knew of it. He had been around enough of the sailors on their boats to hear about the ways of Barbados and even though his grandfather had never told them details of his life before he had married his grandmother, he did confess that he was deeply ashamed of it. He had admonished them never to misuse women as he had, no matter what colour they were, and never to bring shame to their wives when they got married. Although just a teenager at the time, James took his words to heart. He and Harriett had come to their marriage pure and he had never so much as looked at another woman since then. Even during these last two years, it seemed as if all physical desire had died with Harriett and the thought of lying with another woman intimately was enough to turn his stomach.

Forcing his mind away from images that the slave had stirred up, he looked about and was happy to see that the room was neat and looked clean. He threw open the windows, one of which overlooked a garden in the back and the other the road he had just travelled. The windows made the room bright and airy and, apart from a comfortable-looking bed flanked by two bedside tables, there was a chest of drawers with a basin and a jug on top and a chair near the window where he could sit and observe the activity on the road if he cared to. He remembered how his mother and grandmother had talked about having to get used to the noise of living in the city when they had first moved there, but he had no such problem. In any case, it seemed to be fairly quiet around the inn. He was looking forward to exploring the town and even to helping out at the school but, first of all, he wanted to visit The Acreage, where it all began.

Chapter 2

"How do you like your room, Mr. Fairfax?" Sally Perch asked him when he ventured back downstairs with the money to pay her.

"It is very comfortable, thank you." It was far from what he was used to, as the house he had lived in with his parents was quite luxurious. Even the smaller one he had shared with Harriett had been elegantly furnished, but he was not so over-indulged that he needed to live in luxury to be contented.

"If you desire a bath, I can get Rufus to bring up a tub for you."

"I would greatly appreciate that. Thank you."

"Now that you are here, I will take back my girl Jemima to cook and wash," she informed him. "Sometimes I'm forced to rent out my girls when things are a little slow," she confided in him.

"You rent out your girls?" he repeated, trying to grasp the idea of renting out a person.

"Oh yes, it is quite common, especially here in town."

He assumed that Jemima was a slave and he couldn't help but be curious about where Mrs. Perch was taking her back from.

"If you need anything, don't hesitate to ask. Anything at all." There it was again. That offer to provide anything he wanted. They were certainly hospitable in Barbados.

"Well, now that you mention it, I would like to visit a plantation called The Acreage. Are you familiar with it?"

"Of course, I know of it. It is one of the biggest on the island. How did you come to hear about it?"

"I heard about it from some people who used to live here in Barbados." She didn't need to know who the people were or that his grandfather had owned it and his mother and grandmother were once slaves on the plantation.

"Indeed? What is their name?" Her eyes opened with interest. James could see her practically salivating for new information to gossip about, for it took little discernment to see that she relished accessing and sharing information not of her own business.

"Edwards," he shared, watching her face.

Her brow furrowed with concentration. "I can't say I know of any Edwards." James was relieved to hear that.

"Do you know who owns the plantation now?"

"A gentleman named Lord Samuel Bailey. He married Mary-Ann Gordon whose father, Sir Francis Gordon, owned it before. I understand that Sir Francis came from England and bought the plantation, but he had no sons, so the plantation was his daughter's dowry and it was said that he arranged for her to marry Lord Bailey. It seems that Lord Bailey had hit upon hard times even though he was a Lord and all. Word has it that he isn't the best at managing the plantation," she said in a whisper as if anyone else could hear. James was not surprised that she saw nothing wrong with sharing that information with relish.

He had heard of Sir Francis Gordon who had bought The Acreage from his grandfather, but he did not know that he had given it to his daughter for her dowry. If Mrs. Perch was to be believed, it seemed that The Acreage was once again the setting for an arranged marriage. He wondered if Lady Bailey was suffering the same fate as his grandfather's deceased wife, and his great aunt, Elizabeth. Perhaps the visit would reveal whether Mrs. Perch's rumours had any truth to them.

"Is there a way that I can send correspondence to The Acreage and perhaps arrange a visit?" he asked.

"Yes, I can get one of the boys in town who do errands to deliver it for a few coins. If you bring it down when you finish preparing it, I will have it delivered for you."

He would make sure it was well sealed, for he believed that she would have no qualms in reading its contents before she sent it. Had she known that he was the descendant of the man who had once owned The Acreage and the slave who had been his mistress, she would no doubt be horrified. It would probably not be enough for her to turn him out even if she knew, for his money often opened many doors that would be closed because of his ancestry. However, he would leave that revelation for another day. It would serve him no use to reveal who he was too early, and he would have to be especially careful in what he revealed to Mrs. Perch in particular.

He felt a fresh stirring of excitement as he went back up to his room to write the letter to Lord and Lady Bailey. Barbados was bringing him back to life and this was only the first day. Surely, it was for this very reason that he had been led to come here.

ꙮ

The Royal Inn
Bridge Town
March 28, 1726

Dear Father and Mother

I hope this letter finds you in good health. I reached Barbados safely and I have taken a room at The Royal Inn just on the outskirts of Bridge Town. It is a pleasant enough boarding house and the proprietress is a widow by the name of Sally Perch. She is a source of information, mostly about other people, so I am very cautious in what I tell her. I am happy to report that the water has not affected me as it did you, Father, when you first came to Barbados. Or perhaps Mother really did try to ptomaine poison you by not warming up your meal enough. I am joking, Mother.

Barbados has surely changed considerably since you left here, in terms of the development, at least. There are many stores and boarding houses in Bridge Town and everything one desires is available. In fact, I have been offered anything I want by both Mrs. Perch and her negro Rufus, and I believe that I heard undertones in their suggestion which make me inclined to believe that their offers are nefarious in nature. Naturally, I have declined.

I am sure that you will be happy to hear that I now have an excitement in my spirit which stirred as soon as I laid my eyes on Barbados. I cannot explain it, but I feel as if I have come home. These last two days I have been eager to get out of bed in the morning and I can even think of Harriett without grief overcoming me. It is as if Barbados is somehow healing and restoring me already.

Mrs. Perch arranged for me to send correspondence to The Acreage to request permission to visit and I am delighted to have been invited to spend a few days there by the new owners, Lord and Lady Samuel Bailey. I am going tomorrow. I am surprised at how hospitable they are, considering that they do not know me. All I mentioned in the letter was that I had heard of the plantation from an acquaintance in England who used to live in Barbados and that I wished to pay a visit to see the property. Perhaps they are starved for news from England, so I am delighted to accept their hospitality.

You will be happy to hear, Mother, that I found your school and met Cassandra Brown and gave her the supplies you sent. I have promised her to come and help when I return from The Acreage.

Mother, I hope you (especially) appreciate this lengthy letter, for you know that, like Father, writing letters is not something I am pleased to do. This is a warning not to expect many letters while I am here, but I will write you again and let you know of my stay at The Acreage. I am very much looking forward to seeing where it all started. I even hope that your favourite spot overlooking the east coast is still accessible and I can go there and imagine when Father caught you reading Shakespeare under a tree. I remember how incensed you said you were that day, for after talking with you as though you were a free woman, he then ordered you to get him some food when it was your day off. How much you have changed, Father! Thank God!

I will end here as I begin my adventure in Barbados which I am greatly looking forward to. Give my love to everyone.

Your son
James

ꕤ

It was a good day for making the carriage trip to The Acreage. James had packed a satchel with enough clothes for a few days and had gotten Rufus to arrange for a carriage to take him to the parish of St. James which he was told was about 11 miles from Bridge Town. The sky was a clear, brilliant blue and the sun was unobstructed, making the conditions perfect for it to be a hot day, but thankfully, there was a good breeze and he opened the carriage windows as soon as he settled down to let it blow through. He could have travelled outside with the driver, but he didn't feel to engage in conversation.

The driver took the route through town and James observed that the buildings were close enough for neighbours to shout to each other across the street or on either side of them, making him glad that he had chosen The Royal Inn. As they left town behind them, trees and shrubs were more plentiful and colourful flowers grew wild beside the roads. The roads were better than he had expected, and the traffic was quite heavy as they passed several carriages heading towards town with curtains pulled back so that the occupants could see and be seen. Most of them appeared to be ladies driven by their negroes and accompanied by a female slave who was seated beside the driver. It was no different from England except for the colour of the servants and the fact that they were slaves.

As they drew onto a road which ran parallel to the coast, James was delighted to spot patches of azure water through breaks in the trees. He had already enjoyed the waters at the beach near to the boarding house and he had found them to be quite warm and exhilarating. His visit to the beach had called to mind his grandmother Sarah telling him about the first time she had seen the sea when she was still a slave and how free she felt as she enjoyed the water swirling around her feet and the wind in her hair.

After about two hours, the carriage turned off the coast road and began to climb a gradual hill where the trees on either side of the road came together to form a tunnel, breached occasionally by patches of sunlight. Eventually they parted and the carriage emerged onto a part of the road where palm trees stood tall and majestic as if they were sentries on guard and he knew that he was close to The Acreage even before the driver's announcement confirmed it.

His grandmother had described the driveway and the palms that lined the road, which she had said made her feel almost welcome when she first arrived at the plantation in the back of a cart. He tried to imagine how she must have felt after being torn from her mother's arms and taken to The Acreage, not knowing what awaited her there. All she knew at the time was that the master from The Acreage had paid her master £50 to buy her because he was determined to own her.

He bent his head to peer out of the window at the palms which soared about thirty feet in the air and found that they did seem to be waving their fronds to welcome him. A nostalgic smile teased his mouth and he had a sense of having been there before. How could that be? Yet, it felt familiar. Did his spirit somehow recognise that he was intimately connected to this plantation? The reality that it was no longer owned by their family suddenly filled him with regret.

The carriage drew to a stop at the end of the driveway and he alighted eagerly, only to stop abruptly as he stared at the house. It was foolish to think that it would remain unchanged from the way it had been described in the stories told by his grandmother and mother. But where he had been expecting walls of pale yellow with green shutters, he was dismayed to see stained white walls in need of painting and brown louvred shutters that were missing some of the slats which had rotted and had not been replaced. However, the doors were thrown open as if in welcome. As he paid the driver a lady rose from one of several rocking chairs on the patio which were scattered around a low table.

He straightened his coat and strode towards her with all evidence of his surprise at the condition of the house carefully removed. "Good day, my lady. I am James Fairfax. I assume you are Lady Bailey?"

"Mr. Fairfax, we have been expecting you. Yes, I am Mary-Ann Bailey. Welcome to The Acreage."

She gestured for him to come into the patio and, as he drew closer, he was arrested by her appearance which was in startling contrast to the state of the badly neglected house. She was a strikingly beautiful woman probably towards the end of her twenties with flawless white skin and rich brown hair coiffed in an elegant style. She wore a silky-looking dress in a blue that matched her eyes and enhanced her figure.

"Thank you, Lady Bailey. I greatly appreciate your hospitality."

"You are most welcome. My husband went to Jamestown on business, but he should be home shortly. Do sit down, and please call me Mary-Ann. We are not as formal in the islands as in England." She turned to a slave girl who was standing just inside the doorway and sent her for drinks.

"How was your trip?" she asked politely.

"It was very scenic and surprisingly comfortable. I had expected the roads to be in poor repair for some reason."

She laughed lightly. "Most visitors to the island do not know what to expect of Barbados and often find it to be somewhat of a surprise. I was the same myself when I first came."

"Oh, you are not originally from here, then."

"No, I was born in England and lived there all my life until I got married and moved here." Her story sounded like Elizabeth's story all over again. James hoped that was where the similarity ended. Elizabeth's story was tragic and had repercussions even today. His grandfather's two daughters from his marriage to Elizabeth, had refused to speak to their father after he married Sarah, so he had never met them.

"And is it to your liking?" he probed, bringing his attention back to the present.

"The island or the marriage?" She laughed. "They both have their good qualities and their bad, as everything else."

He was surprised at her candour and wasn't quite sure how to respond. The glimmer of discontentment that flashed across her face was gone as soon as it had come, and thankfully, he didn't have to respond because she continued talking as if she had not just shared very personal information with a stranger.

"Whereabouts is your home in England?"

"I am from Bristol. We have a shipping business based there and I live in the city."

"Indeed?"

Before she could say any more the slave girl returned with a tray and two glasses of a brownish coloured beverage. She kept her eyes discretely lowered, giving James the opportunity to look at her without being observed. From what he could see of her face, she was attractive with smooth brown skin, darker than his grandmother's. She wore a simple dress that was quite shabby from beneath which bare feet peeped and a faded handkerchief covered her hair. James could not help but wonder what her status was in the house. Could she be in the same position that his grandmother had been? Mistress to Lord Bailey? If that was the case, he certainly was not spending money on keeping her well-dressed. He chastened himself for making such a judgement and marshalled his wayward thoughts.

"Are you familiar with mauby?" Mary-Ann gestured towards the drink.

"Indeed. I find it extremely refreshing."

"You must be a Barbadian at heart, for many visitors to the island find it too bitter for their taste."

"Perhaps I am." He smiled, thinking that she had no idea how close she was to the truth.

He had only taken a few sips of the refreshing beverage when a horse and rider galloped up the driveway and headed towards the side of the house where the man dismounted and handed the reins to a raggedly dressed boy who seemed to magically appear.

"My husband has returned," Mary-Ann informed him tonelessly. She did not appear to be overly pleased at his arrival.

James stood as his host entered the patio. He hoped that his face did not betray his surprise on seeing a gentleman who looked to have passed his fortieth birthday some time ago. He was of medium height and he possessed a slight paunch. His sandy hair was thinning at the front and was already liberally streaked with grey. It was pulled back, as his was, with a leather thong. This was her husband? Recovering from his surprise quickly, he took the hand being offered and met the strong handshake with one of his own.

"I arrive at home to find my wife in the company of a handsome stranger. Should I be worried?" he joked in what James thought was a rather inappropriate manner.

"Not a stranger any longer, Husband. This is James Fairfax whom we have been expecting."

"Ah! Welcome to The Acreage. Lord Samuel Bailey at your service. Sorry I was not here to greet you, but urgent business took me to Jamestown."

"That is quite all right," James assured him. "Your wife has welcomed me in your stead and has been entertaining me," he said with a polite smile.

"I am sure she has," came the enigmatic reply.

James wondered at the cryptic comment but before he could dwell on it, Lord Bailey said rather brusquely to the slave girl, "I am parched. Get me a drink, girl. And hurry up."

His wife's evident discomfort with his tone matched James'. They had servants in England, but they were not spoken to in such a rude manner, especially since his mother had been a servant herself.

The girl returned in record time and hurriedly approached her master with his drink. James watched the interaction covertly and was surprised to see that despite the brusque way he had spoken to the girl before, Lord Bailey's eyes took on a lazy, assessing quality as he looked over her in a way that made James feel as if he was mentally undressing her. On chancing a glance at his wife to see if he was alone in his observations, he caught anger quickly followed by a brief look of intense dislike on her face before the polite mask dropped back in place. It appeared that The Acreage had stories to tell and they seemed to be very similar to the ones that he had heard before.

Chapter 3

Dinner was a quiet affair with only the three of them at the table. The girl that served the drinks earlier was joined by another one who was similarly dressed but perhaps not as attractive. Both brought in the dishes quietly, making no eye contact with the diners. James surreptitiously watched his host and once again was privy to the possessive looks he cast over the slave girls.

"I hope your room is to your liking," Mary-Ann Bailey said. Tonight, she wore a deep red dress made of some silky fabric that was cut so low that James feared what would happen if she sneezed. He did not see how it was suitable for a quiet dinner at home, or anywhere else for that matter, save a house of ill-repute. He deliberately kept his eyes on her face, although it was with great difficulty.

"It certainly is. Thank you again for accommodating me." James had wondered if the room he had been given was the one in which his uncle

William had ravished his mother and the same one in which his parents had spent several weeks together before his father went back to Carolina to his fiancée. What a scandalous past his family had!

"What brings you to Barbados, my boy?" asked Samuel. James bristled at being called "my boy" but chose not to take offence as Samuel did not say it in a demeaning way. In any case, though he was long past being a boy, he was surely near enough to being Samuel's junior by twenty years.

"I have acquaintances who used to live in Barbados and they encouraged me to come for a visit and see some of the plantations." That was a bit of a stretch of the truth, but that was as much as he would offer.

"Why The Acreage?" his wife asked.

"My acquaintances knew the people who used to own the plantation." He was really stretching the truth to its limit.

"Indeed? Who?"

"Edwards is their name."

"How extraordinary! My father bought The Acreage from a Thomas Edwards. He was visiting the island when he learned that Thomas Edwards was looking to sell it and he did not hesitate to get his hands on it. Your friends must mean him."

"Yes, that's it. Thomas Edwards, and his wife's name was Elizabeth, I believe." The lying was becoming alarmingly easy, although it wasn't really lying, James told himself. It was more like withholding pertinent information.

"That's right. I understand that she and their daughters moved to England, leaving him here. There was somewhat of a scandal surrounding him when he sold the plantation to my father and left the island."

James could well imagine that his marrying Sarah would have scandalised the planters on the island. He was glad that Mary-Ann seemed not the sort to gossip and did not choose to elaborate on what the scandal was about.

"What made you come at this time?" her husband asked again.

"My wife died a little while ago and I felt the need to get away from England for a time."

"Oh, my dear, how dreadful," Mary-Ann sympathized.

"Yes. Dreadful indeed," repeated her husband.

"It has been two years, so I am no longer officially in mourning."

"Still, I am sure you must miss her dreadfully. We must do what we can to make your stay pleasant and give you something to take your mind off your situation. Perhaps a small party," Mary-Ann suggested.

"Please do not go to any trouble on my behalf. I am quite content to spend a few quiet days here and explore the property, if that is all right with you."

"By all means," invited Samuel. "Although we are in the midst of harvest now and it is a very busy time on the plantation. I may not be able to entertain you as I ought. Even I have to get involved during harvest time, although I do have a very efficient overseer."

"I do not need to be entertained. In fact, I would be pleased to help. I'm not afraid of a little hard work and I often work on our ships at home, doing whatever is needed."

"Help out? Absolutely not!" protested Mary-Ann. "You can keep me company and stop me from dying of boredom. I do detest this time of the year. All my girls are practically taken from me to work with the harvest."

"I would love to see how the canes are harvested and made into sugar."

"I will take you around the fields and show you the mill and the boiling house tomorrow."

"I am sure that Samuel is keen to show you how they keep the slaves producing to make sure that he gets every drop of juice from the canes to make his precious sugar. But I would be happy to entertain you instead." James felt distinctly uncomfortable with her words.

"It is that precious sugar that keeps you in fine silks and bathed in French perfume," Samuel countered dryly. His wife opened her mouth to reply, but James hastily cut in before she could make what he was sure to be a cutting remark.

"I insist on helping in some way. I would feel quite guilty sitting around drinking tea and chatting while others are working," James insisted. "Besides, I prefer to be active."

"That is what we have the slaves for, my dear man, to do the work, so you need not feel guilty. However, it is your choice, of course. Mind you, if you choose to keep my wife entertained and out of trouble, that would be of benefit to me too." He smiled at his wife, but there was more derision than warmth in his eyes. Something was definitely amiss at The Acreage and he was sure that he would discover what it was before he left.

"You say that your father bought the plantation from Thomas Edwards," he prompted, changing the subject.

"Yes. He did quite a lot of business with the planters here and when he met Thomas Edwards and heard that he was selling it, he seized the opportunity to own it."

"Yes, those of the merchant class are now buying plantations in the islands," Samuel said somewhat disdainfully.

"Indeed, as they often have significantly more wealth than some of those of the peerage," Mary-Ann returned with a smug smile.

"One does not speak of one's wealth, my dear. It is rather common to do so."

"Particularly when one has no wealth of one's own to speak of, I would imagine," she parried. James wondered if there was any safe conversation to be had with this couple.

"Who are your closest neighbours?" That should be safe enough.

"The Bowyers live closest to us. Henry and Susan Bowyer. They have two unmarried, but rather unattractive, daughters who would probably be very happy to meet you," Samuel shared with a knowing smirk.

"That is rather unkind of you, Samuel. And anyway, I am sure James is not in the market for a wife," Mary-Ann chided him.

"Definitely not," James said quickly. The last thing he needed was anyone trying to play matchmaker, as he could not imagine anyone taking Harriett's place. He was relieved when the girls came to clear the dishes and Samuel invited him to join him in his office for a glass of brandy.

"Please excuse me," he said to Mary-Ann. "That was a wonderful meal." After the tasteless meals he had endured at The Royal Inn it was truly a welcome change.

"Thank you. I shall tell the cook you appreciated it." She ignored Samuel who rolled his eyes at that.

ꕥ

James looked around at the library and once again had the sense that he had seen it before. It was probably because his grandfather had described it to him and his siblings in such detail during the many times that he talked about the island. James knew that he had missed Barbados terribly as it had become home to him soon after he had moved there from England. It was a great testament of how much he had loved Sarah that he was willing to sell The Acreage and move back to England for her.

Their love had been deep and true. Although Thomas had started out simply wanting to own Sarah when he first saw her at Holdip Manor where she lived, the desire to own her had eventually transitioned into a deep love. So deep that he had been prepared to give her up to another man if it would have made her happy. The pain of regret stirred in the region of his heart as he knew that he would never have that kind of love now that Harriett was gone. He had loved her, but would that love have been strong enough to give up everything the way his grandfather had? Was he capable of such selfless love? One never knew until tested.

"This is my favourite room in the house. It is my place of escape," Samuel confided with a smile as he handed James a glass of brandy.

"There is something peaceful about it," James agreed, taking a seat opposite the desk.

"A man needs a place that he can call his own, without his wife constantly harping on about something." James could not relate to that as he had enjoyed being with Harriett although they had had their own times of being alone as well.

"Believe me, I would give anything to hear my wife's voice again, harping or not," James shared in a sudden bout of annoyance. Samuel's wife was alive and well and he seemed far from thankful for her, while James would do anything to have Harriett back again.

"Forgive me, my boy. That was thoughtless of me." James nodded and let go of his annoyance. "Especially since I, too, lost my first wife several years ago," he continued.

James looked at him in surprise. "Yes, Mary-Ann is my second wife. We have been married ten years. Her father wanted his daughter to have a title and I wanted to get out of England. The promise of a profitable sugar plantation was no small incentive and Mary-Ann is not unattractive." What a great understatement!

He did not know how to respond to the confidence that was shared so openly, so he said nothing. Was it the way of the island to share intimacies with strangers?

"Anyway, that is enough about me. I married Mary-Ann a year after my wife died so, to me, two years is a long time. You may not be ready to consider marriage, but surely you must be in need of some female companionship. I would be happy to send you one of the house girls to relieve you of the physical discomfort you must be enduring."

James coughed as the brandy he was sipping went down the wrong way when he heard Samuel's words.

"I beg your pardon?" Was he hearing correctly? Then again, he should not be surprised; he had heard that this was done in Barbados, but he did not expect to confront it himself.

"You need not be ashamed of wanting to satisfy your needs; you're a virile young man and you must be suffering for relief by now." If he was given to blushing, James knew he would surely be red in the face by now. Thankfully, he was not.

"To tell the truth, my desire seems to have died with Harriett."

"You think so because it hasn't been tested, my boy. Believe me, one of these slave girls will bring it back to life. I can attest to that," he added with a sly smile. James did not have to ask what he meant by that. The image of Samuel and his slave girls that involuntarily sprang to his mind repulsed him and made him feel physically ill.

"And how does your wife feel about that?" he asked pointedly, putting down his brandy.

"Oh, she is probably glad not to have to suffer my attentions quite so often. Besides, I rather suspect that she has her own amusements, both for her pleasure and to repay me for my indiscretions."

"And you are not concerned?" He could not imagine being so nonchalant if his wife was seeking pleasure outside of their marriage. Not that Harriett would ever have done that.

"Well, it must be quite obvious, even on our short acquaintance, that ours is not a love match. Perhaps if we had been able to have a child it may have been different. So, my wife cares not whether or not I lie with the slave women and I care not who she takes a fancy to, as long as she is discreet."

"That is unfortunate. I would rather not marry than to live in such a marriage."

"You are still an idealist, but you are yet young. And being young and handsome, be warned that you may be fair game for my brazen wife."

James could not believe what he was hearing. What manner of marriage was this that he had come across? Would Mary-Ann Bailey really be so bold as to try to seduce him in her own house? And did her husband truly not care? He could not fathom it.

ഌൽ

In spite of the plump mattress on the four-poster bed, James did not sleep soundly that night. His sleep was interrupted by snatches of the conversations and scenes from the day before. Moreover, he was disturbed to find himself dreaming of intimacy with his wife – something that he had not done in some time – and he woke up with a great yearning for her, accompanied by great physical discomfort. If this was what coming back to life meant, he would rather endure the numbness he had lived with than the stirring of desire that he was not able, or rather, not willing to satisfy. He blamed Samuel Bailey for making suggestions that planted seeds in his mind. He needed to kill those seeds before they sought to bring forth fruit.

The sun had barely peeped over the horizon when he gave up trying to sleep and swung his legs over the side of the bed and rested his head in his hands, rubbing his gritty eyes.

Lord, help me to get through these next few days and to be a help to this household in some way. Let me not judge these people but help them to see that there is a better way.

The sound of the door quietly opening caused his eyes to turn sharply towards the doorway. Relief filled him when he saw that it was one of the slave girls from the night before bringing in a bucket of hot water for his basin. He had had a fleeting thought that it might be the mistress of the house and he had no desire to encounter her just yet, especially after his disturbing dreams.

The girl hesitated on seeing him awake and murmured, "Good mornin', sir. I just bringin' up some hot water for you."

"Thank you." James gestured for her to come in. "What is your name?"

"H-Hetty, sir." She looked ready to bolt through the door.

"You don't need to be afraid of me, Hetty," he assured her. She nodded uncertainly and

hurriedly emptied the hot water from the bucket into the basin before fleeing his room. James wondered if she had suffered the attentions of other visitors to the house who had perhaps taken up her master on his offer of her services.

After spending a few minutes more praying for strength, he got up and washed before dressing for the day. He did not feel comfortable to spend the day in Mary-Ann Bailey's company now that her husband had intimated that she might try her wiles on him, so he wore clothes that he could work in.

He was surprised to find Mary-Ann alone breaking her fast on the veranda where he had been directed by one of the slaves. Thankfully, she was dressed a little more modestly this morning.

"Good morning," he greeted her, trying not to groan audibly at finding her alone, although he had delayed coming down until his stomach gave notice that it was time to eat. He hesitated briefly as she gestured to the place setting next to her.

"Good morning. Please join me," she invited. Her eyes shamelessly roamed over the white cotton shirt that sat comfortably on his broad shoulders with its sleeves rolled back to reveal his tanned forearms which were covered with dark hair. He wore a plain jerkin over it but no jacket. She made no secret of inspecting how well his breeches moulded to his thick thighs.

"I had thought your husband would be at breakfast," he said, accepting a plate of food from the slave girl and nodding his thanks.

"He must have had a busy night in the slave quarters, for he is usually up with the sun," she said dryly. "Don't worry, I'm sure he will be along shortly."

She ran her fingers over the hair on his forearm, saying, "I do like to see hair on a man's arms. It's so *manly*," she smiled. James almost dropped his fork but caught himself in time.

"Please refrain from doing that, Lady Bailey," he said firmly, moving away from her touch. He hated how prudish he sounded, but he needed to put a stop to this right away, for it was disturbing to find that her touch stirred feelings in him that had been long dormant, especially after his dreams.

"I thought we had done away with formalities," she teased him, resuming her breakfast as if nothing had happened.

"Perhaps it might be best if we kept them," he asserted.

"We are very relaxed here on the island. Far removed from the restrictions of the motherland. Very relaxed," she repeated in a suggestive voice.

"Good morning," her husband's voice greeted them. James was very relieved to see him and returned the greeting more heartily than he would have otherwise. "You are up early, my boy. You are on holiday. We don't expect you to be up with the sun."

"Habit," James told him. "Besides, I'm not one to lie about in bed when there is work to be done."

"Pity." He could have sworn that he heard Mary-Ann murmur under her breath, but when he looked at her, she wore an innocent smile on her face.

"I see there is no persuading you not to come out. I hope I didn't deter you from staying in last night," Samuel chuckled knowingly.

"Not at all. But I prefer to earn my keep."

"You will hardly be here long enough to be required to earn your keep," Mary-Ann insisted. "But you are free to stay as long as you like," she offered.

"Thank you for your generosity, but I am sure that a few days will be enough for me to see everything." He was determined to get through the time with his values intact, for he had no intention of either lying with any of the slave girls on offer or with his hostess, in spite of the clear signals she was sending him.

Chapter 4

The sun beat down on James' shoulders, making him feel as if he was being branded by its rays. Thankfully, a good breeze blew from the east often enough to ease the sting. He may as well not be wearing a shirt for all the good the cotton did. It was a blessing that he had not offered to cut the canes, but his father had warned him that it was the most back-breaking labour he had ever done when he visited the plantation. Instead, he had volunteered to help offload the canes from the carts that brought them to the mill where they were first washed and then fed through the grinders to extract the juice. The slaves looked at him as if he was mad since he was a white man (at least in their eyes) voluntarily doing work that they were forced to do. No one spoke to him of their own accord but responded briefly if he asked them questions.

He watched the process of the slaves feeding the canes through the grinders anxiously, remembering the incident that his father had recounted where a slave had gotten his hand trapped in the grinder and it had to be cut off to extract him from it lest he lose his life. Years later, there was still a slave on standby with a machete to sever the limbs of anyone being so unfortunate to get caught in the grinders.

He had had a look in the boiling house and as willing as he was to earn his keep, he did not plan to volunteer to help in there. In any case, the slaves who tended the large kettles were experts who knew exactly how to skim impurities from the top of the liquid and when it was ready to be transferred to the next kettle before it was mixed with quicklime to help granulation. Finally, the fire had to be dampened at exactly the right time and the thick liquid, which was a mixture of sugar and molasses, ladled into a cooling cistern. He certainly had no expertise to lend in that area.

"James, my boy, take a break and let me give you a little tour of the plantation," Samuel suggested. James was not sure what exactly he had been doing, for he looked as pristine as when he had come out of the house a few hours ago. He, on the other hand, had streaks of dirt on his breeches, his shirt was sticking to his body under the jerkin and his hair was dark with sweat where the brim of his hat rested. A ride around the plantation on horseback sounded good.

"I must admit that I can do with a break, so I would be happy to accompany you," he confessed with a tired smile, wiping his face and neck with a handkerchief. Working on a ship and even loading and unloading cargo, as he had done before, was nowhere near as back-breaking as working in the cane harvest. He felt sorry for the slaves who were probably at it from six or seven in the morning, but at least the ones in the yard were not under the scrutiny of the drivers in the fields who no doubt wielded whips to get the most out of them.

"You have only yourself to blame," Samuel reminded him. "You are our guest, so we do not expect you to labour like a negro."

"To tell the truth, working hard keeps me from thinking about things that I would rather not think about," he admitted.

"And wine and brandy keep me from thinking about things I would rather not," Samuel laughed joylessly. James had noticed that he had drank rather heavily the night before and he wondered what thoughts Samuel was trying to escape.

"I fully understand that," James commiserated. He had had his share of using similar methods to get to sleep without thinking about the empty side of the bed. "Unfortunately, they help but for a short time and often make things worse."

Samuel laughed without humour. "So true! Especially since the help I need is in the form of several thousand pounds."

"Ah! It is concern about money that occupies your mind. As with most people. It is something that I try not to let occupy mine."

"Spoken like someone whose pockets are lined with coins," Samuel said sarcastically.

"There are more important things in life than money and worrying about it does not draw it to your purse," James insisted.

"I should tell that to my creditors," Samuel laughed cynically. "Perhaps they might be more lenient."

James wondered if the plantation was doing poorly. He knew that the price of sugar had fallen, so perhaps The Acreage was suffering as a result. He recalled the disrepair of the house he had noticed when he arrived and the shabbiness of the clothing worn by the house slaves. However, the Baileys dressed very well and there seemed to be no lack of food, and especially drink, at the table. Perhaps they were living beyond their means and on borrowed money.

"Come let us speak of less depressing things and spend an enjoyable afternoon touring the plantation," Samuel invited. "We can start in the fields and you can see what you were spared by unloading the canes rather than cutting them," he joked.

They rode for a few minutes in silence. James relished having the trees overhead that filtered the brutal rays of the sun. The noisy chirping of the birds in the trees dispelled the gloominess of their conversation and the vibrant flowers that sprung up seemingly everywhere made him appreciate the beauty of the plantation. Eventually, they turned down a small, rough road that was made to accommodate the cane carts and passed small cane plants barely two feet tall.

"We will harvest those when they're between twelve and sixteen months old. Provided we have no fires, hurricanes or pests, of course," Samuel told him.

"I'm sure there is no end to the things that could devastate your crops."

"Thankfully, there hasn't been a major hurricane since I have been here, but I have had more than my fair share of fires, drought and pestilence. Many times I have wondered if I was under judgement like Port Royal in Jamaica."

James was familiar with the dangers of fire on the plantation. His father had been accidentally caught in a fire during a controlled burn and had almost lost his life. His grandfather had once lost acres of canes when one of his slaves had deliberately set them on fire in retaliation for being whipped after he ran away. Fire was something that every planter dreaded as it could totally decimate a crop and even if the canes could be salvaged, the quantity and quality of the sugar could be affected. As for being under judgement like Port Royal, James held his peace on that. Far be it for him to judge any man, but he did not see how abusing one's slaves and indulging in adulterous relationships could result in blessings.

They eventually reached canes which were taller than James with arrows waving in the wind to indicate their maturity. The thudding of cutlasses against hard stalks reached their ears even before they spotted the slaves wielding them. About twenty to thirty men were cutting the canes while a similar number of women loaded the stalks onto their heads and carried them to carts that were waiting nearby. The men's brown backs glistened in the sunshine with muscles rippling as they held the cane stalk in one hand and cut it towards the base with the other. They then quickly stripped off the trash with clean sweeps of the sharp blade. James noted that they wore tattered pants and few of them wore shoes. The women's clothes were similarly shabby. Many times he had to avert his eyes from seeing their bare breasts.

A driver with a wicked-looking whip walked up and down the line hastening those whom he thought were not working as hard as they should with a whip to their exposed back. Apart from a slight arching of the back when the whip landed, they seemed unresponsive and resigned to their task. A white man whose face was shaded by a hat with a wide rim was constantly riding up and down the field, tossing orders to the driver when he took a break from urging the slaves to work faster. James assumed that he was the overseer and noted that he was well protected from the sun by a shirt with long sleeves and long trousers.

"Get on with it. It's nearly time for lunch. You there, get moving or you'll feel the lash this evening," he shouted to a man whose grey hair put him at about fifty or more. The man had a rag for a shirt on his back and pants that had seen many washings. A surge of anger and indignation rose in James and he barely restrained himself from jumping off the horse, grabbing the whip from the driver and administering a good whipping to the overseer. He now knew how Moses felt when he killed the Egyptian, in anger, for beating the Israelite slave. How easy it was to lose yourself to anger and other emotions without thought of the consequences until it was too late.

"I've seen enough," he said abruptly, turning his horse in the direction they had come. His blood was boiling and he fought to control his anger which was dangerously close to spilling over upon Samuel. His grandfather would turn in his grave if he saw the state of the slaves on The Acreage and the way they were treated. The old man may even have been there when Thomas Edwards was the master and would have known better days. He would have still been a slave, but he would surely have had better clothes and, no doubt, better food to eat. The fact that Samuel seemed oblivious to the storm raging in James was a testament of his iron self-control and his face that gave little away.

"Let us visit some of the more scenic parts of the plantation," Samuel offered.

"I've had enough for today," James managed to push past his lips, as he could barely bring himself to speak to his host. *And more than enough of you*, he added silently, before abruptly turning his horse back in the direction they had come. He gave no thought to whether his action was rude or not, for he knew that if he stayed in Samuel's presence any longer, rudeness would be the least of his offences.

Rather than return to the house and encounter Mary-Ann, James turned his mount towards the east of the plantation, hoping to discover the spot that had been his mother's favourite place. He eventually came upon a grassy expanse at the end of which was a steep cliff whose edge was obscured by trees and shrubs that disguised the depth of the drop off. It looked like it could be the place that the same slave who had burned his grandfather's canes had jumped to his death. His grandmother had witnessed it, for he had tried to take her life there as retribution for his own suffering.

Today, there was no evidence of the tragedy that had happened years ago. Instead, it was blanketed in peace that was like a balm soothing his anger until it eventually faded away. From the back of the horse he could see the sea far in the distance. The foamy waves that topped the turquoise water were the only indication that it was rougher than it looked from so many miles away. This was in complete contrast to the calm seas of the west coast that he had seen as he was driven to the plantation.

A solitary tree, with branches that provided much shade, rose from the grass with a trunk smooth enough to invite a person to lean back against it and escape between the pages of a book. This, he figured, was the same place that had become his mother's favourite spot on the plantation. The place where she would escape to read the books secretly borrowed from his grandfather's library. The place where his father had first conversed with her and discovered a slave who could read and who had spirit. A slave who was not like a slave. His father had acknowledged that it was here that he realised that his mother's beauty and spirit drew him like no other woman's had.

Emotions battled in him. He could not explain exactly all of what he felt. Joy was one of the emotions, and peace, but he also had a desire to weep for some unknown reason. His spirit felt connected to this place where his father and mother had first met. The two people who had been purposed to come together and, in so doing, to conceive him. As he looked at the view from the cliff, at the solitary tree and then towards the house in the distance, he wondered whether he had been destined to come to Barbados to restore the legacy of The Acreage to the Edwards and Fairfax families. For surely Samuel Bailey did not deserve to own it after allowing such ruin to come upon it.

ꕥ

"How was your day?" Mary-Ann greeted him as he joined her and her husband at dinner. He had deliberately waited until he was sure that Samuel had gone down before he left his room as he did not want to be alone with his wife again. If she made any advances to him, he would have to be brutal in turning her down. As beautiful as she was, he was not in the habit of sleeping with other men's wives or any but his own, in fact, and he was not about to start now.

Thankfully, when he had come in from touring the plantation she had been resting in her room and he had stayed clear of her for the rest of the day. As he approached the table, his traitorous eyes zeroed in on the neckline of her emerald-green dress which was as low cut as the one the night before. He concluded that she had no modest dresses or chose not to wear them while he was there. Dragging his eyes to her face, he found a satisfied smirk waiting for him. He steeled himself and made sure he kept his eyes well north of her bosom.

"The work was back-breaking. However, I thoroughly enjoyed the tour of the grounds. The Acreage is a beautiful plantation."

"Yes, it is beautiful, but I rather miss the English countryside and the milder weather," she complained.

"My dear, you know that you may take your leave at any time," her husband invited.

"Believe me, that is very tempting."

Before the conversation degenerated, James mentioned his visit to the fields where the slaves were cutting the canes.

"I also saw the canes being harvested," he told Mary-Ann. "My work was not nearly as hard as what the negroes do in the fields. I find the treatment of the slaves to be intolerable and I was disgusted to watch them being whipped to work harder." He cared not if he offended Samuel.

"That is the way it is on a plantation. The slaves are a lazy lot and the only way to make them work harder is to apply the whip," Samuel insisted.

"Is it? We have many men on our ships who work hard, but it is because they are well paid to do so. The better they are paid, the better they are able to provide for their families and so we do not have to beat them to make them work. I am sure that is true for anyone, negro or white," James pointed out.

"My dear boy, you have no concept about running a plantation, so excuse me if I do not subscribe to your notions."

"I may not know about running a plantation, but I know about working with people, and negroes are people too."

"Yes, yes, of course they are," Samuel agreed dismissively. "Girl, pour me some more wine," he instructed the slave girl, Hetty, who was nearby. James barely refrained from making a scathing comment that the "girl" had a name. Samuel had already quickly emptied his glass twice and was on his third, and they had barely got to the main course. He supposed that Samuel was once again drowning his thoughts in alcohol. He wouldn't be surprised if he had downed a few drinks before dinner as well. Perhaps, if he consumed less of the expensive wine and brandy, he would not be so consumed with worry about how to pay for them.

"I believe I will have a small dinner party in your honour before you leave. It has been ages since we entertained," Mary-Ann told James, changing the subject. "We can invite the Bowyers and the Maycocks who are our closest neighbours."

That name Bowyer had sounded familiar to James before. Now he remembered that his uncle had spoken about a Henry Bowyer who had been his good friend when he lived at The Acreage. It was ironic that they were planning a dinner party for him. If they knew who his mother and grandmother were, they would not even welcome him at their table. He smiled to himself.

"A dinner at this time of the year is out of the question, dear, as everyone is busy harvesting their canes."

"I am supposed to die of ennui because it is harvest time?" complained Mary-Ann.

"It is the harvesting of the sugar that we sell to provide you with your bountiful wardrobe and jewellery," her husband reminded her.

"And to buy the wine and spirits that you so heavily indulge in," she smiled coldly.

Samuel, to his credit, did not reply but simply drained his glass of wine and deliberately held it out for the girl to refill.

The poor girl stumbled as she came forward to pour the wine and some splashed onto his dark-coloured breeches. He immediately jumped to his feet and slapped her about the face and head, calling her a clumsy negro and much worse. James was shocked into immobility for a few moments before rising to his feet and grabbing Samuel's hand as it was raised to hit the girl again.

"Lord Bailey, stop!" he insisted.

Samuel Bailey was so surprised at the unexpected intervention that he stared at James blankly for a moment before trying unsuccessfully to free his hand. "You forget yourself, Mr. Fairfax! How dare you interfere with how I discipline my slaves. They are mine to do with as I please."

"How well I know that," muttered his wife, looking embarrassed at the scene. "Return to the kitchen, Hetty," she instructed.

"Yes, mistress," she sniffed, practically running from the room.

James released Samuel's hand and he stormed out of the room, leaving James and his wife alone.

"Do excuse my husband's manners. It is obvious from his behaviour that a title does not a gentleman make." James nodded in agreement.

"I am sorry if I overstepped my authority, but I could not stand by and see that poor girl abused. I will retire to my room now. Perhaps it would be best if I left tomorrow, for I do not feel inclined to stay here after tonight. And I am sure your husband would prefer me to leave."

"Tomorrow? But I was looking forward to you staying for several days. I would certainly not be happy to see you leave, for I have not even had the opportunity to get to know you. If you feel that you must, promise to come again before you leave the island."

"I am not sure if your husband would welcome me back, but perhaps you can be my guests for a meal in town one day before I leave."

"My husband tends to ruin most things, curse the man. I do not know why I stay with him. I would love to return to England. Would you not like a travelling companion on your return voyage?"

"That would be highly inappropriate, my lady. And what would you do in England if you were to leave? Do you still have family there? Please think carefully before you make any sudden decisions," he advised. "If you will excuse me, I believe I will retire for the night. Good night."

"Good night, James." He thought he heard her mutter "for now" under her breath, but he hoped that he was mistaken.

Chapter 5

James searched through his satchel for the small journal that he had brought with him to Barbados to record his observations and adventures. He unwrapped his quill and ink from an ink-stained cloth and prepared his quill for writing.

Saturday, March 30, 1726

I am excited to be at The Acreage, the place where it all began, but yet somewhat distressed. I am excited because I have finally gotten to see for myself the places that my family spoke about: the palms lining the driveway, the mill and boiling house and my mother's favourite spot where my father discovered her reading Shakespeare.

I am distressed because the plantation is showing signs of disrepair and the slaves are practically dressed in rags and are poorly treated. Lord Samuel Bailey, who owns the plantation, makes no secret of the fact that he lies with the slave women and his wife seems to have her own liaisons. She has already tried her wiles on me, but I am unmoved, for the most part. To tell the truth, it is sad that their marriage means so little to them, but it was an arranged marriage and there is no love between them.

Tonight, I stopped Lord Bailey from striking a slave girl about the face and head for accidentally spilling a drop of wine on his breeches. I know not what to make of him. He seems to be a man not given to strong emotions, but after drinking a fair quantity of liquor he became quite violent. He does not see his negroes as people and is only interested in getting the most out of them to increase his profits. But this is the basis of the plantation system so I am not surprised.

The plantation seems to be in some financial difficulties and I would not be surprised if it not only had to do with earnings from the sugar but also to do with the spending by the Baileys. Mary-Ann Bailey dresses in the finest clothes and Lord Bailey drinks the best wines and brandy. Perhaps he gambles as well. I do not know, but something seems to be draining the profits.

Anyway, I am leaving tomorrow. I have been here for only two days, but I fear that I will be unwelcome after the altercation with Lord Bailey. In any case, his wife has made known her interest in me so I think it best to remove myself back to town where I will spend some time exploring the rest of the island.

When my father suggested that I should visit Barbados, something stirred in me and I now wonder if I have been destined to restore the legacy of The Acreage to our family. Is that even possible? I know not.

A soft knock interrupted his writing and the door was quietly opened and closed. At first, he thought it might be Hetty bringing in something, but a wave of perfume caused him to snap his journal closed and stand up quickly.

"Lady Bailey," he stated obviously.

"James, have I not spoken to you about being so formal?" she purred, gliding across the room to where he stood by the bed, making him wish that he had moved closer to the door. She was wearing a silky dressing gown belted at the waist and seemingly little else.

"Is there something I can help you with?" he asked and, even as the words left his mouth, he wished that he could recall them.

"I am so glad you asked. There certainly is. I am feeling terribly neglected by my husband. Even now he has gone to the slave quarters again. It is shameful and distressing." She looked so distraught that had he not had privy to the state of their marriage he would have believed her tale of woe.

"I am sorry to hear that, but I do not see how I can help you. Perhaps you should retire for the night as well." He circled around her and was about to head for the door, but before he could take two steps, she moved swiftly to grab his arm and stop him.

"Wait! There is something you can do to help me. I cannot remember the last time I had a hug. I would dearly love a hug." She sounded very forlorn, but he hardened his heart.

"I do not think that would be appropriate, my lady."

"Please don't call me that. You make me feel positively ancient and I cannot be more than a few years older than you."

"Very well, my– Mary-Ann," he corrected himself.

"That's much better. One little hug. What harm can that do? Don't be so pious." She did not wait for his reply but moulded herself to him and wound her arms around his neck. He could feel ever contour of her body under the thin robe.

"Mary-Ann, please desist," he started to say while seeking to remove her hands. He was not able to utter a further protest, for she used the opportunity to seek his lips with hers. James froze for a moment as he felt the softness of her lips, but the stroke of her tongue prying at his sealed lips caused him to push her off hurriedly.

"Don't be bashful, James. I saw you looking at me tonight. At my décolletage, to be precise," she laughed seductively.

"I apologise. It was not my intention to look. And I did not mean it as an invitation to my room. I am still grieving for my wife and even if I was not, I would never dishonour your husband by lying with his wife, far less under his roof."

"He dishonours me every time he lies with the slaves," she retorted hotly. "Why should I not take my pleasure where I choose, as he does?"

"Two wrongs do not make a right, Mary-Ann," he said gently. "Perhaps you should speak to your husband about his habits."

She laughed mirthlessly. "Do you think he cares? I have no desire for him anyway, not when I can have a young, strong man like you." She sought to draw close to him again.

"But you cannot. You had better go," he advised, putting space between them and hurrying to open the door. "Let us forget that this happened."

"If you think you can forget, please go ahead and try. But I'm sure when you're lying in that big cold bed tonight, you will be sorry that you did not take what I offered." He did not reply, closing his eyes instead as he waited for her to leave.

She stopped in front of him, making his eyes fly open. "You ought to be glad that I do not hold grudges. Until next time," she whispered in his ear before licking it. Her soft laughter taunted him when she felt the tremor he could not restrain and she pressed closer to him to confirm that he was not as immune to her as he pretended.

The door closed behind her with a soft thud and he let out a breath that he did not realise he was holding.

"Help me, Lord," he whispered, for he had had to fight against a surge of desire that had taken him by surprise. Maybe two years was too long. *Forgive me, Harriett. I did not intend to respond to her. I feel as if I have betrayed you. How weak I am!*

James turned the key in the lock and slowly readied himself for bed. He was sure it was going to be another long night and he looked forward to the morning. Although he was coming to love The Acreage, he could not wait to put some distance between himself and the plantation or, to be more specific, himself and the Baileys.

He ran a hand over his face as he recalled the last few minutes. Mary-Ann Bailey had not been in his room for a very long time, but her short visit had shaken him to his core. She had shown him that he was not as immune to the need for female companionship as he had thought and he was disgusted with himself. She was very beautiful, but he could not even claim that he had affection for her or knew her well, and yet he had responded to her like a stallion during mating season at the sniff of a female. He groaned aloud as shame at his body's betrayal washed over him. He needed to make sure that he did not find himself alone with her or any other woman for that matter. His desire was obviously not as dead as he had believed.

ꕥ

James brought his satchel down to breakfast as he had every intention of leaving the plantation as soon as he could. He was glad to see that he was the first to come down and was well into the meal that one of the slaves had set before him when Mary-Ann sailed into the dining room in a very modest but fashionable dress and her hair in an elaborate style.

"Surely, you are not leaving already," she stated by way of a greeting. Gone was the seductress of the night before and in place was a gracious hostess. Maybe he had imagined the whole incident.

"Good morning. Yes, I had hoped I would be able to ask for a ride in your carriage back to town."

"I'm afraid that we attend church most Sunday mornings, so we will be using the carriage. You are welcome to attend with us and return to town this afternoon instead."

"You attend church?" James could not disguise the surprise in his voice.

"My dear boy, everyone attends church here. It is somewhat of a social event," Samuel informed him as he joined them.

James looked from one to the other in disbelief. This was not the aggressive, intoxicated man of the night before nor the seductress who had come to his room. If Mary-Ann had not told him that Samuel had been to the slave quarters and if she had not pressed her body up against his wantonly and kissed him, he would believe that they were the perfect couple. He squirmed guiltily to know that he was acquainted with the feel of Samuel's wife's lips on his even though he had not been a willing participant. But then again, Samuel was more than acquainted with one or more of his slaves, as he had admitted, and he seemed to feel no shame. James immediately chided himself for that thought. Two wrongs do not make a right, he reminded himself as he had said to Mary-Ann the previous night.

"I would be happy to go. My wife and I used to attend regularly before she passed."

"Why am I not surprised?" Mary-Ann said wryly.

"I must admit that I have not gone as much in the last two years." James had been angry with God for some time because he had not been able to understand how God could take Harriett away after only a year of marriage and at so young an age. In fact, it was only when he had spent weeks on the ship with little to do but gaze at the soothing waves and the beauty of the sunrises and sunsets that he had been able to release his anger and had started to pray again.

"Well, you are welcome to come with us," her husband added. "We shall be ready to go shortly."

"You can put your bag back in your room," Mary-Ann instructed with a satisfied smile.

"Only until we return from church," James assured her.

In about half an hour they were on their way in the carriage with Mary-Ann seated too close to James for his liking and Samuel sitting across from them. James didn't know if he preferred to be next to Mary-Ann or if he would have welcomed her being across the small space and observing him. He eased a little closer to the window and took great interest in the passing scenery.

"Do you know anything of the history of the island?" Samuel asked him, bringing his attention back inside the carriage.

"Probably not as much as I should," James admitted. He knew a fair amount, but a lot was more about his family than the island itself.

"We are going to the St. James Parish Church. It is one of the oldest churches in the island as the original wooden structure was built in 1627 by the first settlers. It was built on one of the oldest consecrated plots of land in the island which is often called 'God's Acre'." James had known that. "The original building was destroyed in the hurricane of 1675 and it was replaced with a beautiful building of limestone and coral stone."

"I look forward to seeing it," James said.

"I don't think you would have passed through Jamestown on your way to the plantation, I take it?" James said no. "It is where the very first settlers landed and they called it Jamestown after King James, but it is now more commonly known as Holetown."

"Alas, that is a boring part of our history," Mary-Ann interjected airily. "Have you heard about the happenings at the plantation that is now called Nicholas Plantation?" she asked.

"I can't say that I have," James admitted.

"Well, two gentlemen by the names of Sir John Yeamans and Colonel Benjamin Berringer owned properties next to each other. They were called Berringer Plantation which was in St. Peter and Greenland which was in St. Andrew. Colonel Berringer built a wonderful great house in the Jacobean style on his property. Next time you come to The Acreage we must take you to see it."

James was not sure that there would be a next time. He would certainly love to visit the plantation again, but he did not want to have to suffer Mary-Ann Bailey's advances or see the brutal way their slaves were treated.

"Well," she continued, "it is rumoured that Yeamans had an affection for Colonel Berringer's wife, Margaret, and that he arranged for her husband to be poisoned so that they could be together. She did not grieve her husband for too long," she said, looking pointedly at James, "and they married just a few months later. The two plantations were merged and the name was changed to Yeamans Plantation. They eventually moved to Carolina in America but returned to the island a few years later and lived at the plantation until he died in 1674. The plantation eventually passed to Berringer's granddaughter who married a George Nicholas and they changed the name to Nicholas Plantation."

"That is quite a tale," James marvelled. "I am sure it must not all be true."

"It is certainly true that John Yeamans married Margaret Berringer in an indecently short period. Furthermore, she was pregnant at the time, supposedly with the Colonel's child, but who knows? I would not be surprised if he had neglected her and she sought comfort from Yeamans and became pregnant with his child," Mary-Ann speculated.

"My dear, you would do well not to speak ill of the dead. And besides, there is no proof that the Colonel was poisoned by Yeamans. It is said that he fell ill and died at a friend's house while he was on a visit to Speightstown."

"Perhaps it was his wife who poisoned him before he went out so that she could be with her lover and they could join the plantations."

"I cannot imagine that any lady would do such a thing," James disputed.

"Dear James, do not underestimate a woman or what she would do to get what she wants, lady or not," Mary-Ann advised him with a calculating look. He met her eyes briefly before looking away, remembering her visit to his room the night before and her parting words. He was not sure what she meant now, but he was certain that it did not augur well for him. He would have to be on his guard.

ഌ

The Baileys were well acquainted with many of the church attendees particularly, James noticed, those who were well-dressed and arrived in fancy carriages. They graciously introduced him to them as a friend who was visiting from England. He thought the word "friend" to be a little inaccurate in that they had known him but three days, but he did not think to suggest otherwise as that would have been somewhat rude.

They took their seats at the front of the church as befitting one of the largest plantation owners in the parish, according to the Barbadian custom. Samuel gestured him to enter the pew first, followed by Mary-

Ann and then he entered and sat down. James was happy that Mary-Ann kept a respectable distance between them as he felt guilt return to him now that he was in the house of the Lord. He sought to assuage his feelings of guilt by concentrating on the beautiful coral stone walls of the church, the stained-glass windows and the plaques on the walls.

Soon, the server bade them to rise as the processional hymn was sung. It was one that he knew so he was able to sing along with the congregation. Mary-Ann had a wonderful voice and he wondered again that on the surface she seemed all that was perfect. He was happy when they were invited to sit after singing another hymn as he was tired from lack of sleep the night before.

When the priest shared the story of David and Bathsheba, the guilt returned in full force. David had been the king of Israel when he saw Bathsheba bathing and sent for her to come to him. After she had lain with him, she became pregnant and David sought to get her husband, who was at war, to come back and lie with her so that the child would be believed to be his. However, when her husband refused to lie with his wife while he was still on duty, David arranged for him to be killed in the next battle to cover his deed.

As the priest talked about David's sin and the lengths he went to cover up his wrongdoing, James felt as guilty as if he had lain with Mary-Ann the night before and could only imagine how much worse he would have felt if he had given in to her. The sermon, on the heels of the story about the Berringers and Yeamans, seemed to be a little too uncanny to be a coincidence. What did it mean? Was the Lord warning him to be wary of the Baileys or was his imagination getting the better of him? He was very relieved when the service ended and they made their way to the door where the priest greeted them warmly.

"That was a very interesting sermon in light of what we were discussing earlier," Mary-Ann began as they settled in the carriage to wait for Samuel who had been waylaid by another planter. "It just shows that men and women having liaisons outside of their marriages has been going on for thousands of years."

"And with dire consequences, as pointed out by the minister," James reminded her.

"That is only if they get caught," she laughed dismissively. "Some things are worth the risk, James. Life is to be lived to the fullest. You of all people should know just how quickly it can be taken away."

James knew that only too well. He deeply regretted that he did not have more time with Harriett, but that was not enough cause for him to cast all reason aside and succumb to Mary-Ann Bailey and her desires. Thankfully, Samuel entered the carriage before he could reply, which was timely, for he was not sure what he would have said to Mary-Ann in hopes of changing her way of thinking. She would likely have dismissed whatever words he would have spoken anyway. It was a good thing that he would soon be on his way back to The Royal Inn and away from temptation.

Chapter 6

The journey back to town seemed to take much less time than when he travelled to The Acreage. He could not believe that it was only two days earlier that he had left on the trip, for so much had happened in that brief visit. Samuel seemed to have forgotten the incident of the night before, or else he was very forgiving, and both he and Mary-Ann had tried to persuade him to stay longer. However, James was adamant in his decision to leave, saying that he needed to get back to town. There was truly nothing pressing for him to return to, but he could not stay another night under their roof, especially if Mary-Ann was to be believed when she said "until next time". He had half-heartedly agreed to consider another visit before he departed the island and reciprocated by reminding them that they were invited to be his guests for lunch one day in town.

It was a great relief to cross the threshold of The Royal Inn after the long carriage ride, on top of his sleepless night and the hours they had spent sitting on the hard pew of the church. When he had declined their offer of lunch, Mary-Ann had insisted that she would get the cook to pack something for him to take on the trip, for which he was very grateful. He was now satiated and would be fine until dinner which was still a few hours away.

He was greeted warmly by Sally Perch who seemed to live behind the desk, as if always on the lookout for customers.

"Mr. Fairfax, I did not expect you back for another few days," she exclaimed. "Not that I am sorry to see you, of course. I do hope your visit went well."

James could see the curiosity all over her face, but he would not humour her or give her cause to gossip about the Baileys, or The Acreage for that matter.

"Yes, it went very well. I even attended St. James Parish Church for service this morning. I wanted to get back and do a few things here in town."

"Anything I can help you with?" she asked eagerly.

"No, not at all, but thank you for offering," James replied politely.

"Well, I am happy to tell you that Jemima has just returned so you will be getting a good dinner tonight. I am so glad that I fetched her back today now that you are here. The girl is an excellent cook, if good for nothing else."

This was the second time he had heard about this Jemima and he couldn't help but wonder where she had gone. He did, however, look forward to enjoying a good meal as he had been spoilt by the few meals he had had at The Acreage.

"That sounds wonderful. I will retire to my room and come down in time for dinner."

James could not wait to take off his boots, shed his jacket, waistcoat and breeches and sink into the comfortable mattress. After securing the door to his room the night before, he should have rested well, but it was the thoughts tormenting him that rendered him unable to sleep. Tiredness now overcame him and he blissfully succumbed to a much-needed rest. He felt as if he had barely been asleep for a few minutes when a commotion roused him from his slumber. He looked around groggily, trying to ascertain the source.

"You thieving girl, where is the rest of my money? Major Lawrence was supposed to pay me six shillings a day for your services. The money is short!"

"That is all he gave me," the girl insisted. "Ask him how much it was and you will see."

"You think I would question him, you insolent girl?"

Identifying that the quarrelling was coming from the yard below his window, he staggered out of bed to look out. Mrs. Perch was scolding a slim girl who was partly obscured by the clothes she was hanging out, but he caught glimpses of, pale, olive-coloured skin as the clothes blew in the wind. Mrs. Perch grabbed one of her shoes from off her foot and approached the girl menacingly with it in one hand. The rage on her face made it nearly unrecognisable, but the girl stood her ground, seemingly undeterred by her mistress' approach.

"You are a liar. That looks like a new dress you are wearing. You must have bought it with my money. I am working too hard to keep this boarding house to let you steal from me!" She launched at the girl suddenly and hit her across the face with the shoe before she had chance to react. The girl grabbed her cheek before turning to stagger away. Mrs. Perch managed to grab the handkerchief from her head, releasing a long plait of vibrant reddish coloured hair before her victim slipped away and ran. This only served to increase her rage and James was surprised to see the speed with which Mrs. Perch took off after her. The poor girl tripped on her skirt and fell on her hands and knees. Sally Perch, who was close behind, was on her in an instant and started to hit her with the shoe anywhere she could reach. A surge of outrage equal to that which he had felt the previous night at The Acreage caused James to shout, "Mrs. Perch! Stop that at once!"

He was glad to see that his shout caused her to halt in mid-strike and she looked back towards the window, startled, as if she suddenly remembered that he was her guest and ashamed that he had caught her at her worst. Without waiting to see if she would heed him or not, James drew his head back, grabbed his breeches and threw them on hurriedly before running down the stairs and out the front door in his stockings, having not stopped to put on his shoes or anything else.

By the time he reached the yard, Mrs. Perch was nowhere to be seen but Rufus was already there, as if he had been nearby, and was helping the girl to her feet. As James drew close, he was horrified to see the bruises on her face and blood running from a cut on her forehead that mixed with her tears, leaving watery red streaks down one cheek. Her eyes widened when she saw him and he caught what looked like shame on her face before she quickly wiped away the tears with her hand.

Her lips, where the first blow had caught her, were beginning to swell so that he could not tell what they had looked like before. Regardless of the bruises that were now marring her face, he was struck by her exotic beauty and the abundance of wild curly red hair that had worked its way from the plait and tumbled about her shoulders.

"Are you all right?" James asked and immediately felt stupid, for it was obvious that she was not. However, she nodded quickly and slipped away, disappearing through a side door that he had not noticed before.

"What the devil was that about, Rufus? Who is that girl and why was Mrs. Perch beating her?"

"That be Jemima. The mistress beat she because she t'ink that she t'ief some of she money."

"I believe I heard her saying something about a Major Lawrence owing her money. Who is he? Was he a guest here?"

"No, sir. Major Lawrence is who she rent out Jemima to for these last three months when things was slow."

"Mrs. Perch had mentioned renting out one of her girls. Was it to cook and clean for him?"

Rufus laughed mirthlessly. "Cook, clean and anything else he want she to do," he insinuated.

Realisation dawned on James and anger resurged in him. Mrs. Perch was nothing more than a degenerate woman, making money from a vulnerable slave girl in addition to running her boarding house. Rufus was just as bad, for had he not suggested that he could provide a girl, probably like Jemima, for him if he wanted one? He had only been on the island five days and already he had witnessed the abuse of vulnerable women like Hetty at The Acreage and the girl Jemima here and who knew how many countless others were suffering on plantations all over the island or here in town. It was enough to turn his stomach. Once again, he was confronted with his dual heritage and, at that moment, he hated the one which his appearance made him out to be.

"What will happen to her?" James asked Rufus, carefully making his way back to the front of the boarding house. It was only then that he noticed the rocks pushing through the thin fabric of his stockings. Funny how he had not felt them when he raced into the yard to stop Mrs. Perch from beating the girl.

"Mistress Perch goin' cool down and be back to she self soon. Jemima goin' to be all right. She could handle she self. This ain' the first time it happen."

But it is going to be the last, James vowed to himself as he climbed the stairs to his room. Mrs. Perch seemed to know to make herself scarce because he was still very tempted to give her a sample of what she had been dishing out and he had never in his life contemplated using violence against a woman. What was happening to him? Was the island bringing out a baser side that he did not know he had?

If he had thought staying at The Acreage had its challenges, he now realised that The Royal Inn also had its share. His visit to Barbados no longer appeared to be the quiet retreat he had imagined that would help him overcome his grief and come to terms with his life. Instead, it seemed as if the visit was somehow destined to challenge him in ways that he had never known.

ꕤ

Jemima closed the door to the small room that she shared with the slave girl, Ruth, who also worked at the boarding house. She was glad that it was empty so that no one else would witness her shame. It was bad enough that the man had seen Mrs. Perch beating her as if she was a dog. He must be the new guest that had caused Mrs. Perch to call back for her. Despite him seeing her shame, she was thankful that he was staying there, for now she was needed to cook and would no longer have to endure the vile attentions of the Major. She shuddered at the memory of his touch.

Wetting a small rag with water that she found in the jug they shared, she cleaned her face as gently as she could. Hatred for Mrs. Perch and her life at the boarding house consumed her and she swore to herself that another year would not find her there. She would get her freedom somehow. She was sick of Mrs. Perch hitting her for real and imagined offences. The only thing that stopped her from retaliating was the threat of being truly beaten by the town whipper who was paid to discipline slaves and servants or of being sent to jail for injuring a white woman.

A picture of the man with his brown hair loose about his shoulders and his shirt hanging out of his breeches, as if he had hurriedly put his clothes on, flashed into her mind. He was tall and the breadth of his shoulders could not be disguised by the loose shirt. She compared him favourably with Tobias who had been her benefactor for about a year. He had lived at the boarding house while he was on the island before he was transferred to another island and Mrs. Perch has been kinder to her then, for business was better. He had promised to buy her freedom from Mrs. Perch when he returned, but it had been a year since he had left and she had not heard from him, so she did not know whether or not he would ever return.

She combed her hair and plaited it, securing it under her handkerchief before having a quick wash and changing into another dress. Tobias had been very generous to her so Mrs. Perch had no cause to accuse her of stealing her money to buy dresses, and the one she had been wearing was not new anyway. In fact, they were all now beginning to look a little worn and she could do with some new ones.

Although her face throbbed where the shoe had hit her, she had no more time to nurse it, for she had to go and prepare dinner for the man before she incurred Mrs. Perch's wrath again.

ꙮ

James was the only guest in the dining room. Before he had left for The Acreage there was an older couple who had come to visit relatives on the island, but they had since left. He could well understand the financial challenges that Mrs. Perch was facing, but he certainly did not approve of her renting out the girl's services (Jemima, he corrected himself) to supplement her income. If it was to cook and clean, fine, but if she was truly expected to provide sexual services, that was totally unacceptable. He would see if he could help the business by encouraging the crew from their ships to patronise the boarding house, although it was probably a little outside of town for them.

As if his thoughts drew her, Jemima emerged from the kitchen with a bowl of soup that smelled better than anything he had had during his stay at the boarding house. Her hair was once again covered with a handkerchief. His eyes sought her face and found that her lips were still swollen, but the cut on her forehead had stopped bleeding although it had not formed a scab yet. He hoped she wouldn't have a scar to blemish her otherwise perfect skin. She was quite tall for a woman and he figured that if he stood up the top of her head would be level with his cheek. She wore another dress which was far superior to what the house slaves at The Acreage had worn and showed off her figure to good advantage, although being quite modest. He chided himself for noticing such a thing.

"Good evening, Mr. Fairfax."

"Good evening, Jemima," he said in surprise.

"I should thank you for stopping the mistress from beating me this evening. Although if I had not tripped, she would never have caught me," she boasted.

She said that she should thank him, but it seemed to be a challenge for her to do so, which told him that pride was one of her close associates, and therefore she resented that he had seen her shame.

"You are welcome," he said as if she had really thanked him. The slight narrowing of her eyes let him know that his deliberate answer was not lost on her. Her greenish-brown eyes shone with resentment as if she was angry with the world and he with it. She was as fair as his mother, but her hair was a rich red and much curlier from what he remembered. Even in her anger she was beautiful.

"I am sorry you were beaten at all. She has no right to abuse you like that." He tried to soften her, unsuccessfully.

"I am indentured to her so she owns me," she said as if that explained everything. "For now," she added defiantly. "I made split pea and eddo soup for you to start." She got back to business as she put the steaming bowl in front of him and bid him to enjoy it before retreating to the kitchen.

James found himself wishing that she had stayed and talked to him while he ate. It was not that he needed company to eat for he had eaten alone many times in the last two years, but he found himself intrigued by her. He wondered how she came to speak so well and wondered if she could also read and write. Could she be one of the students who had benefitted from the school? He wondered how much longer she was indentured for. Was she stealing money, as Mrs. Perch was accusing her, in hopes of buying her freedom? And how had she come to be indentured to Mrs. Perch in the first place? As he took the first sip of the soup and almost moaned with pleasure, he also wondered where she had learned to cook.

The soup was smooth and creamy although she had said it contained split peas, so she must have cooked them until they were soft and then crushed them somehow. It was a little saltier than he was accustomed to at home, but in the few days he had been in the island he already realised that their food was more seasoned than in England. He found that he enjoyed the more highly seasoned food and wondered how he would readjust when he went back home. He looked forward to the next course with unabashed eagerness. He drained the bowl and was hard-pressed not to tip it to his mouth to catch the last drops. No wonder her services as a cook were in demand. Although, from what Rufus had suggested, that was not all that was demanded of her.

When she returned, she was carrying a plate on a tray with the contents steaming as if it had just come off the stove.

"The soup was delicious!" James praised her, earning a quick smile followed by a grimace as her swollen lips reminded her, too late, of the abuse they had suffered earlier.

"Thank you," she said, surprising James after her earlier rudeness. "This is snapper and yam pie with plantains. I hope you like it too."

"I am sure I will," James assured her. "But what is snapper?"

"It is a soft white fish that lives in our waters," she answered.

Once again, she retreated to the kitchen, taking the soup bowl with her. James could not help but notice the sway of her hips as she walked. She was truly a beautiful woman. The thought of her being forced to provide the Major with other services against her will turned his stomach and made him clench his fists around the knife and fork he had just picked up. After what had been done to his mother, and even to his grandmother initially, the thought of any woman enduring such misuse angered him greatly.

He focused his attention on his plate with an effort and began to eat. He was rewarded with a delightful mouthful of soft, white yam crushed until it was smooth and mixed with shredded pieces of the delicately seasoned fish. His mouth delighted at the texture of the food and the burst of flavours on his tongue. He popped a piece of plantain in his mouth and the sweetness of the fruit provided a wonderful contrast to the savoury dish. In just a few minutes the plate was clean and he leaned back contentedly.

Jemima must have been watching him from the kitchen, for as soon as he put his cutlery together on the plate she approached his table. He watched her cross the room with confident strides which were so at odds with her status as an indentured servant. There must be a story as to why she was in this position, for she certainly did not act like the slaves at The Acreage, although for all intents and purposes that is what she was.

She did not wear silks like Mary-Ann Bailey and her dress was free of trimmings and covered her completely, but she exuded such grace and poise that she could well have been the lady of The Acreage. His gaze brushed and quickly passed over her surprisingly abundant bosom that was in his line of sight and dropped to where her skirt swept the floor. He wondered if she was wearing shoes and hoped that she was as he remembered the sharp rocks in the yard.

"Dessert is bread pudding with rum. I did not think to ask if you like rum," she said almost apologetically, which was quite a feat for her.

"I am more of a brandy man, but I am sure that your rum bread pudding will be as delightful as the rest of the meal."

He was happy that he had accurately predicted how delicious the bread pudding would be. It was not too soggy as some people made it, nor was it too dry. It was just the right texture, nice and creamy and flavoured with cinnamon and, of course, rum. He had barely put down the spoon when Jemima appeared to remove the dish with a slightly expectant look on her face.

"That was one of the best meals I've ever eaten! I think I'll take you back to England with me," he joked thoughtlessly.

The eyes that flew to his were filled with such hope that he immediately regretted the careless words he had spoken. While it was true that he would not mind eating that well every day, taking her back with him was not at all a consideration and he cursed himself for saying such a foolish thing. He opened his mouth to retract what he had said and to dispel any seeds of hope that his words may have planted, but he closed it again when he saw the fresh light that glowed in her eyes and he realised that they had already found fertile ground.

Chapter 7

James could have slapped himself for giving Jemima hope that he would rescue her and take her back to England with him. He had come to the island to see the place his roots had sprung from and to be healed of his grief. He had even committed to helping at the school while he was there. He did not come looking for either a wife as Samuel Bailey had suggested, a brief liaison as his wife wanted or a servant as Jemima now hoped, if indeed that was what she believed he had meant. A woman in his life was the last thing he needed. He steeled himself against the light in her eyes. He was happy to see the anger and resentment depart from them, but he needed to make it clear to her that he was not there to save her.

"I am sorry, Jemima. That was thoughtless of me. I was only joking, of course," he apologised.

"That was not at all funny! Can you not take me back with you, Mr. Fairfax?

"No! I am sorry. That is out of the question."

"Why?" she asked boldly.

"You are owned by Mrs. Perch, and besides, I have no need of a cook as I live alone. Or anything else," he added hastily in case she had other suggestions. "I think I'll take a turn on the beach to walk off this meal," he said and hurriedly made his exit, putting as much distance as he could between himself and Jemima.

His feet took him towards the beach which was a short distance from the boarding house. The moon, although not yet perfectly round, bathed the sand in light and created a shimmering path across the sea. A surprisingly cool wind blew across its surface, lifting the hair that was escaping from its leather thong from his face and cooling him down. The tranquil setting was at odds with the regret that his words had caused.

He hoped he had been able to crush her hopes gently, although he acknowledged that it was somewhat of an impossibility to crush anything gently. He certainly couldn't take her back to England. Besides, she still had to work out her time with Mrs. Perch. In any case, the last thing he needed in his house was a beautiful, quadroon girl whom he was drawn to. He brought his walk to an abrupt stop, as if to halt his thoughts. Drawn to? No, he wasn't drawn to her. Yes, he felt protective of her and she was certainly beautiful, but he wasn't attracted to her in that way. He remembered how she looked with her eyes alight with hope instead of anger and something stirred in his heart to know that he had put that light there.

He pushed the thought away before it could be fully explored and he deliberately called Harriett's face to his mind. He smiled slightly as he pictured her with her delicate pixie-like face and soft blonde curls, so different from Jemima's. Jemima again! He immediately brought his thoughts captive and turned back towards the boarding house. He hoped that neither of the women was about as he had no desire to encounter either of them. Perhaps he should find somewhere else to stay. That would certainly solve his problem, although it wouldn't solve Jemima's or Mrs. Perch's. Not that he owed Mrs. Perch any favours, and anyway, he had already paid her for the month.

Luck was not with him for, as he pulled open the door of the boarding house, he found Mrs. Perch seated in her usual place.

"Mr. Fairfax, I was hoping to see you."

"Were you? I am surprised to hear that," he said in a hard tone. He could hardly reconcile this woman with the madwoman he had seen earlier and she obviously hadn't wanted to be seen, for she had disappeared even before he reached the yard.

"I want to apologise for my unseemly behaviour this afternoon. Things have been very hard since my husband died, leaving me with the running of this boarding house. I am in danger of losing it if I do not get more business, so I am afraid that my fears overcame me and I took out my frustrations on Jemima."

"Mrs. Perch, it is not me that you should be apologising to, but Jemima," James reproached her. "And from what I understand, this is not the first time it has happened so forgive me if I doubt the sincerity of your words."

"You would not understand how hard it is for a woman, especially with no man to help her," she whined. James did understand, for his mother and grandmother had faced many challenges when they started their businesses, and they were even more disadvantaged by their colour. However, they overcame their challenges and managed to operate thriving businesses without abusing the two slaves that his grandfather had given Sarah when he freed her.

"On the contrary, I understand well, but difficulty and frustration do not give you license to abuse your servants. I do not want to add to your financial troubles, but I believe it would be better for me if I found another place to lodge. You, at least, have money for one month's stay which I would not expect to be refunded. I have come to the island for peace and tranquillity, and I have experienced neither today." Besides, the school was a fair distance away from the boarding house. Perhaps it would make sense to move closer to it.

"Please, Mr. Fairfax. Give me another chance. Your leaving will only make things worse." She looked so distraught that James could not bring himself to go through with his plan to leave right away, although he was prepared to walk away from the money he had paid to stay a month.

He sighed heavily. "Very well. I will continue as agreed, on the condition that you will cease your abuse of Jemima."

"Indeed, I will! Thank you, Mr. Fairfax. I am forever in your debt."

"Good night, Mrs. Perch," he said in response, heading for the stairs.

He suddenly felt very weary. Was it only that morning that he had been at The Acreage? He couldn't believe that the next day would make a week that he had been in Barbados. So much had happened in just six days! What would the rest of the trip bring? He was glad that he had agreed to stay for the month if it meant that Jemima would be granted a reprieve for that time, not that she would be grateful to him. He regretted that he had had to crush her hopes, but under no circumstances was he prepared to take her to England with him when he returned. Hope deferred was said to make the heart sick and if it was Jemima's hope that was deferred, why did his heart feel so sick?

ꟼ

James shut the door behind him. The moonlight that shone through the open windows gave enough light to the room for him to undress by, but he lit the lantern next to his bed so that he could write in his journal. Although he was very tired, he now felt that sleep was far from him. It was concerning how much worse he was sleeping in Barbados in the last few days than he had been in the bed that he and Harriett had shared. He needed to get his life back in order and marshall desires that he had thought dead but were stirring to life again. There was something about the island that seemed to cause rational men to come under its power. Or so he tried to tell himself. He dressed for the night and took out his writing utensils, intent on capturing all that had happened that day.

Sunday, March 31, 1726

I am back in town and, though I thought The Royal Inn would be a refuge from being at The Acreage, I have found myself in the midst of turmoil yet again. This afternoon I was awoken from sleep by a commotion in the yard. When I looked out, it was Mrs. Perch beating her servant Jemima whom she had fetched back from a Major Lawrence to cook and help clean. Of course, I was forced to intervene, for I could not simply ignore the abuse that was going on beneath my very window.

Jemima is a mystery! She is an indentured servant which makes her practically a slave, but she is not like the slaves at The Acreage. For one, she is much better dressed and I am quite certain that it is not at the expense of Mrs. Perch, for she is in financial difficulties. Therefore, I assume that she has or had a benefactor who clothed her. I know not if it is the same Major Lawrence to whom she was rented out. I cannot believe that the slaves and servants here are rented out, but it is so.

Whether or not she is required to do more than cook and clean I am uncertain, but Rufus suggested that she provides other services. I have to confess that the Major would have to be blind if he was not tempted by her. Only a man of the greatest honour and fortitude would be able to resist such a temptation. However, to force her to do anything against her will would be inexcusable. I would never do such a thing or approve of such being done, but the woman is without equal in beauty. Mayhap the fact that we share a common ancestry makes her so attractive to me (I have stopped denying it) and I am deeply distressed by my traitorous thoughts as I feel that I am betraying Harriett.

Tonight, I did a very cruel thing, though it was without thought. After the meal she served me, which was among the best I have ever eaten in my life, I told her I would love to take her back to England with me. I quickly regretted being so careless with my words, not only because she is not free to leave and go to England but because I gave her false hope. I need no woman in my life at this time. Mayhap never. No, I cannot lie to myself. I confess that my body is beginning to desire female companionship once more and I fear that I will have to battle to bring it under subjection.

I think it might be best if I visit some of the other places on the island in the coming days and begin to help out at the school, for the less time I spend here the better. Needless to say, I will ensure that I am back in time for dinner, for I am not that much of a martyr to deny myself Jemima's wonderful meals. It is her company, however, that I must not indulge in, for I am intrigued to know how she came to be owned by Mrs. Perch, for she speaks as one who is well educated. I wonder if she is one who benefitted from the school. I know nothing at all about her save that her skill at cooking is truly a gift from God, but I find myself wanting to know more.

Enough about Jemima. The day seems so long that I have almost forgotten that I attended church with the Baileys this morning. I tried hard not to judge, but I confess I was hard-pressed not to express my disbelief when Mary-Ann Bailey told me they were going to church. The trip to church was quite an education with Samuel telling me about the parish church and how it came to be founded and Mary-Ann taking pleasure in sharing the scandalous history of a plantation called Nicholas Plantation.

The rumour surrounding the plantation is that a Colonel Berringer who owned one plantation was poisoned by John Yeamans who owned the adjoining plantation and who was believed to have had a liaison with Berringer's wife. I could not help but feel as if Mary-Ann took particular delight in retelling that story. While I wonder if I am to bring The Acreage back into our family somehow, I certainly would not resort to poisoning Samuel in order to get it, and I certainly would not wish Mary-Ann to be a part of it.

I would also never contemplate having a liaison with her, though she came to my room last night and made her intentions plain. I asked her to leave, which she did, but not before promising with her parting words that there will be another time. She has given me fair warning, but she will be disappointed, for when I return to The Acreage, I will ensure that I do not find myself alone with her and that my bedroom door is locked. I say "when" and not "if" for already I find myself longing for my return to The Acreage and I fear that it has already found its way into my heart.

ꟷ

Jemima settled down on her pallet on the floor. Ruth was already asleep so she was free to lose herself in her thoughts about the day. She shifted to try to make herself more comfortable. While she hated being at the Major's house, at least she had a comfortable bed to sleep in, but the hard pallet she endured now was more preferable than the Major's attentions. She resented the fact that there were several unoccupied beds upstairs with plump mattresses and yet she was denied their use because she was now a servant. It had not always been this way.

Her father had been a school master who had come to the island from England. He had met her mother, who was a mulatto houseslave of one of the plantation owners whose children he taught and had convinced her owner to sell her to him and he had subsequently freed her. Therefore, Jemima had been born into freedom and her father made sure that she could read, write and speak well. Unfortunately, her father had died of a fever, leaving them almost destitute and with no means to support themselves. Her mother had indentured them to Mr. Perch for five years and became the cook for the boarding house. It was from her that Jemima had learned how to cook.

Her mother had died a year later when Jemima was seventeen. By the time the indenture finished in another two years, she would be one and twenty, unless she was able to pay for the remaining years, which she was determined to do soon. She could not endure this form of enslavement for even two more years. It had not been so bad when Mr. Perch was alive, but since he had died the business had declined and Mrs. Perch had become quite abusive.

She had not stolen any money from Mrs. Perch; it was the Major who refused to pay all that Mrs. Perch was due. He would never do that if Mr. Perch was still alive because no one would take advantage of him the way they did to Mrs. Perch. Then again, if Mr. Perch was still alive she would not be rented out. Although she hated the way she was treated, she knew that Mrs. Perch was nearly as helpless as she was.

Many times, guests had departed without paying her, until finally she became bold enough to demand payment upfront. Why was it that women suffered from these dishonest practices so much more than men? Somehow, she knew that James Fairfax would never do that. There was something about him that seemed honourable. Perhaps it was because he had rushed downstairs to rescue her from Mrs. Perch. She smiled in the darkness as a warmth stole over her body. For the first time in a long time she felt protected. It made her feel safe and warm. She quickly chided herself, for she could not allow such feelings to soften her. She could not rely on him to be there to protect her all the time. Besides, she could protect herself if she needed to, which is why she carried a knife in the pocket of her skirt when she ventured out.

She could tell that Mr. Fairfax had been sorry for the words he had spoken about taking her to England with him and he had left quickly after making his apologies. She did not want his apologies; she wanted him to get her off the island. She did not see why he could not take her with him. Surely, he had enough money to pay Mrs. Perch for the last two years of her indentureship, if he really desired to help her. But why would he? He did not seem to be interested in her or he would have made her a proposal. If he was not willing to help, she would find someone else who would.

Chapter 8

April 5, 1726

Mrs. Perch tallied up the books and the number at the end of the page looked horribly dismal. She sighed heavily as she saw that even with the money from the couple who had left a few days ago and Mr. Fairfax's payment for the month in advance it was going to be a hard month. If it was true that Jemima had not stolen the money, then the Major had paid her short. She should have insisted on him paying every week rather than sending the money on Jemima's return, but she had been desperate and did not want to put pressure on him. She fumed at his dishonesty and vowed never to rent out Jemima to him again. How she missed Mr. Perch who used to take care of the financial side of the business while she looked after the comfort of the guests.

She needed more guests to stay there and for longer periods. Maybe she should start serving lunch as well as breakfast and dinner and not only to guests but to the public. She was sure that Jemima's food was far superior to what they served in some of those places in town. Surely, she could get patrons to come just for the food. It would also be good if she could get Mr. Fairfax to stay another two or three months. It did not make sense for him to travel all the way from England and stay for only a month. He was so tight-lipped that she was not even sure what he had come to the island for, although he had said it was to visit. He had gone out several mornings that week, but he never said where he went.

One thing was clear though, judging by the quality of his clothes and his ability to pay for the month without a thought, he was not short of money. How could she get him to change his plans and stay there longer? As she pondered, an idea took shape in her mind and she immediately put away the ledger in the drawer and hurried from her room.

She found Ruth cleaning the kitchen and was told that Jemima was washing clothes in the yard. Hurrying to the yard, Mrs. Perch found Jemima bent over a tub of clothes which she assumed belonged to Mr. Fairfax as he had asked her earlier how he might get some clothes washed.

"Jemima are those Mr. Fairfax's clothes?" she asked.

"Yes. He said that you told him he could get his washing done for extra money."

"Yes, I did."

"He said he would pay you himself to avoid any trouble," she added defiantly.

"Yes, yes. I have no doubt that he will pay. He seems to be an honest man."

Jemima watched her curiously, wondering what she wanted.

"He agreed to stay for the month provided that I do not hit you again," Mrs. Perch admitted, a little put out. Jemima bent over the wash tub to hide the smile that threatened to show on her face as Mrs. Perch humbled herself. She waited for her to continue.

"I need him to stay for another two or three months." She looked over Jemima's flawless face, save the small cut on her forehead. "So, I want you to treat him well," she told her.

"Am I not treating him well now by cooking and washing for him?" Jemima was no fool; she knew what Mrs. Perch meant.

"Yes, but I am talking about taking care of his other needs. He is a young, healthy man. I am sure you can convince him to stay longer if you tried. He could become to you what Tobias was."

Jemima felt disgust that Mrs. Perch saw her as nothing more than a possession that could earn her money. She said nothing but scrubbed at a stubborn streak of dirt on one of his white cotton shirts. She wondered how he managed to get it so dirty.

"You heard me, girl?" Mrs. Perch sounded annoyed.

"Yes."

"Well, girl, you will do as I say! I still own you for two more years. Besides, you can keep any extra money that you get from him," she added slyly.

Jemima's head snapped up. "I can keep any money he gives me?" she repeated.

"Yes," Mrs. Perch confirmed. "I just need the money from his room for two or three more months."

"OK," she agreed. "I will do what I can to try and get him to stay longer."

"I will leave it to you and I will give you leave to go with him about the island if he so desires, as long as you get your work done." Jemima nodded in agreement.

Mrs. Perch left in high spirits, confident that Mr. Fairfax would soon be coming to her to extend his stay. She had confidence in Jemima's abilities.

Jemima frowned at the shirt. It was now pristine, which should have made her glad, but the whiteness of it somehow made her think of Mr. Fairfax. He seemed spotless like the shirt. When she served him these last few days, she had seen no sign of interest in his eyes as he looked at her. Even when he had said he would take her back to England with him, she was sure he had meant for no other reason than her cooking. He had even apologised for saying it. What manner of man apologised to a servant?

He was a mystery to her. He was very polite to her and the other slaves, yet he was a white man who obviously had money. Something did not add up with him. She wondered what he was really doing in Barbados, for he disappeared after breakfast several days and came back at dinner, not saying where he had gone. Not that she expected him to report his activities to her, but she couldn't help but be curious about where he went and what he was doing.

Mrs. Perch might think that she could convince him to stay longer and although she had agreed, she was less than confident. Worse yet, why did she feel that it was somehow wrong to use her wiles to get him to stay? But she wanted her freedom and money from him would help, or she may even be able to convince him to pay the remaining value of her indentureship. Besides, he would certainly benefit from the arrangement as well. And as he was tall and handsome, it would certainly be no hardship for her to lie with him if she could convince him. She ignored her conscience as she rinsed the shirt. She would do it.

ꕥ

James decided that he would keep his contact with Jemima to a minimum and think about her even less. He couldn't avoid her at meals for she served him breakfast and dinner, but he determined that he would take a book with him to his meals and keep his eyes firmly on the pages instead of watching her as she gracefully crossed the room. He would not notice the smoothness of her skin or the way her simple dresses displayed her figure perfectly without revealing too much of herself. It was intriguing how a modest dress could make one so much more curious than a dress that displayed everything. And he was intrigued; he admitted it.

He had been distinctly uncomfortable when he handed his clothes to her for washing. His shirts, breeches and jacket were not an issue, but the thought of her washing his drawers was a little too intimate for his liking. She had not seemed to share his discomfort but, then again, part of her work was to wash so it would seem as nothing to her. Her life could not be easy, with having to prepare the meals twice a day and do the washing when she wasn't cooking. He wondered if she had a day off for, if she was the only cook, he did not see how she could. Then again, when she was at the Major someone had cooked, or attempted to.

Today, he planned to take a trip out to Needham's Point where his parents had lived and where he had been born. He would probably find it much changed from how they had described it but he still looked forward to seeing it. He decided to walk into town and find a carriage to take him, for he did not want Mrs. Perch asking him any questions about where he was going. The woman was by far the nosiest person he had ever encountered and he did not want to give her any more information than was necessary.

He had promised her to stay for the month, which he would, but he would begin looking for another place to stay. It would be a sacrifice to forgo Jemima's meals, but a man could not be governed by his belly. He knew that the Baileys would welcome him there, but that would be more detrimental to his wellbeing, not to mention too far to travel to the school the days he had agreed to help out. Tonight would be the first night that he would teach slaves and he would have to leave after dinner which was the only time they could sneak out.

As he descended the stairs, he caught sight of Mrs. Perch coming in from the yard by the side door that he had not noticed the day of the incident. She had a pleasant expression on her face for a change and James wondered what could have caused that rare occurrence.

"Mr. Fairfax, you are on your way out?" she asked cheerfully.

"Yes, I am," he replied.

"If you need someone to show you around, I would be happy to spare Jemima," she offered. Jemima, not Rufus? James was immediately on guard. What was the devious woman up to?

"That won't be necessary. I am perfectly capable of finding my own way." Then to check if she actually gave Jemima a day off, he added, "But which day does she have off? For surely she does not work every day." His disapproval that this could be a possibility was obvious.

"By no means! Why, even the good Lord rested one day." James marvelled that she knew anything the Lord did, for she obviously had none of his love and compassion. "She normally has Sundays off. I am sure she would be happy to accompany you on an excursion. You need not wait until Sunday either, just as long as she gets through her work."

"I will keep that in mind. Thank you," James said politely and tried to make his escape. There was no way he was going on any excursion with Jemima alone.

"Before you go, I wonder if I might ask your advice, as a man who is likely knowledgeable about business. I have no husband to ask these things," she added woefully. James thought she was playing on his sympathy, but he gave her the benefit of the doubt.

"I would be happy to offer any advice I can."

"As I told you, my finances are rather strained at present, so I was thinking about opening the dining room for lunch to the public as well as to my guests. What do you think?"

"I think that would be a very good idea. Maybe you should start with once a week, say Friday, and see how it goes. But you may need extra help in the kitchen or with the serving, for Jemima will not be able to cook additional meals and serve them as well. But her food is good enough to attract diners."

"Yes, I agree with that. I can get Ruth to help her out. I would have to find a way to let people know that I am offering lunch on Fridays. That is my concern."

"I can help with that," James offered. "I have already invited Lord and Lady Bailey to have lunch with me in town. I can arrange to have it here, for I am sure that once they taste Jemima's cooking they will be back and perhaps will tell others about it."

"That would be most welcome, Mr. Fairfax. Perhaps I can start next Friday. Thank you so much for your advice and your patronage." Mrs. Perch was thrilled at the thought of having titled patrons dining at her boarding house.

"Not at all. I would be glad to help. Perhaps as I visit other plantations, I can give my recommendation to the owners about your dining room as an excellent place to dine."

"That is extremely generous of you, Mr. Fairfax. While I very much appreciate your help, I am afraid I will have to add a little more to your bill to take account of the lunches," she said apologetically.

"As I have to pay for lunch elsewhere now anyway, that will not be a problem," he said agreeably.

"And you won't consider staying on for another month or two?" She held her breath.

"I have not decided how long I will stay in the island yet, but I may decide to move to somewhere in town if I stay longer. I will see."

"That would be a great pity," sighed Mrs. Perch. "I do hope we can somehow convince you to stay." James smiled politely but made no comment.

Mrs. Perch knew she would have to rely on Jemima to convince him to stay and she had no doubt that it was well within her power to do so. Between the money from another two or three months' stay and new customers for lunch, her boarding house would be in a good position once again.

ꕥ

James opted to sit next to the driver this time so that he could ask questions as they drove through town and along the coast towards Needham's Point. He was glad that it was another glorious day on the island. When he compared it to the oftentimes gloomy weather in England, he felt that he could quite happily live in Barbados.

"I will take you to see St. Ann's Fort close to Needham's Point before we go to the area that you described to me, if that is all right with you," the driver said. "It was built just over 20 years ago and named after your Queen Anne, though we have dropped the 'e'."

"That would be fine. I have heard that it has an impressive number of cannons," James told him.

"That probably accounts for why the island has had only one attempted invasion and that was back in 1665 when a fleet of Dutch ships fired on Bridge Town and damaged quite a few shops and houses."

They rode on in a comfortable silence with the driver pointing out various interesting sites every now and then. Eventually, they stopped briefly to look at the fort before heading down the hill to the area which had come to be known as Needham's Point after the

Needham families that had settled there in the 1600s. From his parents' description, James was able to easily identify the house which looked as if it had been added to over the years but, based on its location, was still recognisable. He decided against a visit for that would raise questions that he was not ready to answer.

"I would like to take a turn on the beach, if you would be so good as to wait for me," James requested. On the driver's nod, he climbed down from the carriage and walked a short distance to the beach where he took off his shoes and stockings. The sand felt warm and powdery between his toes as he strolled up the beach, looking towards the house in which he had been born. His parents would have walked on this very beach, perhaps with his father carrying him on occasion.

A deep yearning filled his heart. For what, he was not sure. Perhaps it was for the children that he and Harriett never had. Would he ever have children? He would like to, perhaps three like his parents had, or even four. He loved his family and had enjoyed a wonderful childhood. They had lacked nothing in the way of material things but of even more importance, they had never lacked the love of their parents. Because his mother had been born into slavery, she never let them forget what a great privilege their freedom was and that they were blessed with everything they had.

That brought to mind a day when Alexandra was about eight years old and his grandmother had offered to fix her hair. Alexandra had come down afterwards and told him and Charles, in awe, that grandmother Sarah had never had a new, unbroken comb when she was growing up but had had to comb her hair with a piece of one that the mistress of the plantation had thrown out. Grandfather Thomas had given her the very first new comb and brush she had ever owned when she turned eighteen. It had been wrapped up in brown paper and that was the first time she had ever received a real present. Alexandra, who had everything her heart desired, could not conceive of never having a wrapped up present or not having something as basic as a comb.

How different their lives were just one or two generations later. He wanted children and he wanted them to know about their heritage and use their knowledge to make a difference. He was using his knowledge a little to help the students at the school, but he could probably do so much more. And anyway, before he could even think of children, he would have to consider marrying again. His heart protested the idea as soon as his head conceived it. Perhaps the fact that he could even consider such a thought meant that he was healing. Once again, he felt a rightness about coming to the island. It was as if his destiny had been waiting for him to pick it up again here, but he had no idea where it would take him.

Chapter 9

Later that night
School for slaves and coloureds

James left the boarding house directly after dinner so that he could get to the school by eight o'clock, giving him time to get instructions from Cassandra before the slaves got there. They were hungry for knowledge and even the risk of getting caught was not enough to deter them from coming to the school, Cassandra had told him. He was not sure how he would be received by the slaves. Although it was not illegal to teach slaves how to read and write, it was not encouraged by their owners, for they felt that such knowledge would cause the slaves to be dissatisfied with their lives and plan revolts and other disturbances.

Needless to say, it was unheard of for a white man to be teaching them and he knew that they would be suspicious of him, but Cassandra assured him that she would smooth the way. Although he had had misgivings about his ability to teach, he had felt surprisingly pleased at how good he had felt when he helped out with the free coloured men and women the two days he had come. It had taken his mind off his own grief and his lack of purpose and given him a feeling of accomplishment, as if he was doing something important. And he was. He was possibly changing the lives of these people by elevating them to the status of being able to read and write, which meant that they were better equipped to deal with life.

"I have another helper who comes on Friday nights," Cassandra told him. "It is Jemima from the boarding house where you are staying. I did not want to say anything to you before."

"Jemima?" he asked in surprise. He could not imagine her helping slaves to read and write, for she seemed to be totally focused on herself and her situation. He felt badly for judging her.

"Yes. She will come after she finishes up dinner and the cleaning."

"But that will be late. Should she be walking here by herself?" James asked worriedly.

Cassandra laughed. "She will be fine. Our Jemima is more than capable of looking after herself. She does not know that you are helping out, though. Do you want to leave before she discovers you?"

"No, why would I? I would ask, though, that you do not explain to her how it is that I am involved with the school, for she does not know of my mother and grandmother."

"I will keep that in my confidence," she promised.

"Was she a student of the school? Is that how she speaks so well?"

"No –" Before she could explain, several slaves came in and stopped abruptly as they saw James. Cassandra ushered them in and assured them that he could be trusted and was there to help. They nodded cautiously at him before shuffling into the back room where several lamps were lit and chairs set out for them. They were about eight of them, men and women who were eager enough to learn to steal out and come there at night although they must be tired from working all day. James was moved by their hunger for knowledge and silently pledged to do all he could to help them and others.

He was teaching basic arithmetic to one of the slaves using a piece of slate when the door opened and Jemima hurried in. She was still dressed as she had been when she served dinner and she was breathing heavily as if she had hurried to get there. Her eyes widened in shock to see him and she hovered uncertainly by the open door, as if poised to flee. He realised that not only was she there to teach slaves, which was forbidden, but that if Mrs. Perch found out there would be no end of trouble for her.

"What are you doing here?" she demanded, her eyes swinging around to Cassandra.

"Sorry Jemima, I did not have a chance to let you know that Mr. Fairfax had kindly agreed to help us out while he is here," Cassandra explained.

"Help us out? Why would he help? Are you sure he is not here to spy and report back what we are doing here? They would have no problem destroying this place."

The students looked from Jemima to James with fear beginning to creep into their eyes. There was a restless stirring as they shifted in their seats as though they contemplated leaving before someone broke through the door and found them learning to read.

"'My people perish for lack of knowledge'," James quoted. "I am here to teach. The same as you."

"Your people?" she scoffed. "What has a rich, white man to do with helping black slaves? They are certainly not your people."

"I see that you are not well versed in the scriptures," James chided her. "I was quoting from the book of Hosea where God said that his people perish for lack of knowledge. Now, are you here to help or to hinder?" he challenged her and waited expectantly to see what she would do. He found himself unaccountably glad when she closed the door to signal that she would stay and help.

The room in which Jemima was usually comfortable suddenly felt too small as James' presence filled it. Cassandra asked her to work with Tibby, a young slave girl who had been coming to the school for several months. Thankfully, she was bright and did not need much help, for Jemima found herself very distracted by James' rich voice with its English accent and his apparent patience as he went over a sum with one of the older men more than once.

She was still in shock at finding him in the school and looking surprisingly comfortable among the slaves. Who was this man? He was not like any white man she had known before. He had rescued her from Mrs. Perch and had apologised to her. Most white people did not apologise to servants or even care if they were being beaten. More confusing, he had not propositioned her or promised to take her to England in exchange for her body. This manner of man was outside of her experience and she did not know how to deal with him.

ᘓᘐ

As the last of the slaves quietly filed out, Cassandra shut the door behind them and turned to James and Jemima.

"Thank you both for your help tonight. Because you were here, Mr. Fairfax, we were able to get through a lot more and the practical examples you gave from your business were very helpful."

Jemima grudgingly admitted to herself that he did have a way of making the sums clearer by giving real life examples.

"It is my pleasure to help you. To tell the truth, I did not think I had much ability to teach, but I find it is coming surprisingly easy. I will be back next week and I will see what supplies I can buy in town to bring."

"I would appreciate that," Cassandra smiled.

"I would like to speak with you for a minute, Cassandra," Jemima said. "Alone." She looked pointedly at James who held up his hands as if in surrender, nodded to Cassandra and left the house. As soon as the door had closed behind him, she turned to Cassandra. "I cannot believe you trust that white man not to betray what you are doing. Do you even know anything about him? How did he come to find out about the school?" She fired off questions.

"Jemima, you are too suspicious. He comes on good recommendation and I trust him. And did you see how good he was with the men? I think it is good for them to learn from another man, rather than a woman. It helps their pride," she laughed.

Jemima shook her head in frustration. "And you are too trusting," she insisted. "Suppose he tells Mrs. Perch that I am helping here?"

"Why would he? What does he have to gain? Jemima, go home and rest yourself. You worry too much. God will take care of everything. Perhaps he sent him here to help us."

"God?" Jemima scoffed.

"Say no more. Let us say goodnight, for I am weary." Jemima saw the tiredness in her face and was ashamed that she had not noticed before. She, too, was tired.

"Sorry, Cassandra. You are a good woman. Get some rest."

"Get home safely. You have your weapon?"

"Always," Jemima patted her pocket, feeling the comforting heaviness of the knife that she travelled with at night.

The door closed behind her, leaving her alone in the street. It was later than usual, probably about half past nine, but she had no way to tell. The quietness of the night made her a little uneasy as she usually left at the same time as the students and would have company for most of the walk home. She patted her pocket again and started down the street. As she was about to pass the alley that separated Cassandra's house from the one next door, a tall figure emerged from the shadows and came towards her.

Jemima's heart leapt in fright, trapping a scream in her constricted throat. She backed away, grabbing the knife from her pocket as she did so. The cold steel glinted in the night. She held it confidently as if she knew how to use it and was not afraid to do so.

"Jemima, it's me!" James' voice penetrated her panic.

She lifted a shaking hand and pressed it to her chest.

"Mr. Fairfax! Are you mad? You nearly scared me to death!" Her breath was coming in short pants.

"Did you think I would leave you to walk back to the boarding house on your own? What kind of man do you think I am?"

"I have been asking myself that question all night," she admitted. "As you see, I can take care of myself." She gestured with the knife that was still in her hand.

Before she could say another word, James lunged at her and grabbed the knife from her hand, flung it to the ground and in the same movement pulled her hand behind her back, trapping it against his firm abdomen with his other hand across her chest. She struggled in vain to release herself.

"Do you see how easy that was?" he said quietly in her ear. His warm breath teasing her ear made her break out in gooseflesh.

"You took me by surprise," she said breathlessly.

"Exactly! You think you can take care of yourself, but if I were of a mind to, I could easily overpower you."

"You have made your point. Please release me."

Immediately, he freed her from his grip and saw her surreptitiously rub her wrist as he picked up the knife.

"I am sorry that I hurt you. It was not my intention, but I want you to understand how vulnerable you are. Do not put yourself in danger like that again. I will wait and walk with you to and from the class at night."

Jemima's anger rose in her, mainly because of how easily he had made a mockery of her claim to be able to look after herself. She was angry to discover that she was more vulnerable than she had believed. Not only did he easily disarm her, to her shame, but now he was trying to dictate to her what she was supposed to do! She ignored him and stalked off.

"Did you hear me?" His firm voice carried to her. She stopped a few feet away and turned.

"I think the whole neighbourhood heard you. Kindly give me my knife back."

"I will return it if you agree not to come here at night alone again."

"I cannot promise that! You will be leaving sometime soon. Who will walk with me then?"

"We will cross that bridge when we come to it. But for now, I will walk with you to and from the class at night. Do you agree?"

"Yes, Mr. Fairfax, sir," she agreed sarcastically.

"Yes, James," he corrected her with a victorious smile. Jemima was almost floored by the smile which transformed his already handsome face.

"Yes, James," she repeated obediently and he gave her back the knife, hilt first. It was still warm from his hand as she slid it into her pocket. She turned to walk again and his presence, as he fell into step beside her, was more comforting that she cared to admit.

ജ൦൫

"How did –"

"How long –"

They both began to speak at the same time, stopped and laughed softly.

"Ladies first," James invited gallantly.

"I am hardly a lady," Jemima demurred, "but I was going to ask how you knew about the school."

James gave careful thought to how to phrase his answer and then said, "The school has ladies in England who support it. They entrusted me with supplies for the students and asked me if I would help out with the teaching while I am here."

"They are English?"

"No. They used to live in Barbados and have always helped the school, so they continued even when they moved to England." He hoped that she did not know much of the history of the school or who started it. He was not sure if he could trust her with his secrets yet.

"What were you going to ask me?"

"I was going to ask how long you have been helping. And did you learn to read and write at the school?"

"I have been helping for a year now. Cassandra knew my mother and she knew that I could read and write so she contacted me secretly, told me about the school and asked if I would help."

"I was surprised when she told me you were coming to help," he admitted.

"Why? Did you think I was too selfish to help other people?"

"No," he denied hurriedly. "I know it is not illegal for slaves to read but it is not encouraged, and if you were discovered it might not go well for you."

"It is already not going well for me," she scoffed. "But I know how being able to read and write can make a difference to a life and as my father gave me this gift, I feel that it is my duty to give it to others."

"I had wondered how you learned to speak so well. Where is your father? Is he still alive?"

"No, he is dead. He was a teacher. I will tell you about him another time, for we are here."

James did not even realise that they had reached the boarding house already. He wanted to continue talking to Jemima and to discover more about her, but that would have to wait for another time.

"I will go in first and see if Mrs. Perch is about. Wait here," he instructed.

"Yes, Master," she replied cheekily. He smiled as he unlocked the front door and peered around. Seeing the room deserted, he gestured for her to come in and locked the door behind them.

"Good night," he whispered.

"Good night," she replied.

They stood for a few moments as if neither wanted to move and then James looked at her again before breaking the connection and heading up the stairs. Jemima followed him with her eyes before heading for her room to get ready for bed.

As she lay on her pallet, exhaustion overcame her and the last thing she remembered before she fell asleep was the way James had easily removed the knife from her hand and how good his body had felt pressed against her back.

Chapter 10

April 6, 1726
Bristol, England

"I wonder how James is doing," Deborah mused aloud as she put down the book she had been reading or trying to read, for it had ceased to hold her interest for a while as her thoughts kept returning to her son. "I hope he has arrived in Barbados safely."

"Weather permitting, he should have arrived over a week ago," her husband assured her. "I am sure he is fine."

Richard and Deborah were spending a quiet evening at home reading together in their sitting room. It was one of the evenings that they most enjoyed with no social events to take them out, so they had given the servants leave to retire early. Richard put down his own book and rose to join Deborah who was sitting on a loveseat with her feet drawn up under her skirt.

He smiled as he thought how appalled his mother would have been at what she would consider improper behaviour, God rest her soul. She and Deborah had never got on during the one visit she had paid them in Barbados when they first got married. He had not seen her since, but she had corresponded with him, even when they moved to England. His father had also passed, leaving his brother Charles to run the business.

"He is a grown man, married and widowed, my love. He doesn't need his mother worrying about him anymore." He pulled her close to lie against his chest. His fingers idly played with her wavy reddish-brown hair that fell down her back and shoulders the way he liked it. The few strands of grey that he was beginning to detect amongst the brown reminded him that she was now forty-eight. With a face that was still firm and flawless, one could be mistaken for thinking her to be no more than forty. His hair was completely streaked with grey at the sides which Deborah teased him about, saying that it made him look distinguished. Where had the time gone?

"He may be grown, but he will always be my son, so I cannot help but worry about him."

He brushed her hair away from her face and kissed her brow.

"I think that Barbados will do him good. Look what good it did me when I went there," he teased.

"You ended up owning me and blackmailing me to come to your bed," she reminded him dryly.

"I hardly call it blackmail. I made you an offer and you did not refuse it. But, my love, I married you and made it all right," he smiled. "The best decision of my life."

"I'm glad you think so because it was the best decision of mine as well." Deborah turned and rose to meet his lips as they descended to hers. She was amazed that after being married to Richard for nearly thirty years his kiss still stirred her. She broke off the kiss as a thought came to her, making Richard groan as he knew that her mind was still on James. "I hope he has managed to go to the school and help out. It will do him good. Maybe he will meet a nice girl who will help him to get over his grief. Harriett wouldn't want him to grieve forever."

"Would you want me to remarry in two years if you died, Lord forbid?"

"That is different. James is young and virile. He needs to marry again."

"Are you saying that I am not young and virile," Richard asked in mock offence. "I'll show you, my dear!" With that, he stood up and swept her off her feet, making her squeal in delight. He headed for the open door and strode down the hall as if her weight was no burden to him.

"I look forward to your threat," she teased him. "It is a good thing that Alexandra and Charles are out tonight," Deborah laughed, trailing kisses down his neck as he mounted the stairs and strode down the hall towards their room.

"Surely, they should be used to their parents disappearing into their bedroom by now," he grinned smugly.

"We are rather scandalous, aren't we?" she agreed with a laugh.

"When you marry a hot-blooded Caribbean woman it is to be expected. Maybe it would do James good to find one of his own," he concluded as he opened the door to their bedroom.

"We need to pray about James," Deborah said.

"Afterwards. We can pray afterwards," Richard told her as he closed the door with his foot.

ꕥ

Charles closed and locked the front door behind him and his sister and followed her towards the sitting room where their parents would normally be found when they were in for the evening.

"The house is very quiet," he remarked.

"Mother and Father have probably gone to bed," Alexandra said, "Although it is not that late. Yes," she confirmed as she reached the room.

They looked at each other, smiled wryly and rolled their eyes as they came to the same conclusion.

"I am sure that none of my friends' parents behave like this. It is rather embarrassing," she complained, flopping down on a sofa.

"I don't see why it should be. I would be happy to have a marriage like theirs where they still desire each other after all these years."

"Men! That is all you think about. I would prefer a man who appreciates me for my mind and who will listen to my opinions."

"Father appreciates Mother's mind and listens to her opinions as well," he insisted.

"Yes, I know," she agreed. "How will I ever find someone like him?" she sighed. "I believe I will remain unmarried and get involved with causes that help women to be more independent."

"By doing what? You are not even independent," he scoffed and quickly ducked as Alexandra rose to aim a cuff at his head.

"I will be. I have asked Father to lend me some money to start my own business."

"Start your own business?" he repeated, "Doing what?"

"I am not sure yet. He has told me that I need to prepare a plan to tell him what I want to do and how much money I will need before he will consider lending me the money."

"Good for him," Charles praised "He didn't become so successful by just giving away his money, so I am glad he is making you work for it."

"Well, I certainly don't want to join the family business like you and James. I want to do something else the way Mother and Grandmother did. I wonder how James is doing," she said, changing the subject suddenly as she tended to do. Charles was used to the way her mind worked by now and wasn't surprised. "I miss him already."

"I do too. I think I will stop at Barbados and see him on my way to Carolina to visit the family there."

"Oh, are you still thinking to do that? Then I will be the only one left at home," she moaned.

"Then you can have all the attention," he teased her, "Just the way you like it." She childishly stuck out her tongue at him.

"Seriously, why would you want to go all the way to America?"

"I don't know. I feel in need of an adventure. Besides, Uncle Charles told Father in his last letter that he would like to concentrate on expanding the rice plantation that his wife's father left to her and that he would love someone to run the shipping business for him. Who better than me? Maybe I will stay there and run it for him."

"You know, Charles, that though you look white, in America, especially the south, they have that 'one-eighth' rule. If anyone suspects that you have a great grandmother who is black, as we do, you will be ostracised."

"How do you know about this so-called 'one-eighth' rule?"

"It was introduced in North America in 1705 and is used to deter interracial marriages and relationships. I am widely read, Brother. Unlike you." She rolled her eyes. She and Charles were very close, being only four years apart, and they often ribbed each other, but the love they had for each other was very strong. Not that she didn't love James, but he was seven years older than her and they had less in common. Besides, he had not lived there since he had married three years before.

"Men don't like bluestockings, Alex. How do you expect to get a husband?"

"Please don't be obtuse, Charles. Is there not more to life than finding a husband? I, for one, do not need a husband. I am quite content with my own company," she insisted.

"That is because you love yourself so well," he teased her, not taking offence at being called obtuse.

"I love you as well, though I don't know why," she retorted. Sobering up quickly, she said, "Please be careful in Carolina. It is not like England. I do not want anything to happen to you."

"Nothing will happen to me. I have angels watching over me, especially since I'm so handsome and charming," he laughed.

She made a face at him and laughed to cover the sense of foreboding that came upon her.

ഇ൬

Next Day

Deborah and Richard were already at breakfast when Charles and Alexandra finally got to the table. A chorus of good mornings were exchanged as the young people filled plates from the dishes on the sideboard.

"You two went to bed very early last night," Charles remarked before he bit into a piece of bacon.

"Yes, we were rather tired," Deborah answered.

Charles looked at his father who had a contented smile on his face and said with a smirk, "You certainly look well-rested now."

"Please desist," Alex begged him. "Charles has told me that he is going to Carolina soon. Are you really going to let him do that?" she changed the subject.

"He's a grown man," her father said. "He is able to make his own decisions."

"But Carolina is likely to be dangerous. Suppose someone finds out about his ancestry? I'm not sure if I trust Ann to be discreet."

"For heaven's sake, Alex. Please do not discuss me as if I am not here. I will be perfectly fine, and besides, from what Father and Mother have said, Uncle Charles and Ann have long been reconciled to their marriage. In fact, Mother and Ann have become good friends and exchange letters. What is the matter with you? You are not usually such a worrywart."

Deborah looked at Alex inquiringly. She knew that Alex could sense things that others could not. She remembered when her mother had decided to sail to Jamaica with her father to visit her half-brother William soon after they got married and the premonition she had had that something bad was going to happen. So true, her mother had caught Yellow Fever and had almost died. Alex had that sort of sense and much stronger than she did.

"I'm sure he will be fine," she reiterated but gave Alex a look to let her know that she would talk with her later.

"Of course I will," insisted Charles. "Who knows? Maybe I will find an heiress who will inherit a rice plantation and get married and settle there," he laughed. "What do you say, Father?"

They knew that their father had been engaged to be married to Ann whose father owned a rice plantation and had wanted Richard to run it. After Ann discovered that he was in love with a woman in Barbados (their mother), she had broken off the engagement and had married his brother instead, who had always had a fondness for her. It all worked out well as they both had happy marriages.

"I say follow your heart. That is what I did and I am the happiest of men." He reached for Deborah's hand and brought it to his lips, winning a smile from her.

"Please," Alex said a second time but also with a smile as she was truly happy to see how much her parents loved each other. Despite what she had said to Charles the night before, she wouldn't mind a husband who loved her like her father loved her mother, provided that he accepted her for who she was and did not try to make her into a dependent female.

As soon as breakfast was over and the men left for work, Deborah sought out Alex to talk. Alex was like her in so many ways, not only the colour of her thick hair but her fierce independence. She loved her daughter dearly and encouraged her not to settle for anything less than what God had purposed for her to do.

"Alex, what is it that you are sensing?" she asked without preamble.

"I really cannot say with any certainty, Mother. I only have an unease in my spirit at the thought of Charles going to Carolina. I know that he looks white, but I told him about the one-eighth rule that is law in North America."

"That should not affect him, and I know that Charles and Ann will watch out for him."

"It will not affect him unless he really does fall in love with an heiress and gets it into his head to marry, for their marriage would be illegal and they would be banished from the country."

"I think you are getting ahead of yourself," Deborah cautioned. "There is nothing to say that Charles will fall in love with anyone. He doesn't seem the least bit ready to settle down."

"Let us hope not," Alex answered.

"And what about you? Any thought of settling down?"

"Mother, I am barely twenty. Why would I be thinking of settling down? What does that mean anyway? Why is it that marriage is referred to as 'settling down'?"

Deborah bit back a smile as she succeeded in causing Alexandra to launch into her favourite pastime which was getting into a good debate.

"When I was twenty I was already married and expecting James."

"That is wonderful for you, Mother, but I have no intention of expecting at twenty."

"I should hope not, as you have no husband yet!"

"Nor am I likely to, for I have not met a man who is not threatened by me in some way."

"You are rather terrifying," her mother teased. "But I am proud of who you are and that you do not intend to settle for just anyone."

"Thank you, Mother. I do believe that I must take after you and Grandmother Sarah who was prepared not to marry until Grandfather wore her down."

"Yes, with a little nudge from me," Deborah laughed reminiscently.

"What did you do, Mother?" Alexandra leaned in expectantly, knowing that a story was coming. She never got tired of the stories about her family and their life in Barbados. It seemed so far removed from their life in England that sometimes it was hard to believe that just over thirty years ago her grandfather had owned her mother and her grandmother. How would she ever find a husband who would not only accept her for who she was but would also accept the shocking family history that came with her?

Chapter 11

April 12, 1726
Royal Inn, Barbados

Jemima wondered what she could do to get James to notice her. It was as if their time together the week before had not happened, for he seemed to distance himself from her after that. Every day Mrs. Perch asked her how she was progressing and she had to admit that she had little to report. She also realised that it was no longer just for Mrs. Perch that she wanted him to stay, but she was beginning to enjoy his presence. Not that he seemed to notice her or even talk to her more than was polite to do.

Every morning she dressed as well as she could, given her limited selection of clothes, and set a scrumptious breakfast before him. All he did was thank her politely and turn his attention to the book he was reading while he enjoyed the food. In the evening it was the same thing. After every meal he told her how much he enjoyed the food, but he never again made a comment like the one he had made the first night. Nor did he give any indication that they had worked together at the school or talked intimately as they walked home that night. She still did not know what to make of him. Indeed, the fact that he seemed not to be attracted to her or interested in her in a carnal way definitely made him unlike any man she had encountered, and she was unsure about how to deal with him. This was a source of frustration for her.

She had little opportunity to speak to him since that night, for every day he left the boarding house shortly after he ate breakfast and returned just before it was time to serve dinner. She assumed that he was spending some of his days at the school and visiting places of interest on other days. Thankfully, Friday had finally come again, for she was eagerly looking forward to the night when they would walk to and from the school together.

James kept his eyes glued to the book that he purposely brought down to breakfast every day so that he could pretend to be engrossed in it. The truth was that he had read the same page several times and still had no idea what he had read. It was certainly better than trailing Jemima with his eyes as she retreated to the kitchen, and it deterred her from making conversation. He was deceiving himself if he thought that would stop him from thinking about her. It was very disconcerting that he was finding it hard to control his thoughts. Since the night that he had taken the knife from her and held her against his body, he could not stop thinking about how good she felt. Worse yet was the fact that she was working for the same cause that he was. That made her even more attractive to him and he was fighting against it.

He was going to be eating lunch at the boarding house today, for Mrs. Perch had wasted no time in starting her plan to offer lunch to the public. She had given him enough notice that he had been able to send a missive to the Baileys inviting them to join him for lunch that day. Although they were still in the throes of harvest, Samuel had returned a note saying that he and his wife would be delighted to join him for lunch. He would be glad for the distraction, to tell the truth.

He had told Cassandra that Jemima would be preparing lunch for the public for the first time and that he did not think she should come to the school that night, for she was sure to be exhausted. Cassandra had agreed with him, but now it was up to him to convince Jemima to stay at home.

"How was your breakfast, Mr. Fairfax?" Jemima asked him with a teasing smile.

"Excellent as usual, Jemima. Thank you."

"Mrs. Perch told me that you will be having guests for lunch today."

"Yes, I invited Lord and Lady Bailey from The Acreage to join me."

"I have never cooked for a lord or lady before," she remarked. "I hope they will like it."

"I stayed a few days at their plantation and while their cook provided good meals, they came nowhere near yours, so you have nothing to fear," he assured her.

"Thank you. I will make a meal that you will not be ashamed of," she promised.

"I am sure that I would never have cause to find fault with any of your meals. By the way, Cassandra has said we are not to come tonight," he added quietly.

"Why not?" Jemima asked disappointedly. She had been looking forward to the time she would spend with James.

"I believe she has something pressing to do." His face did not betray the lie that slipped far too easily from his lips. He excused it by telling himself it was for a good cause.

"Oh." She sounded so disappointed that he almost relented.

"It is for the best, for I am sure you will be exhausted after preparing lunch," he consoled her. "Now, if you will excuse me, I plan to take a short visit to Oistins town to see whether Ye Mermaid Inn still exists."

"What is that?"

"My dear girl, it is where the Charter of Barbados was signed nearly seventy-five years ago. It ended the war between Barbados and England."

"I did not know that. I did not even know there was a war between Barbados and England. I would love to see those kinds of places on my days off, but I have no one to take me about. Mrs. Perch has even given me leave to go as long as my work is finished," she hinted.

James would have to be deaf and blind not to hear and see that Jemima was hoping for an invitation to accompany him, but he knew better than to encourage her.

"I am sorry to hear that," he said, as he picked up his book to make his escape. "Please excuse me."

Not sorry enough, Jemima thought as she stomped back to the kitchen. It looked as if she would have to change her strategy with Mr. James Fairfax as the subtle approach was not working.

ꕥ

"Why James, it is a delight to see you again," Mary-Ann Bailey purred as she devoured him with her eyes. He had been waiting in the reception area to greet them on their arrival. Mary-Ann was dressed elegantly in a green and white striped dress with a jaunty little green hat that matched it perfectly. The neckline of her dress covered a bit more than her usual dinner wear, for which James was grateful. Samuel was equally well turned out in a dark-green coat, tan waistcoat and cream breeches. The two of them looked like a well-matched and prosperous couple.

"The pleasure is mine," James replied politely, knowing that Mrs. Perch's ears were no doubt tuned to their conversation. "Samuel, I am glad that you could take a little time away from the harvest to join me for lunch."

"My dear boy, from your enthusiasm about the meals you have been receiving here, I could hardly let even the harvest prevent me from joining you. Besides, I couldn't possibly let Mary-Ann dine with you alone," he added with a knowing smirk.

"Let me introduce you to the proprietress," James said, turning in the direction of Mrs. Perch who had risen from behind her desk in anticipation. "Lord and Lady Bailey, I would like to introduce you to Mrs. Sally Perch, the proprietress." He was surprised to see Mrs.

Perch look flustered by the titled couple. James could not help but think that if she only knew what a potential source of gossip they were she would not be so impressed by their titles.

"I am honoured to have you at my establishment for lunch," she gushed. "If you are ready to be seated, please come this way."

"Thank you," they murmured politely.

All three followed her to the dining room and James was pleasantly surprised to see that all the tables were covered with pristine white tablecloths with a flower arrangement in the centre of each. Shiny cutlery and sparkling glasses dressed the tables in anticipation of diners. James hoped that she would manage to fill at least three of the six tables for the first lunch.

"My girl will be here shortly to pour you a refreshing drink. I do hope you enjoy your lunch," she said before retreating to the kitchen. Almost immediately the slave girl, Ruth, brought out a pitcher and filled their glasses with a drink that he enjoyed which was made from water and oranges and sweetened with sugar. Samuel looked as if he could use something stronger.

"What have you been doing to keep busy?" Mary-Ann asked him. Why was it that everything she said seemed to have an undertone of suggestion? Or was it his imagination?

"I have seen some of the interesting sites nearby such as St. Ann's Fort. The farthest I have been is Oistins, which I visited today."

"Lovely," Mary-Ann said.

"Speaking of lovely…" James looked at Samuel to find him staring across the room at Jemima who was gracefully approaching their table. She was wearing a dress he had not seen before that showed off her figure to perfection. Glancing at Mary-Ann, James noticed that she, too, was assessing Jemima. "And who is this lovely specimen?" Samuel asked James in an undertone.

James found himself unaccountably annoyed with the question and tried to convince himself that it was because Samuel referred to Jemima as a specimen and not because he was looking at her with keen interest.

"Do stop drooling, Samuel," Mary-Ann reprimanded even as she straightened her posture to display her own assets more favourably.

"Good afternoon," Jemima greeted them. "I am Jemima. Today I will be serving a cream of split pea and eddoe soup followed by grilled red snapper with potato pie, fried plantain and vegetables in a special sauce. For dessert there will be guava tarts."

"That sounds delicious, Jemima," Samuel answered with a gleam in his eye. "I am certainly looking forward to it." She rewarded him with a warm smile which James found a little too friendly, especially as his wife was sitting next to him.

"Thank you, Jemima," he said rather shortly and turned to Mary-Ann who had put a hand on his arm to draw his attention. Jemima gave a brief, tight smile to him, far less warm than the one she had given Samuel and returned to the kitchen.

Mrs. Perch had warned her to display her best manners as she had said that Mr. Fairfax's guests were very important. The husband was a little obvious in his attention to her, but she was accustomed to that from men. All men except James Fairfax! Yet he did not seem to mind the intimate way that Lady Bailey was touching his arm to get his attention. Did he find her attractive? After all, she was free, white and beautiful, everything that she was not. Well, she was beautiful too but that did not seem to be enough to attract James' attention. She suddenly felt dejected, as if she had lost the battle before the war had even begun.

James was appalled to admit that he was jealous of the smile that Jemima had given Samuel and that he felt quite possessive of Jemima when he had seen Samuel's eyes assessing her. He had no right to feel jealous; after all, he had no claim on her. Nor did he want to! But he knew full well of Samuel's leaning towards brown-skinned and coloured women, and therefore Jemima, with her pale olive skin and curly hair, would probably be to his liking. And now, thanks to him, Samuel knew where to find her. He was sure that The Royal Inn would become Samuel's favourite place to eat every time he was in town and that Jemima might possibly be in danger of advances from him. Well, hardly danger, for she did not seem opposed to his interest.

A few minutes later, during which they chatted about some of the places he had been and others the Baileys recommended that he should visit, Ruth came out bearing a tray with three bowls of steaming soup. She did a fair job of serving them without incident, for which James was glad, but she was certainly not as pleasing to look at as Jemima and Samuel looked a trifle disappointed that Jemima had not made another appearance.

"This soup is delicious," Mary-Ann pronounced when she had taken a few sips.

"Maybe we should try to steal her away," Samuel suggested with a smile.

"I am sure you would like that," his wife said dryly.

"But, my dear, I am thinking of you as well. Wouldn't you like to eat like this every day?"

"Yes, but it's the nights that you have in mind, I am sure."

James cleared his throat and cut in. "I have to confess that I had the same thought after my first meal."

"About eating like this every day or the nights?" Mary-Ann laughed.

"I'm sure you know I mean her cooking, for I have told you that I am not looking for female companionship." He left it up to Samuel to determine if he meant the singular or plural version of "you". Mary-Ann did not look at all perturbed that he had possibly revealed that she had made advances to him.

"Every man that I know is looking for female companionship," she retorted. "You probably have not met the right female yet. One who will not be so easily deterred by your claims." She threw down the gauntlet.

Before James could reply, Ruth came to remove the bowls. Unlike Jemima, she was not so bold as to ask how the soup was enjoyed, but Samuel spoke up.

"Give my compliments to the cook."

"Yes, sir," she agreed demurely.

Shortly afterwards she came out again wheeling a cart with three plates on it. James was as disappointed as Samuel looked when he saw that Jemima had once again remained in the kitchen. What was he thinking? He was glad that she had not presented herself for Samuel to lust after. For if she thought that working for the Major was bad, Samuel would be no better. The scent of the delicious food wafted under their noses as Ruth placed each plate before them and scuttled back to the kitchen. There was silence for a few minutes as they savoured the food and gave murmurs of appreciation as the flavours melded on their tongues.

"My goodness, this is truly exceptional," Samuel declared. "I will be a regular here when I come to town."

"I am sure Mrs. Perch would appreciate the patronage," James told him, biting his tongue to stop himself from saying what he really wanted to. "And, of course, if you told other people about it that would help her tremendously." He had invited them for that reason, hadn't he? When he went back to England, it was not his concern if Samuel frequented the boarding house or not. It would certainly help Mrs. Perch and no doubt Jemima too.

"When will you come to visit The Acreage again?" Mary-Ann asked him. "We would be happy to take you around to see Nicholas Plantation that we talked about as well as to visit some of our friends in the north of the island."

"That is very kind of you. Perhaps in another week or so. I will send you correspondence to see when is convenient for you."

"My dear boy, anytime is convenient. If you bring the girl, Jemima, that would be a wonderful treat for us as well."

"I am sure that Mrs. Perch would not be able to spare her, especially if her dining room grows in popularity."

"No doubt she rents her out when things are slow. I would be happy to make it worth her while."

"I am sure you would, Husband, but we already have a cook."

"Not of this calibre, I am sure you would agree, my dear." *Nor beauty*, Mary-Ann thought. It was a good thing that she had no love for her husband or she would truly be hurt by his obvious interest in the girl. However, if she could get James at The Acreage again, she was sure that she could wear down his resistance. She would make sure that the key for the door to the guest room mysteriously disappeared. She smiled in anticipation.

"Yes, indeed, Samuel," she agreed. It would be good to have him occupied with Jemima so that she would be free to pursue James.

Finally, Jemima appeared from the kitchen bearing a tray with three plates of dessert on it. She removed each lunch plate from before them and deftly replaced it with the dessert plate.

"Thank you for your compliments. I hope you have enjoyed everything so far."

"This is beyond anything I have had before," Samuel declared. "I wonder if that will be true for everything you do," he added suggestively.

"I have found her cooking to be very consistent," James cut in, stressing the word "cooking". He signalled with his eyes for Jemima to return to the kitchen, but she ignored him.

"My desire is to please my customers," she replied, "so I am glad you enjoyed it." She smiled again at Samuel in what James considered a very inviting manner. Did she not care that his wife was there? She was truly playing the harlot, but perhaps that was what she was at heart and not the victim that he had previously thought. Well, Samuel was welcome to her, if that was the case. So why did he feel repulsed at the thought of the two of them together?

After the dessert that was as exceptional as the rest of the meal, they retired to the reception area where Mrs. Perch offered the men a glass of brandy and the lady a glass of sweet wine.

"That was a most outstanding meal," Samuel praised Mrs. Perch who preened as if she had prepared it herself.

"I am very glad you enjoyed it. I do hope you will come again."

"Most certainly, but my wife and I were wondering if we could hire your cook for a week when James comes to visit us again."

"Yes, indeed. We can have that party I was planning then," added in Mary-Ann.

"I thought you said that harvest time was not the best time to have a party," James said to Samuel. He thought Jemima going to The Acreage to be a very bad idea.

"Oh, perhaps it would be good to have a little break since we are just about mid-way through the harvest," the traitor replied, looking pleased with himself.

Mrs. Perch looked at James, in vain, to try to assess what he thought of the idea. Her mind worked quickly to consider the proposal. How was she to grow her business if she hired out Jemima again? But, then again, Mr. Fairfax would be at The Acreage so she would not need to feed him and it would only be for one Friday which would be Good Friday, if he went the following week, and she was not sure if she would get patrons if she opened on the sacred day. Besides, time at the plantation would hopefully give Jemima some opportunities to persuade Mr. Fairfax to stay a few more months. And she would also get extra money from Lord Bailey, probably more than she would get even if she opened for business.

"Once we can come to a fair arrangement, I would consider it," she said, hoping that she sounded like an experienced businesswoman. James looked at her in surprise.

"Are you sure that you can spare Jemima when you are seeking to increase your diners?"

"It would only be one Friday, would it not?" she looked at Samuel for confirmation.

"Indeed. Although that would depend on when James here would like to come."

"Well, perhaps Monday week after next and I could stay until the Sunday so that I could attend church with you again."

"Why wait so long? You could come this Monday and stay the week. It will be Easter next weekend."

"That is true and I will not open for business on Good Friday," Mrs. Perch added as if she was ever so pious and not driven by mammon. James almost rolled his eyes.

"And that would give Mrs. Perch some time to begin to let people know about her dining room before Jemima comes back." Mary-Ann seemed quite keen for him to come sooner rather than later.

"That seems like a very good idea, my lady," Mrs. Perch said, looking at James expectantly. James knew that she was thinking about the certain revenue she could get from Samuel, especially if she really did not intend to open on the Good Friday. But could Samuel spare the money to pay her? He hoped that it would not turn out to be another case like the Major's. Well, it was her decision, so she would have to face the consequences.

"I have no fixed plans for next week, so there is no real reason why I cannot come then." He would have to tell Cassandra that he would not be at the school next week.

"Wonderful! It is settled then," Mary-Ann exclaimed happily. "I can send out invitations to our friends this weekend and we can have an early party next Saturday, for the following day will be Easter Sunday and we will need to be up early for church." James marvelled at how religious she was even while plotting to seduce him if she got him under her roof. "Jemima can cook and that would give many more people a chance to taste her cooking which would be good for your business, Mrs. Perch," she concluded, smilingly triumphantly.

"Oh, that would be wonderful, my lady!" Mrs. Perch agreed excitedly.

"It has been ages since we had a party. I am already looking forward to it," Mary-Ann enthused. "I am very much looking forward to having you as well, James."

Surely, she meant she was looking forward to having him stay at The Acreage. He glanced at her briefly and saw the look of satisfaction on her face, like a cat which had cornered a mouse. No, she had meant exactly what she said. Well, she would be disappointed.

Chapter 12

There was tremendous excitement in the boarding house over the next two days. Mrs. Perch hoped that renting out Jemima for the week would result in her business improving significantly when all the planters at the Baileys' party partook of her food. She was extremely kind to Jemima, giving her all kinds of advice about what to cook and insisted that she take the Sunday off. The money that Samuel Bailey had agreed to pay to have Jemima for the week was also a source of great satisfaction for her. If she had filled the dining room for lunch she could not have made as much. She also confirmed that she would be paid up-front and Lord Bailey had promised to send her money when the carriage came to pick up James and Jemima, so she was happy.

For the first time, Jemima was looking forward to being rented out by Mrs. Perch. She was going to spend a week at a big plantation house where she would be responsible for preparing the meals. In addition, the party would give the opportunity for other people to sample her cooking and maybe help her find a new benefactor. Most exciting of all, she would have two or so hours with James travelling to The Acreage and she hoped to be able to find ways to spend time with him during the week. Surely, she would have some time off in between preparing the meals.

James had mixed feelings about the upcoming week. He desired greatly to be back at The Acreage and to find out more about the plantation, but he had no desire to travel there alone with Jemima and, worse yet, deal with Mary-Ann Bailey who had all but declared her intentions to pursue him once he was back under her roof. Not that she could force herself upon him the way a man could on a woman, but he was concerned that if she caught him in a weak moment she might not need to. He would have to be fully on his guard.

He was also concerned about Samuel's intentions towards Jemima, although she seemed not to mind his attention. He felt responsible for her since she was going there because of him, to some extent. He had no doubt that Samuel would try to use the opportunity to lie with her while she was under his roof, but he felt that she was under his protection and he might need to warn Samuel that she was off limits. Or was it even his business to do that? Everything was getting rather complicated. He had never expected all this when he decided to come to Barbados. Lord, help him!

Monday came almost too soon for James. When the carriage arrived, he put his burgeoning satchel in the carriage himself while the driver placed Jemima's trunk on the floor of the carriage before she climbed in. Mrs. Perch came to see them off and was horrified when she saw him close the door behind Jemima and head towards the seat next to the driver.

"Mr. Fairfax, what are you doing?" she exclaimed.

"I am riding up front with the driver."

"That is unheard of! The servant is supposed to ride with the driver, not the guest. What will the Baileys say when you arrive thus?"

"Mrs. Perch, I care not what they will say. I prefer to ride outside the carriage," he insisted, climbing up beside the driver. No way was he going to subject himself to two hours of temptation by being in close proximity to Jemima, especially as today she had shed her handkerchief and was looking like a lady with a smart hat perched on her curly hair which she had swept up into a bun. He wondered where she had gotten such fancy clothes. "It will do me no harm."

The darkening of the sky belied his words as clouds that he had been watching since early morning thickened. He hoped they would be able to reach The Acreage before they released a torrent upon them.

"It looks to rain, Mr. Fairfax," Mrs. Perch stated the obvious.

"Well, if we leave now, we may be able to get there before it does. Good day, Mrs. Perch." He tipped his hat to her.

"Good day, Mr. Fairfax," she repeated, shaking her head as the driver shook the reins to start the horses moving. "Have an eye to Jemima," she added. James nodded in agreement. Now she was thinking about Jemima after renting her to the Major?

Jemima's dismayed eyes met Mrs. Perch's through the carriage window. She had been looking forward to using the time in the carriage with James to move forward her plan, but she had not anticipated that he would sit up with the driver. She would pray for the rain to fall and drive him inside. She smiled a little at that before sobering. It had been quite a long time since she prayed, so she was rather out of practice. Would her prayers even be answered? Especially for the reason she wanted to get him inside the carriage?

James was happy that, as they moved towards the west coast, the clouds that seemed so threatening in town were being left behind. He hoped that was in part due to the prayers that he had offered up asking the Lord to hold off the rain. He had added in a prayer about "leading us not into temptation" as well, and it seemed as if his prayers had been heard.

The overcast sky made the trip quite pleasant and although the sea looked rather grey because of the reflection of the clouds on the water, the day was still much warmer than it would be in England under similar conditions. He found it strange that he did not miss England more. Of course, he missed his family, but for some reason, he was not longing to go back home. Even after one week, Barbados felt comfortable to him, as if it could easily become home to him.

Perhaps he was more like his grandfather than he realised, for he, too, had taken to Barbados quickly when he came. Was he like him in his attraction to brown-skinned women as well? Not that Jemima was brown, but they clearly shared some African heritage. Harriett had been the total opposite to Jemima and he had loved her dearly, but now he felt unwittingly drawn to Jemima's pale olive skin and exotic features. Not to mention the mass of red, curly hair that he had seen loose about her shoulders that day in the yard. Yes, his decision to ride beside the driver had been the right one. He trusted the Lord to keep the rain in the heavens until they reached The Acreage.

James' prayers were answered, for although the clouds seemed to follow them, the heavens held back the rain for which he was very grateful. The journey passed quickly and enjoyably with the driver pointing out places that James had noticed on his last trip but had no knowledge of the history associated with them. He was amazed at the rich heritage the small island enjoyed, and it had barely been settled a hundred years.

He was told that the Portuguese had been the first Europeans to discover the island and they called it Los Barbados (the bearded ones) after the fig trees they saw on the island which had a beard-like appearance. They had also released some hogs there to breed in case they ever came back and were in need of food. However, it was the English, under the command of Captain John Powell, who landed in 1625 and claimed it for King James I. He returned in 1627 with 80 settlers and 10 slaves to occupy the island.

Barbadians had even colonised Carolina when a group of settlers left Speightstown in 1657 for America and established Charles Town. He had known that already, for his father's father, whom he had been named after, had come from England and, not being able to find an affordable plantation in Barbados, decided to continue on to Carolina with the Barbadian settlers. His sister, Elizabeth, had married Thomas Edwards and settled at The Acreage. That made Elizabeth his great aunt. So, he was related to his uncle William and his aunts from both sides of the family.

He was happy when they emerged onto the palm-lined driveway of The Acreage, for raindrops were finally beginning to sprinkle him and the driver.

"Good timing, sir," the driver remarked, urging the horses to take the hill a little faster.

"Yes, indeed," James agreed.

By the time they pulled up to the house, the rain was beginning to fall in earnest and he had to climb down quickly and open the carriage door for Jemima who hurried out, leaving his satchel and her trunk for him and the driver to deal with. He hurriedly grabbed his bag and ran out of the rain into the patio where Mary-Ann and Samuel Bailey were waiting with matching smiles to greet them. Their smiles reminded James of hungry wolves who had just spotted easy prey.

"Welcome, James. So happy that you are with us again," Mary-Ann greeted him. He thanked her as she turned to address Jemima. "Jemima, Hetty will take you to your quarters. We are looking forward to experiencing your delights."

"Thank you, Ma'am," Jemima replied before following Hetty who was hovering in the doorway.

"James, you should get out of those wet clothes right away," Mary-Ann advised.

"Indeed," agreed her husband. "I will see you for lunch in about an hour. I will be in my office."

"You are in the same room as before," Mary-Ann said. "I hope you'll be very comfortable there."

"I am sure I will be," James replied as he took his leave. *Just as long as I have no visits from you.*

ꕥ

James closed the door behind him and dropped his damp satchel on the floor. Before he even shrugged out of his soaked jacket and breeches, he glanced at the lock and was unsurprised to find that the key had been removed. He did not have to guess who had removed it, for it was evident on Mary-Ann's face that something was afoot when she had told him of his room. He shook his head at her audacity and silently awarded her points for the move. If they were playing chess, his king would be under threat, but it was not checkmate yet; he could still challenge her queen. It did mean, however, that he would definitely be sleeping with one eye open.

By the time he had changed and made his way back downstairs, the rain had stopped, as he had found happened so often in Barbados, and the sun was pushing through the remaining clouds. Not seeing Mary-Ann or Samuel, he decided to take a turn about the yard and walk over to the east of the property which he knew would become his favourite spot, as it had been his mother's.

When he stepped out of the patio, he was surprised to see that a ladder had been propped against the front wall of the house. A negro man was working on taking off one of the shutters which needed repairing and a man was below him waiting to receive it. It looked as if The Acreage was getting a sprucing up. Could be it for the party?

"Good day. Doing a little repair work?" James asked them.

"Yes, sir. We got the shutters to fix and then we goin' paint up the house."

"When are you looking to get it finished?"

"Before the party Saturday."

"Very well, then. Let me not stop you."

Just as he had thought, The Acreage was getting some attention for the party. The Baileys obviously did not want to appear destitute in the eyes of their friends. Did that mean that the plantation was not unprofitable as he had thought? He wondered how he could find out what the true position was. Perhaps he could chat with the overseer to see if the crop had been providing a good yield in the last few years. He knew that the price of sugar had dropped, but the plantation also produced molasses for rum and was apparently renting out the mill to other planters. Perhaps it was the bad years together with the Baileys' lifestyle that had depleted the finances. Could the plantation be profitable if it was run properly and the non-essential expenses cut out?

The remaining clouds had dispersed by the time he reached his destination, but the grass still glistened with rain drops that had not evaporated as yet. A slight chill accompanied the wind that blew from the cliff, and James marvelled at how he had become so acclimatised to the weather in just three weeks that it felt chilly to him.

Peace descended upon him and once again he felt a deep sense of belonging to The Acreage. It disturbed him somewhat, for he knew that coveting another man's property was wrong, yet he had a secret longing to own the land that he stood on. He wondered how much it was worth and whether Samuel would be prepared to sell it. Mary-Ann had already expressed her desire to return to England, so perhaps Samuel could be persuaded if he could get a handsome sum for it.

Property in Barbados was incredibly expensive and to be able to afford to buy The Acreage, assuming that Samuel would even sell it, he might have to sell his house as well as most of his investments. He needed to find out how much the property was worth. Perhaps his father would be willing to invest in it as well. He smiled to himself at how far ahead he had gone with his dreaming before he even knew if any of this was possible.

Turning, he walked back to the house where the men had managed to get two shutters removed and lowered to the ground. While one of them prepared to carry them to a work shed, the other stirred a bucket of whitewash that he had not noticed before. He wondered why Samuel had not seen it fit to keep the place in better repair until now but yet seemed to spend much in other areas. Perhaps he lived well by borrowing against the sugar crops as he knew many planters did. He needed to find out the state of the plantation's finances and wondered how he could broach the subject without offending Samuel.

ꕥ

James entered the house just as Samuel appeared from the direction of his office. He had hoped to catch him in his office so that he could start to make discreet enquiries about the plantation and to discover how Samuel would feel about selling. That would have to wait for another time, but he was a patient man. He had all week.

"Good timing, my dear boy. I was just coming to search for you. Lunch should be ready to be served just about now."

"Yes, indeed," Mary-Ann confirmed, joining them in the foyer. "We won't be having any of Jemima's cooking, of course. Not before tomorrow, at any rate."

"How has she been received in the kitchen?" James asked, knowing that cooks could sometimes be territorial.

"Very well," Mary-Ann told him happily.

"Well, of course she would be. That will mean less work for the cook," Samuel commented dryly.

"That's true," Mary-Ann conceded. "Anyway, I've gone over some menus with her for the week as well as for the party on Saturday and I am looking forward to having her here immensely."

"So am I," Samuel agreed. James followed them into the dining room where plates were quickly set before them.

They had hardly tucked into their meal properly before Mary-Ann began to question him.

"James, we hardly had time to get to know you on your short visit last time. Tell us a little about yourself," she invited.

"What would you like to know?" *That I would be willing to share*, James finished in his head. He hoped she would not ask too many probing questions.

"You had said that your family is in the shipping business?"

"Yes. We ship cargo from England to Barbados and America and bring cargo from both countries back to England."

"Indeed? How many ships do you own?"

"Three at present."

"Three?" Samuel chimed in. "You must be doing very well. Does your cargo include slaves, if you don't mind me asking?"

"No, we do not transport slaves. Nor do we own slaves," James responded. They were doing well, so he was not keen to sell his ship to contribute to buying The Acreage, if he had the opportunity. He would have to liquidate other investments. "And how is the plantation doing? Especially now that there is competition from Jamaica and other islands?"

"Needless to say, we cannot compete with the vast lands of Jamaica and their level of sugar production, but we are holding our own. This looks as if it will be a good harvest."

"So, the plantation is doing well?" James persisted. "I remember you saying that you have had more than your fair share of problems."

"As I said, we had several challenges in the last few years, but this year looks to be good, thank God!" Samuel informed him. "Our sugar is called Muscovado Gold, as you may know, and sometimes it seems as difficult to get that gold as it is to mine real gold. Many times I have felt to give it up and move back to England." James' ears pricked up at that confession.

"Then we are in agreement for once, my dear," Mary-Ann looked at him in amazement. "I can hardly believe that such a thing is possible." Samuel ignored her sarcasm.

"But I have come to love the island," he told James, "So I would find it hard to leave. It would really have to be worth my while."

"I can well understand that, as I am coming to love it too, and I have only been here for three weeks."

"Really? You would consider living here?" Mary-Ann eyed him carefully.

"If I was able to make a good living, I would certainly consider it."

"Hmmm," was all she said as she turned back to her meal, but James was sure that her mind was working through the new information she had just received. He would love to know what she was thinking, especially as he saw a slightly devious look cross her face before she flashed a smile at him.

"Do you have siblings?" she went on.

"Yes. A brother and a sister. I am the oldest."

"And your parents are alive?" James wished she would stop the inquisition, for she was getting close to a topic that he did not wish to discuss. He had no desire to lie, but neither was he ready to disclose his background and the connection to The Acreage. Already he had deceived them by not making known his connection to Thomas and Elizabeth Edwards.

"Yes, they are." He did not elaborate and hoped she would change the subject.

"How long were you married? I cannot remember if you said."

"My dear, give the boy a chance to eat his meal. He has not been able to put any food in his mouth for your questions."

Mary-Ann pouted slightly at his reprimand but did not ask any more questions. James politely answered her after swallowing the food he had managed to get into his mouth.

"I was married just about a year," he told her.

"That is tragic," she exclaimed. "That is why I believe that life is to be lived to the fullest, for you know not when you will be gone."

"Yes, but perhaps it is more important to know where you will be going than when you will be gone," James cautioned her.

That seemed to shut her up, giving James a chance to mull over all he had learned. He had not even had to speak to the overseer as he had thought he would have to do, for Samuel was very forthcoming with information. He wondered how he could broach the subject of how much the plantation was worth. Obviously, he would have to join him for a few brandies after dinner to find out. With any luck, Mary-Ann would be well asleep by the time they were ready for bed.

Chapter 13

James groaned as he turned over in his bed. He and Samuel had drunk a large bottle of brandy the night before and, while he welcomed how it had loosened Samuel's tongue, he regretted nearly matching him glass for glass. He did not often consume large quantities of liquor, but he could hold it well enough and unlike many people of whom "in vino veritas" could be said, he tended to become quieter and more introspective when he had been drinking.

Thankfully, much truth was found in Samuel after the brandy and he now knew that Samuel was deep in debt and was somewhat behind in paying the mortgage on the plantation. He had also borrowed against the current sugar crop as James had suspected. James found it ironic that he had complained about the cost of Mary-Ann's wardrobe and how her expenses were draining their finances even as he continued to pour glass after glass of imported brandy for them.

By the time they both left the office and made their way upstairs, with Samuel swaying dangerously along the way, James was happy that he had acquired a good amount of information about the state of the plantation and only lacked actual numbers to determine its value. He had also been relieved to see that Samuel was in no state to visit the slave quarters and Jemima that night.

He had undressed quickly and tumbled into bed, not giving Mary-Ann a second thought, for it was well into the night by that time and she was sure to have fallen asleep by then. Thankfully, he had enjoyed a dreamless night and felt quite rested, apart from the pounding in his head. Belatedly, he realised that he should have drunk his fill of water before going to sleep, for the brandy had dehydrated him and left him with a headache. He was sure that Samuel must feel worse than he did and knew that there would be no working on the plantation for either of them today.

He would spend a quiet day around the house or maybe he would take his journal out to the cliff and write, for it had been quite a few days since he made his last entry. He rolled to a sitting position and sat with his throbbing head in his hands. A gentle knock at the door and his summons to enter brought in a hesitant Hetty with a jug of hot water in one hand and what looked like a glass of juice in the other which she offered shyly.

He took the glass gratefully and thanked her before downing the contents in a few gulps. By the time she had poured the water into his basin he had finished.

"That was exactly what I needed. Thank you, Hetty." She smiled and left as quietly as she came in, closing the door silently, as if she knew the state of his head. Perhaps the fact that Samuel had not visited the slave quarters the night before gave away what they had been indulging in. Would he have to keep this up every night to keep Samuel away from Jemima? He smiled at the thought. Not likely. Martyrdom was not his gift.

He washed before the water got cold and dressed for the day in a clean pair of breeches, another white cotton shirt and a royal blue waistcoat. He did not bother with a jacket as it was quite warm. He could certainly use a cup of hot coffee with his breakfast today. His stomach didn't take kindly to the thought of food in it, especially nothing fried. He would ask for some porridge instead.

He met one of the house slaves at the bottom of the stairs and put in his request for coffee and porridge. Her slight smirk told him that the slaves somehow knew of the amount of brandy they had consumed the night before. Perhaps it was the empty bottle on the desk that had given them away. His stomach roiled at the thought and he quickly made his way to the patio where he chose to sit to catch the cool morning breezes.

The slave, whose name was Dottie, burst out laughing as she entered the kitchen.

"Wha' happen to you?" Hetty asked her.

"I just see Mr. Fairfax and he ain' look so good." Hetty's giggles joined hers.

"What is the matter with him?" Jemima asked, butting in. She was getting on surprisingly well with the house slaves and they had welcomed her warmly and already given her all the gossip about the Baileys.

"When I went in to take hot water this morning, he was sitting down on the bed with he head in he hands,"

Hetty told them. "I did feel sorry for he, to tell the truth."

Light dawned for Jemima. "Oh! He had too much to drink?"

"Girl, he and the master like they drink a whole big bottle of brandy last night 'cause I see it 'pon the desk in he office," Dottie told them.

"That is why he didn' come down by we last night," Hetty told Jemima. "I wish he would drink so every night," she sighed.

"And Mr. Fairfax is in a bad way this morning?" she asked.

"Yes, he say he want coffee and porridge. I don't think he stomach could tek fry egg and fry plantain this morning." Dottie laughed again. Jemima had to smile, for she could not picture Mr. Fairfax indulging in that amount of liquor. She was happy to know that he was not perfect. Something that Hetty said finally registered with her.

"You said that you took up his water?" Hetty nodded. "You do that every morning?"

"Yes, why?"

Jemima smiled broadly. "I will do that for you while I am here." Hetty looked puzzled that Jemima would take on more work than she needed to, but she was quite happy to let her do that task.

"All right. If you want to. You could start from tomorrow mornin'."

"Let me get the porridge for the poor man. Pour some coffee for me there, Hetty," Dottie instructed.

"Let me take them out for him," Jemima offered. "I have not seen him since we arrived."

"Oh, you sweet 'pon he," Dottie teased her. "I ain' blame you. He look good; tall and good-looking."

"And he real nice too," Hetty chimed in. "He does tell me good morning and thank you and everything. And he stopped the master from beating me one night when he was here last time."

"He did?" Jemima asked sharply. Did he go around rescuing all women? She had thought she was special in some way but now Hetty was saying that he had done it for her too. Suddenly she felt dejected. Maybe she wasn't special after all and maybe that meant that she had no chance of getting him to change his mind about staying at the boarding house or anything else for that matter. Would she have to endure the next two years after all? For it seemed she was as far as she ever was from having enough money to buy her way out of the indentureship.

Dottie put the bowl of porridge on the tray and a big mug of coffee.

"You still want to carry this out? I think he 'pon the veranda."

Jemima debated it for a second but found that she was eager to see James, even if he wasn't eager to see her, for he had not enquired after her since they had arrived the day before.

ജ്ഞ

"Good morning, Mr. Fairfax," Jemima greeted him, although her customary smile was absent.

He swung around quickly at the sound of her voice, only to regret it. His head was still painful, but his heart leaped in response.

"Jemima! I didn't expect you to be serving me. It is Mr. Fairfax again, is it?"

"Yes. I don't want to be too familiar here."

"Yes, you have a point. Is everything all right? You do not look very happy."

"I am fine," she said shortly and not very convincingly.

"Is everyone treating you well?" he probed, wondering if she was having problems with the house slaves or if Samuel, by some miracle, had managed to get to her the night before.

"Yes, everyone is good to me." She put down the tray in front of him.

"Good. I am glad to hear that. Mrs. Perch asked me to look out for you," he said with a slight smile.

"I can look out for myself," she insisted.

"Yes. I saw how well you did that last week," he reminded her dryly.

"You caught me by surprise, but I have had to protect myself since my mother died."

"How long ago did you lose your mother?"

"Three years, but I still miss her," she said sadly.

"I know what you mean. My wife died two years ago and I miss her too."

"I am sorry. I did not know you had been married."

Jemima felt some of the defences that she had just put up begin to crumble. He looked so sorrowful that her heart hurt for him, for she knew well how that grief felt. Without thinking about what she was doing, she laid a comforting hand on his shoulder and squeezed it gently. It felt rock solid under her hand. She was surprised when his hand came up to cover hers, making a jolt of awareness go through her. Before she could respond, he quickly removed his hand and shifted slightly on the pretence of leaning forward to eat, so that her hand slid from his shoulder. She mumbled an excuse before bolting back inside the house with her face burning with shame at his rejection.

James was surprised by his response to Jemima's hand on his shoulder. He had instinctively covered hers without even thinking about it and it had felt so natural that he had quickly removed it and shifted away from her, for he did not want to send any wrong signals. However, he imagined he could still feel the warmth of her hand through his shirt and the comfort of her touch. It had been a long time since he had felt the touch of a woman. He didn't count Mary-Ann, for he had not invited her touch. He wondered how Jemima's hands would feel in his hair or massaging his throbbing temples. He groaned at the direction of his thoughts and deliberately focused on his porridge.

"Was that Jemima that I just saw running through the house?" Mary-Ann asked loudly as she joined him. He wondered if she did it deliberately.

"Please, Mary-Ann. My head is aching somewhat this morning." He deliberately did not answer her question.

"Oh, you poor dear. Did you and Samuel drink yourselves into oblivion last night?" She laughed softly. "No wonder he is not up yet and you look so pained. So, what did you do to make Jemima run away?" She obviously had not forgotten her question.

"Nothing that I am aware of."

Mary-Ann watched him carefully before saying, "She is a lovely little thing. Has she succeeded where I have not, yet?"

"What on earth do you mean?" James asked.

"Have you sampled what she is so obviously offering?"

James closed his eyes as his head started to pound afresh. If anyone was obviously offering anything it was his present company.

"Mary-Ann, does nothing else occupy that pretty head of yours?"

"I am happy that you think it's pretty, even though you have cleverly avoided my question."

"There was never a question about your beauty. It is undeniable. However, I have no intention of doing anything more than admiring you from afar. Unlike Mr. Yeamans in your tale, I would never pursue another man's wife, far less lie with her under his roof."

"What about *not* under his roof?" she laughed, totally without shame. James could hardly maintain a straight face in the light of her question. He shook his head at her audacity and took a sip of his coffee.

"What am I to do with you, Mary-Ann?" James asked rhetorically.

"If you have to ask, then I would say you are sadly out of practice. But I'm willing to make allowances, for you have been celibate for two years, if you are to be believed."

James laughed aloud and realised that it had been quite a while since he had laughed. It felt good. He could even forgive Mary-Ann for her outrageous behaviour, for it was helping him to feel alive again. And how much more so Jemima, whose simple touch on his shoulder and shared grief somehow lifted the darkness from his soul and let in a tiny shaft of light. That light was enough to cause something in his heart to stir to life again. Was it only desire that he felt for her? For that seemed to have been resurrected from the dead.

ꟸ

By the time he had finished his porridge and coffee, his headache had abated slightly and he excused himself and left Mary-Ann to her breakfast which Hetty had brought out. He collected his journal and writing instruments from his room and left through one of the back doors to make his way towards his favourite spot. He preferred to keep his whereabouts secret, for the last thing he needed was Mary-Ann discovering where he had gone and following him.

In a short time, he settled himself against the tree with a sigh of satisfaction. It was a truly beautiful day with few clouds in the sky, but at this time of the day the sun's rays were still gentle. The birds in the trees overhead were undisturbed by his presence and continued their conversation with each other as if he was not there. A feeling of wellbeing came over him and he closed his eyes as if doing so would cause him to hold on to the feeling longer.

The feeling of a presence nearby caused him to quickly open his eyes and his heartbeat increased a little as he saw Jemima walking towards him. The gentle breeze blew her dress against her, displaying her form clearly and he was surprised to see her hair loose and blowing in the wind, for it had been hidden under a handkerchief when he had seen her earlier. He stood up as she came close, as he had been brought up to do so in the presence of a lady.

"I hope I am not disturbing you," she said almost hesitantly.

"Not at all," he lied, for her presence was indeed disturbing to him. His eyes kept straying to her wild hair and her lips. They now drew his attention as if they were beckoning him to test their softness. Which he had no intention of doing.

"I saw you leaving by the back door and wondered where you were escaping to," she teased boldly, making him smile. Jemima grew more confident on seeing his smile. By the time she had reached the kitchen she had reasoned that James was probably not rejecting her as much as he was rejecting the awareness between them, especially as he was still grieving for his wife. She knew that men found her attractive so she figured that he was attracted to her but was likely fighting it. Perhaps that was why he did not want to ride in the carriage with her and why he had so deliberately ignored her after the night they walked home together. Or else she was very vain and was deceiving herself. She hoped not. She would test the waters.

"You caught me! Yes, I wanted some time by myself so I avoided letting Lady Bailey see me leaving."

"Oh! I am sorry. I *am* disturbing you then." She turned to leave, hoping that he would stop her.

"No! Stay." James instinctively caught her by the arm to prevent her from leaving. He immediately dropped it as he realised what he had done, but the silky feel of her skin remained imprinted on his palm and in his memory. "You are welcome to join me." Jemima hid her smile of triumph.

"Are you afraid to touch me?" she asked boldly. "You were not the other night when you took away my knife."

Her bold question took James by surprise, but he quickly recovered. "Why would I be afraid to touch you?"

"Maybe you are afraid that you would be betraying your wife if you wanted another woman."

"I cannot believe we are having this conversation," he prevaricated.

"Two attempts and you have not yet answered my question," she mocked him. "Therein lies my answer. You do not need to be afraid of me," she smiled at him provocatively.

"I assure you that I am not," James insisted.

"Prove it!"

"Jemima, that is beyond childish. I do not need to prove anything."

"Well, you would not mind if I ran my fingers through your hair? I have desired to feel it."

"What?" James exclaimed in disbelief at her brazen request, wondering if she had somehow read his mind earlier.

"Do you object?"

"Of course I object! Ladies do not go around asking men to do that."

"I have told you before, I am not a lady."

Without waiting for his consent, she pulled one end of the thong holding back his hair until it came undone and she put it in her pocket. She ran her fingers through his thick locks, grazing his scalp with her fingertips. Her fingertips tingled with pleasure and she enjoyed the sensation of the soft hair cascading between her fingers. James closed his eyes as sensations he had almost forgotten exploded in his body.

"It is lovely and soft," she praised. James fought to keep his hands at his sides and clenched his fists with the effort. "Thank you for letting me feel it."

"I don't recall giving you permission," he corrected hoarsely. He held out his hand for the thong, which she handed over without their hands touching. Jemima considered that she had won that round and she was pleased to know that James was not as immune to her as he pretended. She saw, with satisfaction, that his hands shook slightly as he tied back his hair again.

"That did not hurt, did it?" she challenged. James thought that was a matter of opinion, for his body was still responding to her touch.

"Is it all right with you if I sit for a while?"

"I am afraid there is only the ground for seating." James hoped that would put her off.

"I do not mind," she assured him.

"I wonder that no one has ever thought to put a bench out here." That was something he would do if he ever managed to own the plantation, he decided.

They settled against the tree with their shoulders touching, for his took up more than his fair share of the back rest.

"Hetty is helping me out, so I have a few minutes before I have to start to prepare lunch."

"Hetty is a good girl," James said as he tried to ignore the curly hair that tickled his neck and made his skin prickle with awareness. He should have left his hair loose to cover his neck.

"Yes. She thinks well of you. She said that you are kind to her."

"Am I not kind to you too?" he asked.

"Indeed. It seems that you are kind to everyone. What a *kind* man you are," she said sarcastically.

"What is wrong with being kind? Do you see it as weak? Weak is a man who beats a woman, even if he owns her. In fact, that in itself is wrong."

"Like Lord Bailey? Hetty told me that you stopped him from beating her. That seems to be a habit with you."

He did not answer, for he did not want to dishonour his host – even though he was dishonourable – and he did not respond to her jibe. She seemed to somehow resent the fact that he had also helped Hetty, though he could not think why.

"Let us talk of something else, like the view. In England it would be the weather," he joked.

"This is a beautiful spot," she breathed, following his suggestion as she gazed on the view of the east coast.

"Yes. It's my favourite place on the plantation."

"Speaking of England, what do you do there?"

"My family owns a shipping business and we ship goods to and from England."

"You own ships?" Jemima sat up and looked at him excitedly.

"Yes," he answered reluctantly, for he knew where her thoughts were going.

"And yet you cannot take me back to England with you? It is not that you cannot, it is that you will not!"

"What is it with all you women wanting me to take you to England?" James asked angrily.

"Who else wants you to take her to England? Is it Lady Bailey? Is that why you did not want her to know where you were going?" she asked suddenly, as she remembered what he had said before.

James hesitated to answer as he did not want to expose Mary-Ann. And, to tell the truth, he was quite reluctant to admit that she was pursuing him, for he felt it would make him seem vain.

"She seemed very intimate with you when they came to lunch," Jemima prompted, settling back against the tree. James was surprised she had noticed since she had been so busy smiling at Samuel.

"Perhaps she would like to be, but I am not of a mind to make a cuckold of another man."

"What is a cuckold? I am not familiar with that word."

"It is the term given to a man who has an adulterous wife," James explained.

"Oh, I think he is already a cuckold," she laughed. "You have taught me a new word today."

"Before you told me about your father, I had wondered how it is you are so well spoken," James admitted, unknowingly giving Jemima a little surge of pleasure that he thought that she spoke well. In fact, that he thought about her at all. Maybe there was hope.

"As I began to tell you last week, he was a schoolteacher who came to Barbados from England. He taught children at several of the plantations. That is how he met my mother. She was a house slave at one of the plantations but when he saw her he fell in love with her and asked to buy her freedom. Fortunately, he was able to do so, so I was born free, but they were never married." James was amazed at how closely her story matched his, except that his parents had married.

"So, how did you come to be indentured to Mrs. Perch?"

"My mother indentured us after my father died when Mr. Perch was still alive," she explained and briefly shared her story. "I have two more years to go, but I feel as if I cannot endure another month. Especially if Mrs. Perch will continue to rent me out to men such as the Major." He felt her give a shudder.

"Did he..." James trailed off, reluctant to ask her what he wanted to know. She nodded ashamed of how she had been used in that way, without her consent. It was not that she was innocent, for Tobias had been her benefactor and there had been other men. However, she had no desire to lie with the Major, but she had no choice unless she chose to kill him and forfeit her own life.

James wanted to offer words of comfort but felt like a hypocrite, for even knowing what she had endured, he still found himself having to fight against the awareness of her pressed against his side and the softness of her hair that blew across his face occasionally before she had time to catch it.

"I am sorry. Please be careful with Lord Bailey. I am afraid that he may try to do the same."

"I am not worried about Lord Bailey. At least he is not as disgusting as the Major, who is old and wrinkled. I must do what I can to earn money to buy my freedom, but it will be on my terms. If he wants to make me his mistress and he has money to give me, I am willing."

"What?" James recoiled in horror. "You would welcome Samuel Bailey even though he is married?" he asked in disbelief.

"Their marriage seems not to be a marriage. Did you not say his wife wants to lie with you?"

"That is no excuse for you to do the same with her husband."

"Well, you are not willing to help me, so why do you care what I do to help myself?"

"Do you not value yourself?"

"Yes, that is why I can no longer be anyone's slave. I will value myself even more after I am free," she reasoned.

"That makes no sense," he argued.

"It is easy for you to say. You, who are free to make choices, to go anywhere and do anything. I have no freedom, so I am willing to do whatever is necessary to get it. It is nothing that I have not done before. I will use what I have to get what I want."

"You are able to cook exceptionally well. Why don't you try using that instead?" he challenged her. "Or had you not thought of that?"

He gave her a hard look before pushing himself off the ground abruptly. "I think I have had enough air. I'm going back to the house." He did not wait for her to reply as he gathered his writing bag and strode across the grass, disgusted that she would sell herself to gain her freedom.

Is that not what your mother did? a voice in his head reminded him.

The words gave him pause and he almost turned back. His mother, whom he loved and admired, had sold herself to his father for her freedom and he did not think any less of her for it. Who was he to judge Jemima? What a hypocrite he was!

Chapter 14

By the time James returned to the house, he had determinedly put off the guilt he was feeling and had promised himself to apologise to Jemima the next time he saw her. It seemed as if he was forever apologising to her for something. He couldn't explain his change of heart, but he could at least let her know that he was sympathetic to her plight. His conscience smote him, for he knew that he could pay for her indentureship and give her the freedom that she longed for. He had the means to do it and it would not make a considerable difference to the money he would need to acquire The Acreage if the opportunity arose. He would give it some thought. *What is there to think about?* his conscience asked him.

When he reached the patio, Samuel was at the table eating a bowl of porridge which seemed to be the breakfast of choice, at least for those who had imbibed vast quantities of liquor. Thankfully, Mary-Ann was nowhere to be seen.

"Good morning," James greeted him with an effort. He was still disturbed by his conversation with Jemima and the thought of her with Samuel was enough to make his stomach churn.

"I don't know what is so good about it," growled Samuel. "My head is pounding and my stomach feels like there is a fight going on in it, hence the porridge. Do sit down."

"Thank you. I am your partner in misery, I assure you. Remind me never to imbibe that much brandy in one sitting again," James told him as he joined him at the table.

"Believe me, nor will I." He held his head in his hands briefly before tackling the porridge again, albeit with little enthusiasm. "I will have a quiet day indoors, for I certainly cannot contemplate being in the sun today, with my head feeling the way it does. I am sure that the harvest will be uninterrupted without my presence."

James could concur with that, for from his observations, Samuel did very little to aid the process.

"I was thinking the same thing," James agreed. "I may spend some time updating my journal, for it has been sadly neglected."

"That's fine. I must say, I do not even know if I can do justice to anything that your girl might cook today," he groaned. James laughed in sympathy.

"I think I will retire to my room. I will see you later."

Before he could push his chair back, loud wailing and shouting that sounded as if it was coming from around the corner of the house arrested him and froze him to the spot.

"What the devil is that?" Samuel demanded, rising from his chair. James stood as well, as a shabbily dressed slave woman tore around the corner, face wet with tears and wild-eyed with anguish. Behind her a fearful-looking slave was trying in vain to hold her back.

"My child gone! My child gone! Wha' you do wid my child?" the first one screamed in the direction of Samuel and James.

"Sorry, Massa. Molly los' she head," the other one interrupted, increasing her efforts to stop the distraught woman from coming any closer.

"I'll say she's lost her head! Get her back to work before she gets a whipping she won't forget! Now go!" he commanded.

The one who was pulling the woman called Molly was joined by one of the men who had been painting the wall and they managed to get her under control and drag her away so that she was prevented from further disturbing the master's breakfast.

"What was that about?" James asked Samuel, although it was not a question that needed answering, for the answer was obvious. His anger began to grow as he waited for Samuel to respond.

"I assume that was the mother of one of the children that I arranged to sell today," Samuel replied nonchalantly as he turned back to his porridge. He grimaced as he put the now lukewarm cereal into his mouth.

"You assume that was the mother of one of the children you sold?" James repeated slowly. "You sold that woman's child, tore her family apart and you *assume?*" James' voice was hoarse with anger and disbelief.

"My dear boy, they should know not to get too attached to their offspring, for sometimes we need to sell some of our excess slaves to generate cash flow. We have had some unexpected expenses and my creditors will extend no more credit at the moment, so I find myself in the unenviable position of having to liquidate some of my assets."

"Liquidate your assets!" James could barely force the words from his mouth as the anger consumed him. He shoved his chair back and abruptly grabbed his bag and left the patio lest he acted on his instinct to liquidate Samuel himself. At the moment, he was entirely capable of thrashing him to an unrecognisable pulp without any qualms.

He stormed through the house and up the stairs to his room where he slammed the door behind him and leaned back against it until his breathing was under control. Striding to the bed, he threw down the bag and took out his writing instruments and paper. His hands shook with the effort not to give vent to his anger.

The Acreage
Tuesday

I cannot even remember what the date is today, for I am so furious that I am afraid of how easily I could lose control. I have never felt the likes of this fury before. Slavery is a diabolical system! And Samuel Bailey is the devil himself! I will get this plantation from him somehow, for he is not worthy of it!

I was sitting at breakfast with him and a slave woman came upon us wailing. Her soul was clearly in agony. Samuel Bailey had sold her child (among others) for a few pounds to meet his expenses and could not care less that he had torn a family apart. He said that they should know better than to get attached to their offspring!

I am amazed that I was able to restrain myself, for I was close to beating him beyond recognition with my bare hands. Had he shown so much as a sign of repentance for the distress he had caused the woman I would have believed there was a heart beating in his chest, but I swear that the man is without conscience and his only god is money. Well, I will show him that his god has clay feet.

I have never before considered invoking an imprecatory prayer on anyone, but at this moment I am angry enough to ask God to send down fire and consume his sorry soul. I do not know how I will even stomach to look at him, but I ask for the grace to do so, for I will be at The Acreage for the rest of the week and I need to find a strategy while I am here to restore it to my family as I desire to do.

I drank far too much last night, but as the brandy loosened Samuel's tongue, I learned that the plantation is in financial trouble to the point where his creditors have begun to cut off his credit. I do not know how they are going to pay for the dinner party or perhaps the situation is not as dire as all that. Although the sale of the slaves today will no doubt help to cover the cost, it is a very poor business decision to sell an "asset" to pay for a party. It is beyond me why they would need to have a party in any case. It is all a façade.

Jemima came out to my favourite spot and sat with me for a while. I have discovered that her mother died three years ago. I also found out that her father was a teacher who came from England to teach the children of plantation owners, which solves the mystery of why she is able to speak so well. She is a bold one and reminds me much of my mother! She asked if I was afraid of her and ran her fingers through my hair! I am not afraid of her, but I am afraid of the desire that consumed me when she touched me, for I cannot and will not act upon it. How can I indulge in the pleasures of the flesh when I am alive while Harriett is dead because of my negligence? Besides, were I to do so it would not be with Jemima, for she is willing to prostitute herself with Samuel Bailey to get her freedom.

I am trying not to be a hypocrite, for my own mother did the same to secure her own freedom, but I have to admit that the thought turns my stomach, especially after the episode this morning.

Perhaps I should give her the money and save her from offering herself to Samuel Bailey. Or maybe I should let her do as she wills, for she has her mind set on it. If I am honest with myself, I have to admit that though I should not even want such a wanton woman, I fear that I do. Help me, Lord!

ᘓᘏ

A firm knock made him pause in his writing and slip his journal back into the drawer. It was not timid like Hetty's so James knew before the door even opened that it would be Mary-Ann. Naturally, she had not waited for him to bid her enter. It was a wonder that she gave him a brief moment before letting herself in.

"Mary-Ann, do come in," he invited sarcastically since she had already entered and closed the door behind her. "Did you not consider that I might have been indecently clad?"

"My luck has been poor of late, so that was not a concern for me," she laughed, before sobering up. "I came out of worry for you."

"Me?" James had no idea what she could mean.

"I was in my room, but I could not help but hear the wails of that poor slave woman. It was horrible for me to hear, so I knew that witnessing it would have affected you too. We are similar in that regard." She drew nearer to where he stood by the bed. "How are you?" she asked, resting a hand against his cheek.

James knew it was highly inappropriate for her to be in his room, but he could not bring himself to care at that moment. He laughed cynically and moved away from her touch. "I believe you are asking the wrong person that question. I am not the one whose child was wrenched from my arms and sold to another plantation. When the poor woman was dragged away, your husband continued eating his porridge as if nothing had happened."

"You know what he is like from the last time you were here. Now you see what I have to live with. I hate this slavery too, and I myself am little more a chattel, for I have nothing of my own except what he gives me."

"Forgive me if I do not see your suffering that you say is so apparent. All I see are silk and satin dresses."

"Do not be deceived. Things are not always what they seem." James wondered if she knew just how bad things were. Apparently not, or she would not have hired Jemima for the week with plans to hold a party.

"I am well aware of that," James replied. "And some things are exactly as they seem." He hoped that she would get the point.

"I need your help," she implored him.

"How may I be of assistance, my lady?"

"James, I wish you not mock me so. I need your help to go back to England, as I told you before, or…" She looked at James intently as if trying to gauge what his reaction was likely to be to her next words. "Or I'll employ the same means that Mrs. Berringer used to rid herself of her husband."

"What? You are mad, Mary-Ann!"

"Did you not say you have come to love The Acreage? Would you not want to own it and have me as a bonus?" Her voice became seductive and she drew closer. "I am sure you would do a better job of running it than Samuel."

"I said that I had come to love the island. I did not say The Acreage," he corrected her.

"And is The Acreage not a prime piece of the island?" she reasoned. James did not need convincing about that, for he had already reached that conclusion.

"Mary-Ann, you must know, even from our short acquaintance, that there are some things I would never consider doing. Owning The Acreage by foul means is one. The other is –" She silenced his words with her fingers.

"James, I would never try to force you to do anything against your will. In fact, I fear that I cannot, for you are a strong-willed man. But even Achilles had his heel," she laughed and ran her hand down his chest. When James realised that she seemed intent on continuing the path her hand was travelling, he quickly caught it in his.

"Mary-Ann, please cease from making these advances. I have no intention of succumbing to you and, although I find your husband to be a despicable human being, I will not join with you in cuckolding him, or worse yet, poisoning him. I suggest you get that idea out of your head before you find yourself on the gallows."

"Don't be absurd, James. There are ways that make death seem like natural causes. Have you not heard of foxglove?"

"Mary-Ann, please do not take me into your confidence, for I may call the authorities for you myself if your husband is found dead."

"Really, James! When you can have the plantation and its mistress?" James wanted the plantation, but he was very wary of its mistress. There was no denying that she was a beautiful woman, but his mind was focused on an olive-skinned beauty with wild curly hair.

"I will pretend that you did not say that. For the remainder of my visit, I will endeavour to be polite to your husband and I thank you for being such a generous hostess. However, please do not come to my room again and please do not try to tempt me to secure the plantation by dishonest means. Is that clear enough for you?"

"Crystal clear. Now let me make myself clear. I always get what I want, one way or the other, and I have decided that I want you. Is *that* clear enough for you?" She turned on her heels and strode to the door, leaving in the same way that she came except that he was now in total turmoil.

James flopped back on the bed and covered his eyes with his hand. How he would love some peace in his life. He was caught between a woman who would willingly sell herself for her freedom and one who would willing kill her husband for hers. How did he get into this situation? His headache, which had abated as he wrote in his journal, was now making its presence felt again. Surely, God had no part in bringing him to Barbados to be tempted by these women. It was said that he didn't give you more than you could bear, but he was beginning to question that, for he felt close to giving in to the temptation of one of them.

Chapter 15

"We couldn't keep Jemima's cooking all to ourselves, so we have invited the Bowyers over for dinner," Mary-Ann announced when James went down to sit on the patio with a book later that day. He marvelled at how she could act as if she had not come to his room hours earlier to try to conspire with him to poison her husband. He was of the mind that she was truly mad, as he had accused her of being.

"I believe you mentioned them before. I am sorry, but their names escape me," James confessed.

"Henry and Susan," Mary-Ann reminded him.

"Oh yes, and they have two daughters. I remember now."

"Indeed. The girls are rather unfortunate to have inherited their father's features, but they are nice girls. So, we will dine a little earlier this evening at about half past five."

"That will be fine. I believe I will take a walk about the plantation for a bit before I get ready for dinner," he told her.

The time for dinner came around quite swiftly and James roused himself sufficiently to dress. He was not looking forward to the evening, truth be told, for he had no desire to dine in the presence of Samuel, but he had no choice as he was a guest for the next few days. Thankfully, he was fully over the effects of the night before and was at least eagerly anticipating another one of Jemima's meals. He was also glad that there would be company at dinner as they would act as a buffer between him and the Baileys.

When he reached the bottom of the stairs his hosts were greeting the Bowyers in the foyer. He glanced over them swiftly before they noticed him and he immediately recognised that Mary-Ann was indeed honest in her opinion of the daughters' features. They were quite plain, with fine hair that was a dull brown. Not much could be done with it, although their maid (he presumed) had apparently done her best to fashion it into some sort of style. Their father was quite portly and what remained of his hair was the same brown colour. Their mother had a pleasant face and was just a few pounds shy of her husband's considerable weight. He was sure that the husband and wife would do justice to Jemima's dinner.

"There you are, James." Mary-Ann spotted him first. "Come and meet our guests. James, meet Henry and Susan Bowyer and their daughters Faith and Grace. This is James Fairfax, our guest for a few days."

"Delighted to meet you," he said politely, shaking hands with Henry and bowing over the ladies' hands elegantly. "And what lovely names." The girls blushed while Mrs. Bowyer exclaimed how charming he was. She immediately began to size him up for her elder daughter, Faith.

"Mr. Fairfax are you travelling alone or is there a Mrs. Fairfax?" she asked.

"I am alone," James replied without answering the latter part of her question.

"Fairfax. Hmm. I seem to remember a chap by the name of Fairfax who stayed here several years ago. He was an American, though, not English," Mr. Bowyer commented.

"Indeed? How remarkable," James replied, praying that he would not ask if there was any connection, for he had no idea how he would respond to that question.

"What a small world," Mary-Ann remarked. "Why don't we go through to the dining room. I am sure dinner is ready and we are all eager to sample Jemima's cooking."

James was relieved that she had changed the subject, but when he caught her eye, she looked at him curiously, making his relief short-lived. He could tell that she had filed away that piece of information for later examination.

"I hope you have recovered from last night, my boy," Samuel told him jovially. He also seemed to suffer from forgetfulness for there was no indication that he remembered their interaction earlier that day. "We imbibed rather heavily last night, Henry, I have to confess."

"I know too well how that goes. And you do always have the finest brandy, Samuel."

"I would be happy to share a glass or two with you after dinner," Samuel offered, the sickness of that morning now forgotten.

The table in the dining room was beautifully set with plates bearing a coat of arms, which must have belonged to Samuel's family, sparkling glasses and shining cutlery. On reaching the room, Mary-Ann organised the seating. She placed Henry to the right of Samuel while she sat at his left with James beside her, Susan opposite James, the older daughter to his left and her younger sister next to her mother. It was a small enough group that they could all converse with each other, if they desired to do so.

Once they were seated, Hetty came in to offer drinks followed by Jemima and Dottie who came in to serve the first course. James' eyes immediately sought Jemima's face, but she made no eye contact with him or anyone else, which was uncharacteristic of her. She was wearing a plain dress and the usual handkerchief that hid her hair. She served each person their soup from the tray that Dottie was carrying.

This evening she seemed rather subdued and did not introduce herself as she had at the boarding house. Perhaps she was taking her cue from the other slaves. James could not help but look around the table to gauge the response of the other diners to her. Susan Bowyer was busy talking to Mary-Ann across the table and did not pay any attention to the slaves, not even acknowledging when the soup was placed before her. Her daughters were the opposite of their talkative mother and made no conversation but focused intently on the soup. Their father, on the other hand, literally licked his lips as Jemima leaned over to serve his soup. James felt his ire rising in him at the blatant lust in his eyes. Samuel acknowledged Jemima with a nod, which was a lot for him as he generally ignored his slaves when they served him.

"Years ago, The Acreage was known as having the best-looking house slaves in the country. Are you trying to regain the reputation, Samuel?" Henry chuckled. James wondered if that was when his mother was there. It was hard to imagine her serving guests as Jemima was now doing. Henry Bowyer would very likely have been one of those guests if he was a friend of his uncle's. Had he lusted after his mother the way he was lusting after Jemima? James had to forcibly restrain himself from making a cutting remark.

"Alas, this one is a rental," Samuel replied regretfully. At which Henry leaned over and said something for Samuel's ears only. Although James could not hear his words, the smug look on Samuel's face said enough.

"Well, let us eat before it goes cold," Mary-Ann announced. James knew that grace was not part of the practices at The Acreage so he silently gave thanks for his meal and added a quick prayer to hold his peace in spite of any provocations. He was, after all, a guest in the Baileys' home and he had no desire to insult their friends or offend them.

There were murmurs of approval as the guests sampled the soup, and James found himself feeling secretly proud of Jemima.

"I understand why you rented the girl," Henry said in praise. "This is outstanding."

"Indeed it is," his wife agreed, making quick work of hers.

"James introduced us to Jemima's wonderful talent when he invited us to lunch at The Royal Inn. That is where she is from," Mary-Ann informed them. "We are grateful to him, for she will be cooking for our party on Saturday. James is such a dear boy," she said in a motherly fashion, but the hand that squeezed his upper thigh under the table was anything but motherly. James discreetly removed it without spilling a drop of the delicious soup that was on its way to his mouth.

"Yes. The proprietress, Mrs. Perch, will be offering lunch to the public every Friday, so if you are in town you should go and have lunch," James informed them.

"Indeed we will," Mrs. Bowyer agreed enthusiastically.

"So, what do you do in England?" Henry asked.

"I'm into shipping," James answered.

"Shipping? That's very strange for I am sure that Fairfax fellow was also involved in shipping. What a coincidence."

"Well, Fairfax is a common enough name," he offered, hoping that would put an end to the conversation.

"Well, you wouldn't want to be associated with him even if you were some kind of distant kin, for he married a coloured woman who used to be a slave here and I believe they left the island, probably to go back to America."

"He married a coloured woman who used to be a slave? A white man? What is the world coming to?" exclaimed Susan. "I did not know that. How scandalous!"

James was trying to decide if to confess that he was the offspring from the scandalous union just to see the look on their faces, but he knew that if he had any hope of buying The Acreage he had to keep quiet.

"She was a real beauty, though, and a feisty one. My good friend William, who lived here at the time, can attest to that," Henry laughed suggestively. Samuel joined his laughter.

James dropped his spoon abruptly as a red haze of anger blinded him to reason. He was not sure what he would have done, but a firm hand on his thigh rooted him to the chair. He cast a quick look at Mary-Ann who seemed intent on her soup, but her hand remained on him as if cautioning him not to react. Did she suspect that he was somehow related to the Fairfax who had stayed there or did she think he would reveal his sympathy to the slaves? He squeezed her hand in thanks as he strove to put off his anger and was relieved when she removed hers and he felt something in him warm to Mary-Ann for the first time. She had protected him from himself. Lord, he needed to get control of this anger before it caused him to do something he would regret. He was normally given to anger, but in Barbados he seemed to be perpetually angry. What was wrong with him?

"That was wonderful. I cannot wait to see what Jemima will delight us with next," she announced, smoothing over the moment.

"I as well," Susann Bowyer said enthusiastically. She looked as if she was restraining herself from tipping the bowl to her head to drain the last of the soup that evaded the spoon.

James was happy that the rest of the meal was uneventful. He relaxed more when Jemima did not come out again, leaving Hetty and Dottie to serve the delicious dishes that she had prepared. The two Bowyer girls could have been invisible for all the conversation they contributed, but their parents made up for their reticence. Thankfully, James was able to learn information about the state of the sugar industry in the island and who was doing what. The Bowyers obviously had no knowledge of the state of affairs at

The Acreage, especially since the front walls, at least, had been painted before their carriage drew up.

It was with great relief that James excused himself when the men announced they were going to Samuel's office for a brandy and the women headed for the patio where it was cooler than inside the house. He took the opportunity to slip out to the kitchen and catch Jemima's attention.

"Jemima, I need to speak to you. Can you slip up to my room when you get a minute? It is at the end of the hallway. Please try not to be seen."

"Why would you want me to come to your room, Mr. Fairfax?" she asked coldly. "Are you not afraid I will corrupt you with my vile behaviour?"

"Jemima, I am sorry for judging you today. That is what I want to talk to you about. I would like to make restitution for my behaviour. Will you come?" He saw her soften slightly, but she was not letting him escape so easily.

"I will try," she agreed.

ꕥ

James paced restlessly in his room as he waited for Jemima to come up. It was still quite early and he hoped she would come while the Baileys were still occupied with their guests. He had made up his mind to pay for her indentureship so that she would not be forced to prostitute herself. His mother had had no one to do the same for her and it still hurt him to think about it. Sometimes he could not believe that his father had been so crass as to blackmail her into his bed and that he had actually owned her. He shook his head at the thought. Although it had all worked out in the end, it was not a part of his family's history that he was proud of. So, he would make sure that Jemima was spared what his mother had not been.

A quiet knock at the door halted his pacing and he quickly crossed to the door to open it. His heart gave a little leap of gladness to see Jemima. Her hair was not covered by a handkerchief, but it was tamed into a plait that hung down her back. James stepped back to allow her to come in, casting a swift glance along the corridor to ensure that no one had seen her.

"I cannot believe you invited me to your room, Mr. Fairfax. Or that I came," she added dryly.

"Jemima, I see we are back to Mr. Fairfax. That could only mean that you have not forgiven me for my remarks this morning."

"I do not recall you asking for my forgiveness." She challenged him with a hard stare. He fought back a smile as he knew it would not go down well with her.

"You are correct. Will you forgive me for judging you harshly? It is just that I think you are too valuable to sell your body to any man who has the money to pay…" he trailed off as he sensed her withdrawal, although she did not move. "I am not doing a very good job of apologising." He grimaced.

"No, you are not," she agreed with a slight smile. That encouraged him. "Nevertheless, I forgive you." She turned to leave, but James caught her arm and halted her exit.

"That is not all I wanted to say to you." James realised that he was still holding her arm and released it somewhat reluctantly. "I want you to know that I understand how you feel." He held up his hand to stop her as she opened her mouth to protest. "I cannot explain it to you now, but I do. So, when we get back to town, I will pay Mrs. Perch the rest of your indentureship and you will have your freedom."

Jemima was speechless. She examined James' face to see if he was joking, but he looked completely serious.

"You will pay off my indentureship?" she repeated in disbelief. "Why?"

"I do not want you to have to sell yourself to earn money to buy your freedom and definitely not to Samuel Bailey. If he comes to your room tonight, turn him away."

"Why are you doing this?" she asked again.

"Should you not be thanking me instead of questioning me?" James asked wryly. The woman was beyond his understanding, for he thought she would be crying with joy, or at the very least expressing her gratitude, but instead she was looking at him with suspicion.

"Forgive me if I seem to doubt you, but I have been promised my freedom before and as you can see, I am still here, so when I have the indenture papers in my hand I will rejoice and thank you then."

"Fair enough. I have given you little reason to trust me."

"That is not true. I believe that you are an honest man. But when you have hoped for something for a very long time, when you get it you still cannot believe that it is yours."

James nodded in understanding.

"Thank you," she said simply and reached up to kiss his lips. He should have stopped her when her lips lingered on his. But he finally got the answer to the question of how soft her lips were and he was not disappointed. In fact, he now found himself greedy for more.

Before any rational thought could form in his mind, he cradled her head in his hands, angling it to access her lips better. While she had initiated the kiss, he now took control and began to devour her mouth like a man who had been starving and had finally come upon a feast. In truth, that well described him, for he had grieved his wife for two years and had had no desire to so much as look at another woman and now it was as if the floodgates had burst open.

Jemima was shocked at the passion that James unleashed, for she had thought him to be somewhat pious; however, there was nothing saintly or staid about his kiss. His kiss left no part of her mouth unexplored and the intensity of it shook her to the core. She had never felt this way before, especially not with Tobias who had been quite lacking in passion. This was the kiss of a man who wanted a woman and she gloried in the fact that she was the woman in his arms.

Her fingers remembered the delight of running through his hair earlier and were quick to reacquaint themselves with the thick strands. He loosened her neat plait and delighted in the thick curls that escaped their confine and sprang around his fingers in fiery abandon. Jemima pressed herself against his hard chest and tugged his shirt free of his breeches so that she could feel his firm back. She was rewarded by a shudder that ran through him, but her delight that she could affect him so was cut off abruptly when he dragged his mouth from hers and put her away from him. His hands were still holding her shoulders and his voice was hoarse with need as he said, "Jemima, we can't do this. I am sorry that I got carried away."

"Why can't we?" she challenged him breathlessly. She wanted him as she had never wanted another man, and he was saying no? What man turned down what a woman was willing to give? "You are no longer married." She saw him wince and was sorry she had said it, but it was true. His wife had been dead for two years. Surely, he was in need of a woman in his bed and she was very willing.

"Nor are we," he said flatly. "Only today I told you that you should value yourself and just a few hours later you are willing to come to my bed? Why? Because I said I would give you your freedom?"

"I am sorry if I mistook your passion for an invitation to your bed," she said sarcastically.

James closed his eyes in shame. "I am sorry. I got carried away, but I do not expect you to pay me for your indentureship by lying with me. It will be a gift. A gift means that you do not have to pay."

"What if I want to thank you in this way? It is the only way I know how," she said quietly.

"You no longer have to do that. You don't have to do it on your own. God can help you."

"Don't talk to me about God. He has never helped me before so why would he help me now? I can do this on my own."

"He loves you more than you know," James insisted. Jemima looked unmoving, so he decided not to press her. "Please know that you are too valuable to offer yourself for a quick frolic in the sheets with me," he reproved her gently.

"I was hoping it would not be that quick," she teased, breaking the seriousness of the moment and was pleased when he laughed at her boldness.

"Believe me, after two years of celibacy, it would be quick," he joked. "Now you had better go to your room before someone discovers you here."

Jemima reluctantly made her way to the door, looking back at him regretfully before letting herself out. James let out the breath that he was holding. He longed to call her back and slake the hunger that kissing her had loosed, like a lion catching the scent of its prey, but he fought for control until his mind won the battle over his body, at least on this occasion.

As he sank down on the bed feeling suddenly drained and despondent, he realised that he had not once thought about Harriett while his lips were on Jemima's. In fact, he had not thought about Harriett very much since the olive-skinned temptress had come into his life. This time, rather than feel guilty, he somehow felt that he was once again becoming whole and that Harriett would want that for him. However, he prayed for the strength to resist Jemima. He would have to make sure that he avoided spending time alone with her. Surely, that should not be so hard to do.

Chapter 16

James' eyes sprang open and he looked around the darkened room trying to see what had awakened him. Nothing seemed out of place. The door was still closed and Mary-Ann wasn't standing over him, thank God. Yet, something had woken him up after what seemed like just a few minutes of sleep but must have been longer. He now felt an urgent need to get up. That must have been what woke him. His mind immediately flew to Jemima and he threw back the sheet and hurried to the chair where he had thrown his breeches. Pulling them on hastily under his night shirt, he raced through the door.

He didn't even stop to light a lamp and ran almost blindly along the dark hallway until he came to the staircase which he ran down and headed towards the back of the house where he knew the house slaves slept. He hesitated, not knowing which door Jemima's was, then he heard a muffled cry coming from behind one of them. He burst through the door into a small room. The light from a lantern shone on Jemima as she faced the door with Samuel standing close behind her. One of his hands was covering her mouth, which explained the muffled sounds, and the other was groping inside the neckline of her chemise. Jemima looked more angry than afraid, but all of James' protective instincts urged him to save her.

"Samuel, what the devil are you doing?" he spat out. Jemima mumbled angrily beneath the hand over her mouth and tried to evade his other hand.

"My dear boy, what does it look like I'm doing? I'm about to sample the non-culinary delights of our guest cook."

James could not believe that Samuel was calmly standing before him touching Jemima in a way that he would never give himself the liberty to do. All the anger that he had recovered from that morning rose in him again and he launched himself at Samuel, pulling him off Jemima, who scampered out of the way, and shoving him towards the door. He was shaking with anger as he sought to restrain himself from punching his host several times in the face or breaking the hand that had dared to touch Jemima so intimately. He begged the Lord for the strength to resist.

"Keep your hands off her," he snarled instead. "She is not one of your slave girls. She is here under my protection so do not touch her again. Is that understood? If you so much as look in her direction inappropriately, I will make sure that you regret it. Do I make myself clear?"

"How dare you speak to me that way?" Samuel blustered. "I will not stand here –"

"Do I make myself clear?" James repeated, approaching him in a threatening manner. Samuel took a step back.

"As crystal. You only had to tell me that she was for your own use, you know. I would never have trespassed on your property."

"See that you do not trespass again!"

James heard Jemima gasp behind him at being called his property, but he did not waver. He would let Samuel think that Jemima was his if that would make him keep his distance.

Samuel held up his hands in surrender and picked up the lantern on his way out, leaving them in darkness. James hoped that he had taken him seriously and had not only left with plans to come back at a more opportune time. He almost considered taking her back to his room, but he didn't think his self-control was ready for another test, especially after seeing her clad in her thin chemise. In any case, he didn't imagine that Samuel would strike again tonight, so Jemima should be safe.

"I'm leaving now. Put something behind the door," James instructed her and left the room without a backward glance. He paused outside the door until he heard her dragging something heavy and pushing it against the door. For once she obeyed what he told her to do. She was learning. Now all he had to do was obey his conscience which was telling him to forget what he saw and he would be fine.

When James reached his room, he was still in a fighting mood and he was sorry that he let Samuel escape so easily. The man was without scruples and so was his wife. They truly deserved each other. He wouldn't be surprised if he was asked to leave the plantation, for this was the second time that he had intervened to stop Samuel from abusing a woman. The only reason he would likely continue to tolerate his presence was so that he wouldn't leave and take Jemima with him before the party. He certainly hoped that it would be the last altercation he would have with his host and hostess, for he was growing tired of it all.

Although he couldn't complain about the comfort of the bed, he found it difficult to get back to sleep. He was puzzled. Why had he woken up and felt to go to Jemima? Was there some connection between them? Was it God who woke him up? He felt so far from God right now, would he even sense his prompting, especially with the thoughts about Jemima that kept tormenting him? Seeing her as he did just now did not help either.

He was behaving in such an uncharacteristic fashion since he had come to Barbados. It seemed he was constantly angry about something. There was nothing wrong with being angry as long as he didn't allow it to make him do something he would regret, like murdering Samuel Bailey. A picture of him groping inside Jemima's chemise caused anger to rise in him again. Surely, killing him for that would be justified, for if he hadn't turned up when he did, he surely would have ravished Jemima. He knew that would only result in his own neck being stretched on the gallows, for while it was no crime to ravish a servant or slave, to murder a white man in Barbados would see him lose his life. Perhaps that foxglove was not a bad idea after all. Even as the thought formed in his mind, he repented of it and prayed what he prayed almost daily since coming to Barbados: *Help me, Lord.*

Next morning

James had barely been asleep for a few hours when he was awoken by a persistent knocking at his door. He groggily called for Hetty to come in, surprised that she had not just knocked and entered quietly in her usual way. He pulled a pillow over his head to block out the light and turned over for some more sleep.

"Are you not getting up today, Mr. Fairfax?" asked a voice that was bolder than Hetty's would ever be.

He threw off the pillow, now wide awake, to see Jemima pouring steaming water into the jug for his morning wash. She tipped the last of it from the bucket she had brought up and turned to face him with a smug smile.

"What are you doing here?" he asked her in a gravelly voice which Jemima found very attractive.

"I brought you hot water."

"I can see that, but Hetty normally does that. You are here to cook, not deliver water."

"You do not like me bringing you water?" she flirted. "I wanted to see how you looked when you have just woken up." Her eyes trailed over his tousled hair as if she remembered running her fingers through it. James' body stirred in response. He, too, would like to see how she looked when she woke up. Dangerous thinking!

"Jemima, please desist. You do not need to flirt with me. I have said that I will pay for your indentureship." He was determined to keep their relationship strictly business.

James turned to arrange the pillows behind him and missed the hurt look on Jemima's face. By the time he had arranged them to his satisfaction and leaned back against the wall, Jemima's face was back to normal.

"How are you this morning?" His eyes searched for any trace of the trauma of the night before and found none. He supposed that what Samuel had done was nothing compared to other abuses she had suffered.

"I am well. After all, you came before he could do much harm. How did you know to come?"

"I do not know, to tell the truth. I was asleep and jumped up suddenly with a feeling of urgency to find you. I suppose the Lord woke me up."

"Why would he do that? He cares nothing for me," she said matter-of-factly.

"Why would he not care for you? He cares for everyone," James insisted.

"So, why would he allow the major and other men to force me to lie with them?"

James had not known of other men. His heart hurt as he thought of her being ill-used by men. He would make sure that it never happened again. But how? Even if he paid for her freedom, how would he protect her, especially if he went back to England? He did not know how to answer but he tried.

"I do not have all the answers, Jemima, but he did say he would never leave us or forsake us."

"Maybe he just means white people," she scoffed as she headed towards the door.

"No, Jemima, he doesn't," he assured her, thinking of his mother and grandmother. "One day I will tell you why I know that."

"I look forward to hearing. Have a good day, James. And thank you for rescuing me once again."

"I am glad I got there in time, although I would that I had been even earlier so that he would not have had the chance to touch you at all."

"Thank you," she said, humbled that he was so concerned when Samuel Bailey had only touched her, when other men had done so much more. He made her feel valuable.

ཤ ཨ

James was deliberately later than usual to breakfast. Hoping not to have to share a table with Samuel, he had taken some time to write in his journal after washing for the day. Unfortunately, Samuel also seemed to have come down later than usual. He immediately noticed a coldness in his host's manner when he pulled out a chair to sit at the breakfast table.

"Good morning. Apologies for my lateness."

"Good morning," Mary-Ann greeted brightly, in stark contrast to Samuel's brief nod. She looked curiously from Samuel to James. "Trouble in paradise?"

She laughed knowingly as if she was aware of the nocturnal happenings. James did not see how she could, but she obviously knew her husband well enough to suspect that he might have tried to pay a visit to Jemima during the night and that James had thwarted it in some way. Neither he nor Samuel answered her.

"How about a visit to one of our friends today, James? I had told the Alleynes at Newlands that I would bring you for a visit during the week. We can also take you around to see Nicholas Plantation, as it's nearby."

James hesitated as he wondered if Samuel would be going as well. Not only did he not desire to go on an outing with Mary-Ann alone, but he did not trust Samuel to be alone in the house with Jemima without his protection.

He saw Mary-Ann look questioningly at him as she sensed his hesitation. The last thing he wanted was her thinking that he was overly concerned about Jemima, for she might wrongly conclude that Jemima had succeeded where she had failed. Although she said that she didn't hold grudges, he couldn't help but remember the words from William Congreve's famous play *The Mourning Bride*: "Heav'n has no Rage like Love to hatred turned, Nor Hell a Fury like a woman scorn'd". Mary-Ann certainly did not love him, but she would not appreciate it if she thought she had been scorned, especially in favour of a coloured indentured servant. That would certainly not bode well for Jemima. While Mary-Ann did not seem to ill-treat her slaves, she would certainly not help Jemima to promote her cooking skills and Mrs. Perch's lunches.

"That sounds like a good idea," he said at last. "I am intrigued to see the property that was worth killing for, for surely no property could be so grand or prosperous that it can equate to the value of a man's life," he added, purely for Mary-Ann's purpose.

"With that I agree," Samuel said at last, breaking the ice. "Certainly, no woman is worth the risk of a man being found guilty of committing murder." James was not sure if that was aimed at him or Mary-Ann, but he breathed in relief when Samuel added: "I do believe I will join you."

"If we set out around ten o'clock and make a brief detour to see Nicholas, we should get there around half past eleven," Mary-Ann said. "Is that fine with you both?" The men nodded and Mary-Ann excused herself from the table, leaving an uncomfortable silence.

James concentrated on eating his breakfast. Eventually, Samuel cleared his throat and said, "I suppose we had better declare a truce, if you are going to be here for the rest of the week."

"I am all for a truce, provided that you maintain your distance from Jemima."

"My dear boy, I take it that you have gotten over your grief and broken your two-year bout of celibacy. But did I not tell you that you had not found the right woman?" He chuckled. "I cannot say that I blame you, for she is an exotic creature."

James said nothing and instead allowed Samuel to think that Jemima was his mistress. He reasoned that if it protected her from Samuel, it would do no harm.

ꟹ

The driveway of Nicholas Plantation was flanked by two solid-looking, imposing walls with its gates open in welcome. The carriage stopped outside the gates from where they could see the house. James was struck by the beauty of it as it sat at the end of the short driveway like a queen attired in white robes on a throne of green. It stood three storeys high and its three curved gables, with decorative ornaments at their pinnacles, resembled crowns. Windows were set in each gable as well as at the other two levels, and there were chimneys on either side of the house.

"I cannot imagine why chimneys would be built here, especially as your kitchens always seem to be detached from the house," he remarked.

"Yes, indeed. It is believed that Berringer brought the house plans back from England and had it built to the specifications without altering them, though he would have been aware that chimneys and fireplaces would have no use on the island," Samuel said with a chuckle.

"Nevertheless, they do give the house a rather charming appearance," Mary-Ann allowed.

"Yes," James agreed. "It is certainly magnificent."

"It is said to be built in 1658," Samuel added.

"And in the Jacobean style, I see," James noted.

"Are you an expert on architecture?" Mary-Ann asked.

"I have an interest in it, but I would by no means claim to be an expert."

"Where does your expertise lie, then?" she asked coyly. James knew he walked right into that one. Mary-Ann did not cease in her suggestive comments, husband or not.

"Oh, I wouldn't want to boast by saying I am an expert in anything, for I believe that expertise becomes apparent when it is demonstrated."

"I am all for demonstration," she agreed, smiling at him. James glanced at Samuel beside her in time to see him roll his eyes in response. He suppressed a smile at the antics of the shameless couple. He should not find them amusing, for it was actually quite sad to see the state of their marriage.

"Mary-Ann, please desist from your insinuations. I would not normally care what you do, but do have some self-respect, especially since James here has formed a liaison with Jemima."

Mary-Ann's head turned sharply to stare at James who almost groaned aloud at Samuel's announcement.

"Is this true, James?" she demanded.

He was trapped by his lie of that morning, or more accurately, his non-confession of the truth. If he denied what Samuel said, he would leave Jemima vulnerable to Samuel's advances and he would also leave himself prey to Mary-Ann's, unless her pride prevented her from pursuing him. Or she may take it as a challenge to supplant Jemima in his bed. He wavered a few moments before he decided.

"Hmm, yes, it is." Forgive me, Lord, for the lies are coming far too easily.

"When did this come about?"

"For goodness sake, Mary-Ann. He is not your son to be questioned like this. Nor your husband," he added dryly. James was glad for the intervention by Samuel, for he had no desire to embellish the falsehood any further. Thankfully, the carriage started up again and James pretended to be engaged by the passing scenery and ignored Mary-Ann's question.

After a while, they came to the plantation house owned by their friends. It was about the size of The Acreage and well-kept with neat hedges flanking the driveway and flowers in profusion around the house. The front door opened and they were greeted by an attractive couple whom James surmised were the Alleynes.

James Fairfax, this is John and Jane Alleyne. James is visiting with us for few days and is from England." Samuel made the introductions.

James greeted them in turn and was pleased to see that the Alleynes seemed very much in love with each other by the way they returned to each other's side and held hands after greeting their guests. For the first time in a while, his heart gave a little pain which he absently rubbed while they were ushered inside.

"And where is that new-born of yours?" Mary-Ann asked. "What have you named him?"

"We have named him Jonathan, after my father," Jane told her. "He is asleep, but I'm sure we will soon hear his voice, for although he is just a month old, he has a good pair of lungs on him and has no qualms about loudly demanding his feed." She smiled indulgently.

"Do come into the living room," her husband invited while his wife instructed a brown-skinned girl who appeared from the rear of the house to bring some refreshments for them. James glanced at her briefly and noticed that she was well-dressed, unlike the slaves at The Acreage.

The room was beautifully decorated with soft couches and fine rugs on the floor. Their hosts allowed them to choose their seats before taking the loveseat where they could sit close to each other. He was surprised to see John take his wife's hand in his once they were seated, but the couple had no qualms about being demonstrative in their presence. With a pang of longing, he realised that even more than physical intimacy, it was that kind of closeness with Harriett that he missed.

"How have you been keeping, Jane?" Mary-Ann asked solicitously.

"I am very well. This pregnancy has left me a little tired, so John is constantly after me to rest." She looked fondly at her husband.

"You know that I am only concerned for you, my dear."

"And where are little Ann and Elizabeth?" Mary-Ann asked, settling into her chair.

"They are in the nursery with their nanny."

"Can I go up and see them? They must be, what, three and four now?"

James noticed that her face softened as she enquired after the other children and wondered if she would have been different if she had been able to have her own, as Samuel had said. He felt a moment of regret for her and could almost understand how the emptiness of her life might drive her somewhat reckless behaviour.

"Yes, that is correct. I will take you up now before we have lunch. They do love their Auntie Mary-Ann."

"I will have to come more often, for I do not want them to forget me. I have brought some gifts for them and the baby too," she added, picking up a bag she had brought with her.

The ladies made their excuses, leaving the men to talk. James watched as John's eyes lovingly trailed after his wife as she left the room, making him jealous for what he no longer had. He wanted a wife to share his life with, have his children and maybe even live at The Acreage with him, if he got his wish. He looked across the room at Samuel who had completely ignored his wife's departure and decided that he was not worthy of Mary-Ann, at least not the woman he had seen today.

He felt his heart further soften towards Mary-Ann. First, she had protected him from giving himself away before the Bowyers and now she was showing a softer side that he found very appealing.

Chapter 17

The room seemed strangely empty after the women left, as though they had taken the life from it. James had no idea why that would be so and he was vaguely disquieted by the idea that he missed Mary-Ann's presence. That was a rather troubling development, especially as he was sitting across from her husband. He was glad for the diversion of John's voice breaking into his thoughts.

"So, James, what brings you to Barbados?"

This was a question that he could answer without too much guilt and he was soon engaged in conversation with John about the various parts of the island he had been.

"We just took him to see Nicholas Plantation on the way here. He was very impressed."

"That is a wonderful property," agreed John. "With an interesting history."

"So I have heard."

"Sir John Yeamans who used to own Yeamans plantation, which Nicholas was called before, was from Bristol," John told him.

"I did not know that," James admitted. "That is rather a coincidence, for I am from Bristol too."

"What a small world! His brother, Robert, was the sheriff, mayor and chief magistrate of Bristol."

"I have never heard of him. But then again, I am ashamed to say that I am not very well acquainted with our history," he confessed.

"Don't be ashamed, my boy. I am learning something new myself," Samuel told him.

"I am sure you would have heard the scandalous tales about the plantation, or rather, its owners," John went on.

"Yes," James admitted.

"Mary-Ann took particular delight in furnishing him with the gory details," Samuel told him.

"Well, that is one thing I need not fear – my wife and a paramour plotting my demise to get my plantation." The men laughed, but James was uncomfortably aware of the fact that Samuel would not be able to say the same with equal confidence.

"Do plantations change hands much here?" James asked, hoping that he wasn't being too obvious.

"They are always people who want plantations, hoping to get rich from our Muscovado Gold. More often than not they have the opportunity to acquire them when the owners are forced to sell because of debt. I've heard that Hope in Christ Church is for sale. And Edgecombe, although that's only seventy-eight acres," John told him.

"Locust Hall and Woodland in St. George are as well," Samuel added.

"And Yorkshire Hall in St. Thomas. That one is quite sizable."

"That is rather a lot of plantations on the market. What sort of price per acre does a plantation go for these days?"

"It varies, as you can imagine. I paid £12,500 for this about three years ago and it's one hundred and fifteen acres. Are you interested in acquiring a plantation?" John enquired.

"I may be. I'm certainly becoming attached to the island. Not that I know anything about running a sugar plantation," James said modestly.

"My dear boy, I had no idea. In fact, I had thought you rather too Quaker-ish to consider owning a plantation. He is too sympathetic to deal with slaves as they need," he offered to John in explanation.

"I happen to believe that negroes are people too, with the same needs and feelings that we have, and we do not need to beat them to make them work," James upheld.

"I don't know how well any plantation would work with that approach," Samuel said.

"Perhaps you should try it and see," James retorted before he could stop himself. "But why are so many plantations for sale? Is the sugar industry experiencing financial challenges?" He changed the subject deliberately.

"There have been some challenges, so quite a few plantations are for sale since they have become much indebted," John told him. "However, sometimes it is not that the plantation is not prosperous, but rather, the owners are living lavishly and beyond their means."

James was surprised at the frankness with which John was speaking, but he was pleased with the information that he was receiving. Samuel made no comment, which was telling in itself.

"Another thing that is happening with greater frequency is that merchants from England are lending money to plantation owners here and when they cannot repay it, they either take over the plantation or sell it." James was sure that Samuel looked rather uncomfortable as John shared that information, suggesting he might be in the same position.

"Interesting," was all he remarked, but his mind was already bent on finding out if The Acreage was in such a position.

Their conversation was interrupted by the ladies returning from their visit to the nursery. Mary-Ann looked somewhat wistful at first, but she quickly smiled and declared that she had got her fill of hugs from the girls, so she was happy. James, however, noticed that her smile faded as quickly as it appeared. Fortunately, Jane announced that it was time for lunch and ushered everyone into the dining room, giving her a chance to recover.

The meal was good, not to the standard of Jemima's but very satisfying. James was even more satisfied with the information that he had learned that day. He now knew the kind of prices that plantations were selling for in Barbados and he knew that merchants were prepared to sell their mortgages. All he had to do now was find out who The Acreage was mortgaged to and if the mortgagor was prepared to sell. All in all, it was a very good day.

The passengers in the carriage were silent as they drove back to The Acreage, with each one seemingly lost in their own thoughts. James had no idea what Samuel was thinking, but from the wistfulness on Mary-Ann's face, he suspected that she was thinking about the children she had never had. His heart ached a little for her and he suddenly felt the need to break the silence and free her from her distressing thoughts.

"Thank you for taking me to meet your friends. They seem like a very nice couple."

"Oh, they are. Very much in love as you can see, and their children are delightful," Mary-Ann smiled at him. She seemed happy for her friends as he could trace no bitterness in her voice, although she had neither a happy marriage nor children. That told him a lot about her character, despite everything else. It was a pity that she found herself in a loveless marriage with Samuel, and he wondered if there was any hope for them.

"Well, I must say that the plantation seems to be doing well. Everything looked well maintained and the spread that they put on was very impressive," Samuel praised. "Although not as good as Jemima's, eh, James." He smiled suggestively. "Our girl is very talented."

Our girl? James thought. The sooner he got Jemima back to town the better, lest Samuel decide that he wanted to share *their* girl.

"Yes, she is," was all he said.

"Well, I for one cannot wait until Saturday. All our neighbours will be in fits of jealousy when they sample Jemima's food. That reminds me that I need to tell her I will need her to help serve."

"Don't you have enough girls to serve?" James asked. He found himself feeling very possessive at the thought of Jemima been exposed to the planters. He sternly reminded himself that he was paying for her freedom, not taking over the indentureship, and therefore he had no say in what she did. He could just imagine the sly offers she would get from the planters, if they were anything like Samuel. The thought of her accepting any of them made him feel like hiding her away and it was not only because he was concerned that she did not value herself. He finally admitted that it was because he wanted her himself.

"Jemima is not only talented but pleasing to the eye. If you know anything about Mary-Ann, you will know that she is all about appearances, so she will want not only the food to be appealing but also the servers," Samuel explained wryly.

"Yes, we know she is pleasing to the eye, don't we, James?" Mary-Ann mocked him. "But I would have thought that your sights were set higher than just a servant, delightful as she may be. After all, she cannot give you what you truly want, can she?"

"What are you on about, Mary-Ann?" Samuel asked irritably. "I have no time for riddles and I am sure James has no idea what you are talking about either."

Mary-Ann continued to scrutinise James even as she answered Samuel. "Oh, I am sure that James knows exactly what I am talking about, don't you, James?" she challenged him.

"I am not certain I follow you. You would have to elaborate," James lied, though he had no doubt that she meant The Acreage.

"Oh, James. I am surprised that a man of your high morals would lie with such ease. Oh, but I forgot, you have cast aside your morals." She laughed mockingly.

James had no answer for her. The shame that he had been trying to outrun finally caught up with him, leaving him feeling dirty. He had tainted his reputation by allowing the Baileys to believe that he was intimate with Jemima and he had told countless lies to everyone. It was time to put an end to the deception and confess who he really was. He would do it after the party on Saturday. On second thought, he would do it after he had The Acreage in his hands, for it was still his deepest desire to restore it to their family.

ꕥ

Saturday, April 20, 1726
The Acreage

Saturday broke out in splendour, giving Mary-Ann a perfect day for her party. She had spent most of the week overseeing the preparations and, thankfully, had had little time to try her wiles on him. Or perhaps she had conceded the battle to Jemima. In any case, he made himself very scarce, spending many hours exploring the plantation and talking at length with the overseer to glean what information he could about operating the plantation. Hetty seemed to have reverted to her role, for Jemima no longer brought in his water in the morning and, in fact, he had hardly seen her since he came back from the Alleynes.

He was glad that the day of the party had finally arrived because it meant that they could soon leave The Acreage. He found that he missed teaching the students and he missed the companionship that he had with Jemima through their shared interest. It was as if she was a different person when she was helping to teach the slaves, not focused on herself and her needs but theirs. At least when she was free she would not have to sneak around to get to the school.

He suddenly wondered where she would live and where she would work. Would she be able to find paid employment at one of the restaurants in town? Would she use her cooking talent to start her own business as he had challenged her? How would she afford it? He was beginning to realise that just paying for her freedom was not going to be enough. In fact, it would only be the beginning of a whole new life for Jemima, and he was not sure if she had thought through what she would do. He would have to ask her about that later.

The party was starting quite early in the evening since the next day was Easter and they would all be attending church. Mary-Ann figured that if the party wound up early, the attendees would have the chance to be free of spirits by the time they went to church. James did not intend to indulge in any spirits, for he wanted to keep a clear head and find out as much information as he could from the planters.

He gave his hair a quick comb and secured it in its usual leather thong. He pulled on a navy-blue jacket over a tan waistcoat and cream-coloured breeches and headed downstairs where the first guests were arriving. The Baileys were standing by the front door to welcome their guests and usher them into the sitting room where they were having the party. It was not a dinner party, but rather, they would be serving light refreshments, all made by Jemima. James realised that she must be exhausted and now she also had to help serve.

Mary-Ann gestured for him to join them so that he was part of the welcoming party. He was happy to see the Alleynes again, less so the Bowyers and he recognised some of the people he had met at church. When most of the guests had arrived, Mary-Ann suggested that they join the others while she made a quick visit to the kitchen to tell the girls to start serving the food.

As soon as her back was turned, a gentleman sauntered through the door. He was as well-dressed as the other guests, but there was something about him that lacked refinement. James felt Samuel stiffen at his side and knew that it was caused by the new guest.

"Good evening, gentlemen," he greeted them. "Samuel, I know that my invitation must have been misplaced, for I was aggrieved to hear that you were having a party and I was not invited."

Samuel seemed uncharacteristically at a loss for words before he collected himself and answered, "I am afraid that my wife was in charge of the guest list, so I do not know how you were overlooked. My apologies."

"That is quite all right. These things happen. I hoped that it was not because you did not want me to know that you were throwing a lavish party when –"

"This is our house guest, James Fairfax, from England," Samuel interrupted. James was surprised by his rudeness and intrigued to know what the man was going to say.

"Hello. I am Augustus Berkshire. Pleased to make your acquaintance."

"Likewise."

"We were just going to join the other guests," Samuel told him, gesturing him to proceed. James could tell that Samuel was quite uncomfortable and he knew that it had something to do with the presence of the man who had invited himself. He decided that he would stick close to the uninvited guest and find out what it was about him that made Samuel so discomfited.

The slaves were well turned out tonight, as if Mary-Ann had made sure they were given new clothes for the party. One of the men who worked in the yard served wine and brandy, but thankfully, there were juices as well, so James had a glass of juice. He found himself engaged in conversation with John Alleyne and two other men whose names escaped him. They were discussing how much they needed to fertilise their soil as it was so depleted by the planting of canes. James listened attentively, eager to learn all he could about operating a plantation. Therefore, he was caught off-guard when one of the men stopped in the middle of his sentence and whistled under his breath.

"Who is that tempting morsel serving over there?" He was almost salivating.

James followed his gaze, though he didn't need to, for he knew that he would find Jemima to be the recipient of the stare. Annoyance mixed with a fierce protectiveness stirred in him when his eyes landed on Jemima. My, but she looked beautiful tonight. She wore a silky-looking dress somewhere between green and blue that showed a lot more cleavage than any he had seen her wear before. Her hair was piled on her head in a bun with two curls falling along her cheek to her shoulders. He wanted to sweep her out of there and away from the lustful eyes of the men. Was he any different? Was it only the lust of the flesh or was something else stirring his heart?

She carried a tray of delicacies that she had made and from across the room he could see the men tasting the treats and making comments which caused a smile to transform her face. He was surprised at the rush of jealousy he felt to see other men flirting with her. Surely, she should move on by now and offer her treats to some of the ladies. What had the salivating man asked again?

"That is Jemima. The Baileys have hired her to cook for the party, but she is the cook at The Royal Inn Boarding House. They will be serving lunch every Friday if you find yourself in town any Friday."

"Indeed, I will," he said with alacrity.

"Is she a slave there? I wonder if she is looking for a benefactor," the other man mused aloud.

"She is indentured," James said sharply, "and I do not believe she is looking for a benefactor."

"I think we should let her decide for herself," he chuckled slyly, making James feel like wiping the sly look off his face. "Ah, here she comes now."

"Good evening, gentlemen. Would you like to try some crab cakes?"

"That's not all I would like to try," the first one said. James watched in disgust as Jemima smiled flirtatiously with the men. Why could the girl not see that they only wanted one thing from her?

"Now, gentlemen, I do not believe your wives would approve of your behaviour," John chided them, much to James' satisfaction. At least John was not of the same ilk as the men, who now laughed somewhat self-consciously at his rebuke.

"Thank you, Jemima. That will be all," James dismissed her, earning himself a hard stare, as if she was enjoying the men's lustful attention. He deliberately ignored her and instead changed the subject by recounting for them his earlier meeting of Augustus Berkshire, asking who he was.

"Oh, he's a merchant who holds mortgages on several plantations. I am surprised that Samuel invited him, for I am sure he must hold a mortgage on The Acreage and they are not exactly friends."

James held his tongue. Now he understood Samuel's behaviour earlier. If he was behind in his mortgage payments, he would not have invited the mortgagor to attend a lavish party. He still did not understand why the Baileys would throw a party if they were heavily indebted, unless Mary-Ann did not know the extent of their debt, as men sometimes kept such things from their wives. But he knew who would know and he would make sure that he spoke to him before the night was over. Jemima was the other person he needed to have a word with.

The opportunity presented itself to speak to Mr. Berkshire sooner than he had expected when he excused himself from the men and stepped out onto the patio for some relief from the hot room, only to find the very man he had just enquired about doing the same. He silently thanked God for the opportunity.

"I hope I'm not disturbing you, Mr. Berkshire," he said politely, approaching him.

"Ah, Mr. Fairfax. Not at all. I felt a little hot, not to mention unwelcome, in the room," he laughed cynically.

"I am sorry to hear that you feel unwelcome," James apologised, as if he was the host.

"Don't be sorry. I was not invited, of course. It is quite amusing to see how people who were so eager to court you when they needed your money, try their best to avoid you when they cannot repay it. Yet they can throw grand parties."

"Yes, that has been my experience as well." He did not want to seem too eager to know about his host's financial affairs and he was happy that he did not have to make any further comments for Berkshire continued.

"Yes, I have extended much grace to him and he looks down his nose at me because I am a merchant." He laughed bitterly. "We will see how proud he is when I demand my pound of flesh. Truth to tell, I have no desire to run a plantation and I would like my money repaid." James' ears pricked up at that revelation.

"Are you looking to sell the debt then?" he asked.

"That I am. Are you interested in buying?" Berkshire asked hopefully.

"I am interested, but it depends on the amount, of course."

"Come to my office on Monday and we can talk more. It is on High Street in town. I look forward to meeting with you. Well, at least the party was not a complete waste of time, so I believe I will take my leave now," he announced.

"Thank you. I will be leaving here Monday morning, so I should be there by noon." James held out his hand with a smile as he and Augustus Berkshire exchanged firm handshakes.

As he turned to go back inside, he was thankful for the divine appointment. He felt a stirring of excitement that things were falling into place. It looked as if the way was being opened for him to get his hands on The Acreage.

Chapter 18

Jemima stomped back to the kitchen with her tray that was now empty after she had made her rounds of the room. Who did James Fairfax think he was? How dare he dismiss her like that? If she did not need him to pay for her indentureship as he had promised she would tell him exactly what she thought of the dismissive way he had spoken to her.

"Wha' happen to you?" the cook asked her on seeing her face.

"That man James Fairfax! He thinks he can tell me what to do!" she fumed.

"Wha' he do to you?" she laughed.

"I was serving some men who were flirting with me. It was all harmless and he told me "that will be all" in this cold voice. As if I am his servant!"

"He jus' jealous."

"Jealous? He doesn't want me himself, so why should he be jealous?"

"You know how these men does be, girl. And don' think that he don' want you. It just that he trying to be decent. You could see that he is a decent man." Jemima reflected on how he had treated her with respect and consideration in the past and the fight suddenly went out of her.

"Too decent for the likes of me," she lamented, suddenly feeling like a dirty rag that many people had wiped their feet on. "I may as well get one of those other men to support me."

"Child, if you could support yourself, don' rely 'pon no man to support you. You could use your cooking to get a job when your indenture done or you could do your own thing. You ain' got to work for that woman all the time."

Jemima had not told anyone that James had promised to pay for her indentureship. She still wasn't sure it would really happen. When was the last time something good happened to her? She would wait and see. But do her own thing? She had not thought beyond being free. Could she start her own business? Where would she get the money?

She automatically took another tray as her mind started thinking about the possibilities and headed back towards the house. She could work for herself instead of Mrs. Perch, or anyone else. She was so deep in thought that she did not see James waiting for her just inside the back door and she almost dropped the tray in fright when he stepped in front of her.

"James Fairfax, you nearly made me drop this tray!" she accused. "What are you doing sneaking up on me?"

"I was not sneaking up on you! I was waiting to talk to you. What are you doing? Why were you flirting with those men in there? You know that they only want one thing from you!"

"Well, maybe I only want one thing from them too," she retorted, moving to go around him.

"What do you mean?" he demanded, stepping in front of her. "Have I not said I would pay for your indentureship? What more do you want?"

"And then what? What will I do? I want to start my own business. I need money for that."

"Money, money, money! Money is your god, for that is what you think about all the time," he accused her.

"And what do you think about all the time?"

"You! This!" He leaned over the tray she was holding and held her face with both his hands as he kissed her thoroughly. Surprise held her in shock before she began to respond. The hands that gripped the tray betrayed the effect of his kiss on her as the tray began to slip. James tore his mouth away from hers and caught it before it fell, silently cursing himself for kissing her where anyone could walk in and see them.

"I am sorry, Jemima. I didn't mean to do that."

"James, you are always sorry. I am tired of your sorries! You say that you think about kissing me all the time, but you are sorry when you do. You do not seem to want me, but you do not want anyone else to have me. You do not know what you want! I will find someone who does." With that, she stalked off to serve the guests.

James was left staring after her. She was wrong! He knew what he wanted. He wanted The Acreage and he wanted her, but neither was his to possess. Yet.

ꕥ

The party finished around nine o'clock so that the guests could sleep off the vast quantities of wine and brandy they had drunk. James made sure that he limited his intake to just one glass of brandy as he wanted to make sure that he had all his faculties intact in case Mary-Ann paid him a visit, for despite her believing that he was having an affair with Jemima, she had been giving him sultry looks all night.

The party was a great success, given the compliments that Jemima had received from both the men and the women as she and Hetty served the guests. True to her word, Mary-Ann made sure that she told her guests about Mrs. Perch's boarding house and the Friday lunch that would be available. James felt somewhat guilty, for he had not promoted the boarding house as much as he had promised, for he was distracted by both the meeting with Berkshire and the kiss with Jemima. Worse yet, now that he had agreed to pay for Jemima's freedom, Mrs. Perch would be out of a cook, for it seemed that Jemima had no intention of remaining in her employment.

He had to grudgingly admire Jemima's singlemindedness, for she had deliberately ignored him for the rest of the night and worked the room like a professional. He was sure that before the party was finished she would have a benefactor who would finance her business. He should be glad, but the thought of Jemima with any of these men made him feel like hitting something or someone. She was right, though. If he didn't want her, he had no right to stand in the way of anyone else. But that was the trouble. He did want her. More than that, he feared he was beginning to love her. But how could he love someone who was willing to prostitute herself with any man?

"Well, that was a resounding success," Mary-Ann announced delightedly. Her voice intruded into his thoughts and brought him back to the present as the door closed behind the last guest. He was tired from standing around so he could not imagine what Jemima must feel like.

"I am glad you are happy, my dear. It is not often that I can claim to have made you happy," Samuel slurred.

"It had little to do with you and much to do with James for finding that amazing girl. I do not want her to leave," she moaned.

"I knew that might be the case," James told her. "However, you can enjoy her meals whenever you are in town." He did not mention that it might not be at Mrs. Perch's establishment.

"Apart from the food, she certainly made an impression on the men," Mary-Ann remarked, looking at James to see how he responded to that. James managed to keep his face impassive and deliberately changed the subject.

"That strange man Mr. Berkshire seems to have left early and rather abruptly."

"I am not surprised," Samuel remarked.

"I did not invite Mr. Berkshire, but I could hardly ask him why he was here," Mary-Ann said curiously.

"He was just trying to cause trouble, but it is nothing to concern yourself about," Samuel assured her. "It is a business issue, but I will take care of it."

"Good. Well, I wish you both goodnight, for I am exhausted and morning will come quickly. James, I take it you will attend church with us?"

"Of course. I will take to my bed as well. See you both in the morning."

ɷɞ

Monday morning

James was glad to see the palm trees of The Acreage waving him goodbye for he had had his fill of the Baileys. He had enjoyed the church service the day before and he was pleased that Mary-Ann had been on her best behaviour, perhaps because it was a holy day, although that would have been a surprise. She seemed to have something on her mind.

A lot had happened in the six days that he had been there and he was pleased with the information he had acquired, but he was also eager to get back to town. This time, he had not avoided sharing the carriage with Jemima, for he was no longer afraid that she would try to entice him. She had suggested at the party that she was moving on to greener pastures.

"How are you feeling?" he asked, breaking the silence.

"I am still exhausted, although I rested most of yesterday," Jemima moaned, covering a yawn. James found himself having to stifle a yawn as well.

"You certainly had a successful night."

"Yes," she smiled contentedly. "Everyone said they enjoyed the food. I should have no trouble getting customers when I start my business."

"So, did you find someone who knows what they want?" James asked her. She looked puzzled for a moment before she remembered the words she left him with at the party.

"Yes, I did. Thank you." She turned to look out of the window, ignoring him. Not that she could bring herself to consider any of the planters as a benefactor now. James had spoiled that for her, although she would never admit it to him.

"Well, who is it?" he asked impatiently, not really wanting to know.

"Who is what?" she asked innocently. It was all James could do not to grind his teeth, for he knew that Jemima knew full well who he meant.

"Who is your new benefactor? I am sure you had no problem finding one."

"I have not decided as yet, although I have had several offers." She looked smugly at him.

James stared back at her with a hard look until she tore her eyes from his and sought refuge in the scenery again. He continued to pierce her with his gaze until she began to fidget.

"Stop staring at me like that!" she complained, turning back to face him.

"Like what?" he asked sardonically.

"Like I have been weighed in the balance and found wanting."

"Now you quote scripture?" he scoffed.

"Forgive me for not being as perfect and pious as you, but I have no rich parents to give me all that I need."

"My parents may be well off, but I will have you know that I worked hard for everything I have!" *Well almost,* he amended silently, for his grandfather had left him an inheritance as well.

"I am happy to hear that! So, why do you judge me for working for what I want?"

"If you want to work on your back then by all means go ahead and do so. You should indeed use all your talents," he said cruelly. Jemima's sharply drawn breath was the only indication that he had severely wounded her. She quickly turned to look out of the window again, lest he see the moisture in her eyes.

"I am sorry, Jemima. That was cruel and uncalled for."

He leaned forward and attempted to take her hand which she pulled away. He easily overcame her resistance and captured it, pulling it towards him. His thumb gently rubbed a callous he found at the base of her little finger before bringing her hand to his mouth. The hot kiss he pressed to her palm sent a shock through Jemima's body and she had to restrain herself from running her hand along his firm jaw to feel the slight stubble of his beard before pulling his mouth to hers. Berating herself, she dragged her hand away from his lips.

"What would you have me do?" she asked brokenly. "How can I start my business with no money?"

"I will lend you the money," he found himself saying. What was he doing? How was he ever going to afford to buy The Acreage if he kept promising money to Jemima.

"You will?" Hope leapt in her eyes. He nodded.

"But you will have to prepare a plan to show me how you will make this business work and how much money you think you will need. And how you will pay me back."

"How am I supposed to do that? I know nothing about business."

"Then maybe you should work with Mrs. Perch for a time and learn all you can before you start your own business," he suggested. "She will have to pay you wages when you are free, but with your cooking you will help her to earn extra money so she should have no trouble paying you."

Jemima deliberated that idea in her head. She hated to continue working at The Royal Inn, but she knew that what James was saying made sense. She could then save up the money she needed to get started. Maybe she could even hire herself out to prepare food for parties as well to earn extra money. She could decide who she would hire herself to and it would not be to the likes of the Major. Some of the women from the party had already asked her if she could come and prepare food for their parties.

"That may be a good idea if I can get Mrs. Perch to agree."

"Leave Mrs. Perch to me. She was trying to get me to stay longer so I will agree to stay there until I leave if she will pay you. With two more months of revenue from me and lunch on Fridays she will be able to afford it. Besides, she will also have the money that I pay for your indentureship."

Jemima almost laughed at the irony of it. James had volunteered to do what she had been trying to entice him to do for weeks and she did not even have to offer herself as an incentive. Maybe she did not need to use her body to get what she wanted. A beautiful peace came over her as a weight fell from her shoulders at that thought, making her feel like a new person. James was right. It was time that she valued herself.

"Thank you, James," she said softly, her eyes shining again. Then she held out her hand to shake his and said, "Hello. I am Jemima Andrews."

"Hello, Jemima Andrews. I am James Fairfax. Delighted to make your acquaintance." James instinctively knew what her introduction meant. The smile that broke out across his face almost made Jemima forget her newly made promise to herself, for she suddenly wanted him with a fierceness that shocked her. And it was not to persuade him to stay at the inn or to get money to start her business. She just wanted him for himself. Never had she met a man like him.

ꙮ

The Royal Inn

James and Jemima climbed down from the carriage and stretched the kinks out of their backs. The time had passed quickly as they talked for the rest of the trip, discovering new things about each other. James now understood why she was so reluctant to trust him, for she told him how she had waited in vain for her benefactor to return and pay for her indentureship. He assured her that he would speak to Mrs. Perch and settle it at the first opportunity. They barely got through the door before Mrs. Perch descended upon them as if she had been waiting expectantly.

"Mr. Fairfax. Wonderful to see you. How was your stay?"

"It was very interesting."

"And I hope the party went well."

"Yes, indeed. Jemima's food was well received so I am sure you will be well patronised."

"That is wonderful news!" she said enthusiastically. "Jemima, you may have a few hours off before you have to prepare for dinner."

Jemima murmured her thanks and gave James a significant look before she headed to her room. She looked as if she would have liked to have said something to him. James nodded discreetly to let her know he would deal with Mrs. Perch right away.

"There is something I need to discuss with you, Mrs. Perch. Do you have a moment now?"

"Why, of course, Mr. Fairfax," she said cautiously.

"Perhaps we could sit down," James suggested, gesturing to the sitting area.

"Certainly."

James allowed her to sit before taking his seat, and then he got to the point at once.

"I find that I am coming to love the island, so I have decided to stay on for another two months here at the boarding house."

"Mr. Fairfax! That is the best news I have had for quite some time. I knew that Jemima would be able –" She stopped abruptly as she realised what she was about to reveal and had the grace to look ashamed.

Obviously, she and Jemima had concocted some plan to get him to stay longer. No doubt Jemima had planned to use whatever means necessary to persuade him. He hoped that she was now truly reformed and she would stop trying to use her body to get what she wanted.

"Speaking of Jemima, I would like to know the value remaining on her indentureship."

"Why would you want to know that, Mr. Fairfax?" she asked, looking at him suspiciously.

"I would like to pay off the amount outstanding."

Mrs. Perch looked astounded. "Pay off Jemima's indentureship?" she repeated, aghast.

James could see her mentally working out the money she could gain versus the cost of losing Jemima's services, especially since she planned to offer additional meals.

"Let me assure you that Jemima has agreed to continue to work for you, but you will be required to pay her wages."

"Pay her wages? How am I to afford to pay wages?" she wailed.

"I do believe that the revenue you earn from my stay for the next two months alone would cover her wages for some time. In any case, the money from the indentureship is enough to pay her for about two years," James assured her unwaveringly.

"I suppose so," she conceded. She had obviously hoped to benefit from Jemima's free labour as well as the money from his stay.

"Do we have an agreement?" James pressed. She nodded reluctantly. "Good. I have an appointment this afternoon. Please have the indentureship documents ready for me to review when I return so that I can arrange to pay you the funds as soon as possible."

"This is all rather sudden. I will have to search my husband's papers to find them," she said, stalling. "And is she to continue to live here?"

"You and Jemima can work out the details. I am sure that you can both come to an amicable agreement. Now, I need to retire to my room and ready myself for my meeting."

James could see that she was dying to ask about his meeting, but he ignored her signals and picked up his satchel before starting for the stairs. In a few hours he would have the papers for Jemima's indentureship which he would hand over to her once he paid the balance, so that she would be free. He felt a burst of pleasure that he was able to do this for her, for he greatly desired to help her in any way that he could. He hoped she would use her freedom to her benefit.

Chapter 19

High Street, Bridge Town

The office of Augustus Berkshire could have been easily overlooked as James walked down High Street, for he had no impressive shingle announcing its location. Rather, a small sign was attached to a door in a narrow building. James opened it to find a young man at a desk piled high with papers. He introduced himself as Mr. Berkshire's assistant and escorted James to a room down a narrow hallway.

August Berkshire was seated behind a desk that was so covered with papers it was impossible to tell what kind of wood it was made from. If the success of a business could be measured by the amount of paper it generated, then his business was doing exceedingly well. James wondered how he could find anything.

"Mr. Fairfax, welcome," Augustus greeted him warmly, extending his hand. The gentlemen exchanged a firm handshake.

"Thank you for making time to see me."

"It is in my interest to do so, to be sure. I hope we can do business together."

"That is my hope as well."

"Well, let us get straight to the point. You expressed an interest in acquiring the mortgage I hold over The Acreage plantation." He shuffled papers on his desk as he spoke until he unearthed a set of documents tied together with a piece of string. James would have thought he would have them at the top of one of the piles in anticipation of his visit. Augustus untied the string and flipped through the papers until he found what he was looking for. It was a legal document.

"Here we are. This is the deed of the original mortgage which was for £10,000. To date, about £4000 has been repaid, but the loan is about six months in arrears, so interest has accrued, bringing the outstanding debt to £6,300. If you can raise that sum you may have the deeds to the plantation. You can call in the debt when you are ready and take possession of it."

James' heart began to beat faster. While it was a lot of money, it was not as much as he had thought it would be. His grandfather Thomas had left each of his grandchildren a sizable inheritance which he had invested and multiplied, so he could sell off some of those investments. That would still allow him to keep his boat which would continue to earn revenue for him. He could also sell the house that he and Harriett had lived in, for he would have no need of it when he moved to Barbados. Perhaps that might also help to bring some closure to that part of his life.

It hit him that he would have to return to England to deal with his investments himself. He would prefer to stay for the two months and then return to England, but he was sure that Mr. Berkshire would not wait around for that long. He was eager to put things in motion right away to acquire The Acreage, but he found himself reluctant to leave Barbados and, he had to admit it, Jemima. In spite of the change he had observed in her on the carriage ride, he wondered if she would be tempted to find a benefactor in his absence or if she would work for Mrs. Perch as she had agreed.

"Needless to say, I do not have that kind of money in Barbados so I would need to return to England to liquidate some investments. Would you be willing to hold off for a few more months? I have just committed to the proprietress of the boarding house I am staying at to remain there for two more months and I would prefer not to cut short my stay, if possible." It was worth a try.

"My dear Mr. Fairfax, the account is already six months in arrears and I have been more than patient with Lord Bailey. I am not a charity; I am a businessman, so I need to recover my investment as soon as possible. I assure you it will not be difficult to transfer this mortgage to any number of people, for The Acreage is a prime piece of property. So, if you want it you need to act now." He did not have to tell James that twice.

"I fully understand. I will make arrangements to return to England next week. Would you be prepared to wait until I return if I give you a written commitment and a deposit?"

"On that basis I would wait for you, but I will need a deposit of ten percent of the debt, and of course, unless Lord Bailey pays in any money, there will be additional interest accrued which will be added to the principal."

"That is fair enough. I will send a letter to England immediately so that I can get the deposit to you as soon as possible and I will get myself ready to leave next week."

"That is acceptable to me. Well, it looks like we have an agreement, provided you can fulfil your obligation in, say, three months. I will, of course, keep this between us."

James nodded, for he certainly did not want Samuel to get wind of the transaction and find some way to bring his account up to date. Augustus rose and extended his hand to James who stood and shook it soberly.

"I will have my assistant draw up an agreement so you may either wait here or come back in a few minutes."

"I will wait," James assured him.

Augustus left to give his assistant instructions about the document that was to be prepared, leaving James with his thoughts. He had just committed to buying the mortgage over The Acreage. Excitement filled him but it was quickly tempered by doubts. Would he really have the heart to call in the debt? What would the Baileys do? What would he do with the slaves? Was he mad to leave everything in England and move to Barbados? With determination, he put the doubts and concerns out of his mind. Surely, this was the reason he had been drawn to come to Barbados by Providence so he did not need to worry. He would restore The Acreage to his family and make it successful once again. His grandfather was no doubt smiling down at him in approval, encouraging him silently. Excitement won the battle over doubt as the realisation hit him that he was truly in a position to become the master of The Acreage.

ЖОС

James was happy to see the foyer deserted when he returned to The Royal Inn. Mrs. Perch must have been having her afternoon rest while Jemima was likely preparing the evening meal. Although he was excited about the afternoon's transaction and wished he had someone to share his excitement with, he had to contain himself, for he could not afford that information to get out lest his plans be ruined. He patted his pocket as he headed to his room, feeling the copy of the agreement. He would have to hide it in the secret compartment of his trunk, for he would not be surprised if Mrs. Perch was so bold as to search his belongings when he was out, for she thrived on knowing everything.

He was not looking forward to breaking the news that he was returning to England as early as next week to either of the women. He had found a ship that was sailing early the next day and he had asked the captain to deliver a letter which he would now write to his parents. His enquiries about a ship carrying passengers to England had born fruit too, as he was told that he could get one the following week. He would need to come up with a good reason for his sudden departure, especially after telling Mrs. Perch he would stay two more months just hours ago.

Of the two women, he was most concerned about Jemima's reaction because she had been deserted, it seemed, by her last benefactor who had promised to return and purchase her indentureship and had not returned. Not that he was her benefactor. He would settle the debt with Mrs. Perch before he left and make sure that Mrs. Perch agreed to pay her wages. However, he could not tell Jemima the truth because he did not know if he could fully trust her. Had she truly changed, or would she once again seek another man, maybe even Samuel, to help her the minute his back was turned?

As it was, he would have to pay for the room for the two months even though he would be leaving, for he was a man of integrity. He also wanted to ensure that Mrs. Perch would have no excuse not to pay Jemima. He shook his head at the thought of making one of the worse financial decisions in recent memory – paying for a room and not using it. Actually, he would let Jemima stay in it when he was gone so it would not be a complete waste of money. Maybe that would placate her somewhat. Jemima was costing him a fortune and they did not even have any kind of agreement. What did he really want of Jemima anyway? He desired her greatly and he admired her, at least some things about her. But was he truly ready for marriage again? And did he want to marry a woman with her past? He took his journal out of his drawer with that thought in his mind.

Monday, April 22

I cannot believe it, but I am going to be the owner of The Acreage! I have just come from the office of Augustus Berkshire who holds the mortgage over the plantation and I signed a document and I am to provide him with a deposit as surety until I pay the rest of the money. This was so much easier than I thought it would be and with no wrongdoing on Mary-Ann's part. But will I be heartless enough to call in the debt? I feel sorry for the Baileys, for I wonder where they will go. But then again, they have squandered their opportunity to make the plantation prosperous. Perhaps Mary-Ann will get her wish to return to England now.

I am torn, for I need to leave for England next week to settle my affairs and liquidate some assets to purchase the mortgage. At the same time, I feel as if Jemima and I are just beginning to get to know each other and I do not want to leave her. There really is no choice, for this is an opportunity that I cannot pass up. I know that she had wanted to leave the island, so she may want to come with me. If that is so, how can I take her with me? I cannot make her my mistress nor am I ready to marry again, although my desire for her is great. She seems to have made a decision to change, but if I leave her here will she learn to rely on herself or will I come back to find her with a new benefactor?

Mrs. Perch will no doubt be put out to hear that I will not be here for two or more months as I had promised her. Was it only today? I will have to pay for the two months even though I am leaving so abruptly, for I have given her my word. Everything has happened so fast; I could not have imagined this when I left England. Surely, this is the reason I was drawn to come to Barbados. My future was waiting here for me.

James closed the journal, too distracted to write any more. Besides, it was more important to write a letter to his parents telling them all that had transpired and asking his father to send a draft for £630 as soon as possible. He and Augustus had agreed not to say anything about the transaction to Samuel Bailey, and James hoped fervently that Samuel would not miraculously find the money to pay off the arrears on his debt before he returned. In any case, he would still hold the debt. He took a sheet of paper from the drawer and began to write to his parents. He included his mother who was very much involved with their business affairs, so she would never be like Mary-Ann who was oblivious to what was about to fall down around her.

Monday, April 22, 1726
The Royal Inn, Bridge Town

Dear Father and Mother,

You must be most surprised to get not one, but two letters from me and before you have even had the chance to respond to the first. Well, you will be even more surprised when you read this, for I am excited to tell you that I have entered into an agreement to purchase the mortgage over The Acreage. I discovered in my time here that Lord Bailey is months in arrears in paying the mortgage and the holder of it, a Mr. Augustus Berkshire, is quite keen to sell it to me.

To that end, Father, I need you to purchase a draft for £630 in the favour of Mr. Augustus Berkshire of High Street, Bridge Town and send it to him forthwith. I will be taking the next available ship back to England to deal with my business interests and I will pay you back then. I will then return to Barbados and pay the rest of the money. If Lord Bailey continues to be unable to pay his debt, I will call it in and so become the owner of The Acreage and bring it back into the family.

I must confess that I do have some concern for what the Baileys will do on the one hand, but when I see how lavishly they have lived while their slaves are dressed in rags, I feel no compunction to take over the plantation. I have not worked through all the details in my mind as to what I will do once I own it, but I will deal with that when I come to it.

Although I am eager to return to England to settle my affairs and of course to see you, I am also reluctant to leave, for I have met a woman whom I have developed some affection for. Her name is Jemima Andrews and she is an indentured servant or was one, for I have promised to purchase her freedom before I leave. She is also coloured. I seem to have taken after you and my grandfather in that regard, Father.

We have made no promises to each other and I do not even know if she will be unattached when I return, but I hope so, although I do not know what we will be to each other. I may be ahead of myself in talking about marriage, for we have not discussed any such thing, but I know that is the only way that I would want to have her.

Anyway, I will see you in about five or so weeks and you can ask me as many questions as you like, Mother, for I know you will be bursting. I hope that Charles is still there. Do not let him leave before I arrive, for I do not know when I will see him again if I do not see him when I return.

Please give my love to all.

Your son
James

P.S.: Mother, you will be pleased to know that I have helped out at the school on several occasions and enjoyed it tremendously. Unknown to me before I visited, Jemima also helps, for she is well educated. You would like her, for I see some of your qualities in her. Cassandra would no doubt wish me to send her love to you.

He sealed the letter and hastened down the stairs towards the front door. He had to get the letter to the captain before the ship sailed for England in the morning. Some delicious smells coming from the direction of the kitchen tantalised his nostrils as he headed out. Jemima must be preparing a feast to thank him for her freedom, not that he had dealt with that yet, for he had more pressing matters to address.

Chapter 20

Later that night

James waited expectantly for Jemima to bring his dinner. He was practically drooling from the smells that were emanating from the kitchen. He was also looking forward to seeing Jemima as well, for he had not seen her since they got back that morning. Funny, but Mrs. Perch had been noticeably absent as well, for she had not been behind the desk as was her custom when he returned from delivering the letter. He wondered if she was deliberately avoiding him in an effort to delay his purchase of Jemima's indentureship.

His musing was interrupted by Jemima who came from the kitchen with a bowl of soup and a plate of crusty-looking bread. She was smiling broadly as she placed the dishes with a flourish before him.

"Dinner is served, Mr. Fairfax," she announced playfully. "I have gone to much trouble to prepare what I hope will be your best meal at this establishment."

"It certainly smells that way," James assured her. "I have been salivating for an hour."

"Well, satisfy your mouth," she invited him. James couldn't help but look at her smiling lips and thinking of other ways he could satisfy his mouth. Jemima seemed to read his mind and her smile became quite sultry.

"Why, Mr. Fairfax, I am shocked at what just went through your mind," she teased him.

"And what would that be?" he challenged her with a smile of his own. There was no denying what was clearly written on his face.

"I will allow you to keep your secrets since you have given me a most treasured gift – my freedom."

"I haven't quite done that yet," he corrected her.

"You have not yet purchased my indentureship? You said you would do that right away!" Her voice sounded a little desperate.

"Mrs. Perch said that she had to locate the papers and I have not seen her since this morning."

"Do you not know how important this is to me? Do you not care?"

"Of course I care, Jemima. Do not worry. I will make sure that I settle the debt before I leave."

"Leave? Where are you going?" she asked with dread stealing across her face. She had gone through this before. James could not let her down the way that Tobias did. Not when she was so close to being free.

"I have to return to England. Next week," he added reluctantly and braced himself for the explosion that was sure to follow. He was surprised when Jemima said nothing but turned and walked back towards the kitchen. "I will sort it out before I go, I promise you," he called after her, but she closed the door behind her without acknowledging if she had even heard him. James stared at the soup and bread before him, but he now could barely face the food and had to force it down his throat. He felt terrible, as if he had let down Jemima. He would not sleep that night without getting the papers from Mrs. Perch and setting Jemima free.

The rest of the meal was wonderful, but it was delivered by Ruth, making it clear that Jemima had no desire to see him. He was almost glad, for he did not know what to say to her, so he finished as soon as he could and went to find Mrs. Perch. She was once again behind her desk and she was reading through some papers.

"Mrs. Perch, I hope those are the indentureship papers that you have located."

"Yes. I managed to find them among my dear husband's papers. I was trying to work out the remaining value to be paid."

"May I?" James extended his hand to receive the papers which Mrs. Perch reluctantly handed over. He read through the documents before handing them back to her.

"It appears that there are just under two years remaining of Jemima's indentureship. The original amount was £50 so that leaves £20 to be paid. I am not sure I see the difficulty. I will pay you the money right away and you just need to sign them to indicate that the indentureship has been satisfied. I will then give the papers to Jemima."

"You will pay me now?" Mrs. Perch asked eagerly.

"That I will. If you will just wait a minute, I will get the money from my room."

James handed the papers back to her and headed for the stairs. He felt a lot lighter than he did a few minutes before. Jemima was going to thank him for her freedom and she would learn that she could trust him. He retrieved the money from his trunk, glad that he had travelled with a good quantity of money, for he knew that the living in Barbados was expensive. He had not anticipated having to spend such a large sum to pay for Jemima's freedom, but he could not bring himself to regret it. What sum could be put on someone's life? After counting out the money, he carefully returned the rest, which was significantly less, to the secret compartment and went back downstairs.

He knew Mrs. Perch well enough to present her with the money before he informed her of his plans to leave the following week.

"Here it is. Please count it to make sure it is correct," he advised, handing her the notes.

"Thank you, Mr. Fairfax," she said, her eyes bulging at the sight of the money in her hands.

"Please write 'Paid in Full' across the top of the document and sign your name. I will witness it."

"Certainly." Mrs. Perch complied.

"By the way, I have discovered that I need to return to England on urgent business next week."

"You what?" The words left her mouth without consulting her tongue. Her eyes opened at the news that she would lose two months' revenue, even though she held more money in her hands than she had probably ever done at one time.

"Yes, it is very unexpected, but I intend to come back as soon as possible."

"But what about the room? You told me you would stay for two months," she protested.

"Never fear. I will still pay you for the two months and I will let Jemima stay in it until I return."

Her face was the picture of satisfaction when she realised she would not be out of pocket. Then she couldn't help but ask, with a sly look, "Jemima is to stay in your room? That is very generous of you. She has obviously made a very good impression on you."

James ignored the innuendo and said, "Since she will now have to provide her own board as she is no longer a servant, I am happy to allow her to stay for two months. See that you pay her fair wages, please."

"But, of course. As if I would do anything else."

James barely stopped himself from rolling his eyes at her assurance, for he knew how she was about money. Just to make sure, he would check around to find out what a fair wage in Barbados was before he left. He knew in England a maid with Jemima's skill in cooking could earn about three to four shillings a week, so he would see what the rate was here.

"Thank you, Mrs. Perch." He held out his hands for the papers which she had not handed over as yet and she almost reluctantly parted with them. He now held the papers for Jemima's indentureship in his grasp. For all intents and purposes, he now owned her. It seemed as if he was acquiring interest in quite a bit of property in Barbados, although it was poor form to call Jemima property. For a fleeting moment he considered how it would feel keeping the papers and owning her himself. After all, his father had owned his mother for a short time and that had turned out well. He chided himself for his selfish and unworthy thoughts and he knew that if his mother were ever to suspect him of such a thought she would slap him soundly.

"Thank you, Mr. Fairfax. Although I hope I will not lose the ungrateful girl now that she is free."

"I don't know why you refer to her as ungrateful when she owes you no gratitude, especially after the way you have treated her."

"You have only been here a month, so you have no idea of all that I have done for that girl," she insisted.

"I cannot argue with that. If you would be so kind as to ask Jemima to come up to my room when she leaves the kitchen, I would appreciate it," James told her.

"I would be happy to do that for you. I am sure you will want to be properly thanked for your very generous gesture," she smirked knowingly.

"On the contrary, Mrs. Perch, I do not expect anything from Jemima," James denied. However, he was dangerously close to accepting whatever thanks Jemima chose to give, especially if she insisted on thanking him the way she had wanted to before.

ൈര

Jemima knocked on James' door. This was the first time she had been to his room, as Ruth was responsible for cleaning the rooms. She had ignored Mrs. Perch's disdainful expression when she told her that she was to go to Mr. Fairfax's room. Who was Mrs. Perch to judge her when it was she who had encouraged her to use her wiles to get James to stay? It seemed as though she was now upset that Jemima had succeeded so well, although, if the truth be known, she had not done as Mrs. Perch had expected. James had decided to stay longer on his own. Although now he had changed his mind and was leaving soon. Her heart ached at the thought. She still did not know what had caused him to offer to pay for her indentureship, but she was grateful. Very grateful.

James opened the door and stepped back to allow Jemima to come in. He noticed that she was wearing a different dress from the one she had served him in earlier. She obviously had not come straight from the kitchen, for he could detect the faint smell of a lemony soap on her as if she had just bathed and her hair was loose. Did she not know what her hair did to him? Very likely she did. The thought that she had bathed for him caused his body to stir and some very carnal thoughts to enter his mind which he fought to suppress.

"Mrs. Perch said that you wanted to see me."

"Yes. I wanted to give you your papers." He turned and collected the papers from the foot of his bed where he had dropped them. "Miss Jemima Andrews, you are now free." He placed the papers in her hands with a slight bow and a smile.

Tears rushed to Jemima's eyes and spilled down her cheeks before she could stop them. She never cried but she could hardly believe that she held her freedom in her hands. She began to sob, as if the dam that had been holding her hopes in check had broken. James drew her to his chest and held her for several minutes as sobs shook her body. He rubbed comforting circles on her back and tried hard not to think about how soft she felt against him.

"Jemima, I thought you would be rejoicing, not crying," he teased her gently, putting a bit of space between them so he could look at her.

"Sorry," she smiled through the tears. "These are joyful tears, but it is just that I had all but given up hope that this would ever happen." Her eyes and nose were red and her face was splotchy, but to him she looked beautiful. Her hair beckoned his fingers to bury themselves in the thick curls.

"I am glad that I was able to do this for you. I also told Mrs. Perch that I have to return to England. You can imagine her reaction to that." Jemima smiled as she pictured Mrs. Perch hearing the news. "I had given her my word that I would stay for two more months so I have promised to still pay for the room and you can stay in it until I return."

"What? You are an amazing, generous man, James Fairfax. I do not know anyone who would do that, and for someone who is almost a complete stranger."

"I would hardly call you a stranger, Jemima. I feel that I know you well, although I have not known you for a long time. Besides, I do not go around kissing strangers," James said teasingly, trying to dispel the discomfort that her praise brought. As soon as the words left his mouth, he knew that she may misconstrue them as an invitation. Maybe he had meant them to be, if he was honest with himself.

"I am glad to hear that, Mr. Fairfax," she returned his teasing. "Joking aside, I cannot properly put into words what this means to me, but I can show you."

The transformation from teasing to seductive was immediate and caught James off guard. Before he could respond, Jemima clasped her hands around his neck and pulled his mouth to hers. He tasted the saltiness of her tears that lingered on her lips as she kissed him. Her kiss was as bold and exciting as she was, stirring his body in seconds. Her fingers playing in his hair caused shudders to shake his body. When she pressed herself so close against him that he could feel every contour of her body, he released the last hold he had on his restraint. He buried his fingers in her hair as he had been itching to do and took the dominant role in the kiss, releasing all the passion that he had held in check for two years.

Jemima felt as if she was being swept away by the wave of James' passion as he frantically searched for the buttons on her dress. She eagerly pulled his shirt off before he changed his mind, but when their skin touched, it was obvious that he was past the point of being able to pull back. James had one pang as Harriett intruded into his mind briefly before he quickly closed the door on her memory. He lifted Jemima from where her dress was pooled around her feet and carried her to the bed before he hurriedly divested himself of the rest of his clothes and joined her. Minutes later their laboured breathing filled the room and it was her name that he called at the height of his passion.

James groaned silently as passion gave way to reality. What had he done? He had lain with Jemima without any thought of conception of a child, without the sanctity of marriage and without allowing the guilt about Harriett's death to stop him from giving in to the fulfilment that his body craved. He knew that inviting Jemima to his room was asking for trouble. Maybe this was what he had wanted all along. Shame and remorse filled him, making him cover his face with his forearm as he lay back on the pillows.

"I am sorry, Jemima," he mumbled from beneath his arm.

"Sorry again? That it was so quick or that it happened at all?"

"Both," he admitted. "More so that it happened at all. It was wrong. We are not married and I am still grieving my wife."

"Stop using your wife to keep me at a distance. It was not her name I heard you call a few minutes ago," she added harshly, climbing down from the bed and pulling on her clothes angrily.

"I did not intend to use you in that way, but when you kissed me, I lost my head."

"Yes, I kissed you. I wanted you and at least I am honest about that. I am no hypocrite!" With that she stormed out of the room, leaving him alone with his guilt and shame.

ꕥ

The next few days were hard. The atmosphere at The Royal Inn was tense, for Jemima was not speaking to James and Mrs. Perch was sour faced, as if she was upset that she had not asked for more money for Jemima's indentureship. Added to that, she was not happy that she had to pay Jemima wages and, despite Jemima's silent treatment, James had made some enquiries to ensure that she was paid fair wages.

James was glad to escape the depressing environment and head to Cassandra's school to help with the slaves by the middle of the week. Although he would be gone for a few months, he hoped that Jemima would continue to assist. She was doing it before he started anyway, so there was no reason why she wouldn't, and she would certainly have the freedom to do so now. He was glad that he at least had helped her in that way.

Guilt haunted him again as the night that was ingrained in his mind forced itself to the forefront of his thoughts for the hundredth time. He had prayed and asked for forgiveness, but he found it hard to forget the way that Jemima's body had looked and felt against his. The fact that she was now ignoring him only made him feel worse, but perhaps it was just as well, for all he wanted to do was to have her again and again. He would be glad when an ocean separated them, for he felt that was what it would take to rid him of this desire for Jemima Andrews.

Cassandra was delighted to see him as he had not been to the school since his return from The Acreage. As he worked with the students, he realised that he would miss coming to help them. Maybe when he came back he would have some time to visit and lend a hand before he acquired The Acreage. He waited until the students had left before he approached her.

"Cassandra, I am afraid that I have some bad news for you," he began.

"Bad news? What has happened?" she asked worriedly.

"I have to return to England next week as some urgent business has come up."

"I am sorry to hear that. I thought it had something to do with Jemima."

"Why would it have anything to do with Jemima?"

"Well, she came here to see me on Tuesday and she was not happy with you." James cringed at the thought that Jemima had discussed what happened with Cassandra.

"I am not happy with me either. It should never have happened. And I feel badly that I have to go back home at this time. But I will return. I just hope there are no repercussions from our actions, for she is at the start of a new season of her life and needs to be completely free."

"For Jemima's sake I hope there are none," Cassandra agreed. "Please give my love to your mother and grandmother."

"I will. Look after Jemima until I return and make sure that she does not return to her old ways. When I come back, I will do what needs to be done."

Chapter 21

Five weeks later
The Fairfax Residence
Bristol, England

James knocked at the door of his parents' house and was let in by the housekeeper who beamed on seeing him. It was Saturday, so he hoped that his family would be at home. He silently pointed to the living room and was answered by a nod and smile. He gestured for her to be quiet so that he could sneak in and surprise them. He was very much looking forward to seeing them again after being gone for over three months. The journey home had seemed without end and because he had little to do during the day, he was not very tired at night. Sleep often evaded him and when he did manage to sleep, his dreams were filled with a curly-haired beauty who seemed to have taken up residence in his mind.

Jemima, he discovered, did not let go of an offence easily, so it was only on his final day that she thawed out enough to wish him a safe journey. He had tried to apologise again, but she dismissed it as well as his assurance that if there were any consequences of the night they had shared he would help with the responsibility. She assured him that there were none, so at least he did not have that on his conscience, provided she was telling the truth.

He felt almost guilty for not sending a note to tell the Baileys he was leaving, but since it was for the purpose of acquiring their plantation that he was leaving, he thought it would be in poor taste to tell them anything. Besides, he did not want to deal with Mary-Ann who might still have it in her head to go to England with him. As an afterthought, he realised that it might have made it easier to call in Samuel's debt if she was not there to suffer with him.

Walking stealthily down the corridor, he poked his head into the sitting room where he found his family.

"Did anyone miss me when I was gone?" he asked playfully.

Alexandra squealed and dropped the book she was reading to dash across the room and throw herself on him, making him stagger back under her weight. His mother was not too far behind and although she didn't squeal like Alex, she threw her arms around him and hugged him tightly. His father joined the group by the door, hugging James and patting him on the back once Deborah let go of him.

"Where is Charles?"

"He went out with some friends," his mother explained. "Do not worry. We got your letter and we have forbidden him to leave any time soon."

"I am glad to hear that."

"How are you, Son?" his mother asked, looking him over.

"I am well."

"Come and sit," she instructed. "You have a lot to tell. Would you like something to eat and drink? Alex, go and tell Mrs. Stratton to have some food and drink sent for James."

"All right, but don't say a thing until I get back," she warned James, who laughed as he basked in the pleasure of being home with his family. Was he really prepared to give this up to go back to Barbados? He looked at each of them. His parents had each other. Alex might get married in a few years if she could find a man strong enough to handle her and Charles was about to embark on his own adventures. What did he have? Harriett was gone and instead of her face, a picture of Jemima flashed across his mind. Not that he really had Jemima. They had lain together, but did it mean anything to her or was it just her way of saying thank you? She had been angry with him afterwards for saying that he was sorry it had happened. To be honest, he was only sorry that he had dishonoured her in that way, but he was not sorry about what had happened, far from. Well, he was sorry that it had been so quick, for she had not been completely fulfilled. When he returned to Barbados would she have someone else or would she be waiting for him?

"We got both your letters. My goodness! When we saw you off to Barbados we had no idea that any of this would happen."

"Neither did I, but I cannot explain the feeling that came over me when I saw The Acreage. It was –"

"James Fairfax, did I not say not to start until I got back?" Alex interrupted. James laughed in delight at his little sister who was never shy about making her demands. He hoped there was a man out there who would appreciate her boldness and independence and who would not try to change her. He thought about Jemima. Had he not tried to change her? But then he reasoned that he was doing it to make her value herself more, although he had ended up doing the same thing that he had rebuked her for doing. Shame made him nearly squirm in his seat.

"Yes, missy. Where was I?" Thinking about Jemima had made him lose his train of thought.

"When you saw The Acreage…" his father reminded him.

"Oh yes. I was by your favourite part of the plantation, Mother, that overlooks the east coast and I was suddenly overcome with emotion as I realised that I was standing on the exact spot where father first spoke to you."

"I remember that well," Deborah reminisced. "I had just sat down to let my hair dry and enjoy the story of Romeo and Juliet when your father came striding out to interrupt my day off. I can laugh about it now, but I was less than happy."

"All I can remember is that I couldn't keep my eyes off your hair. It was the first time I had seen it loose and it was wild and beautiful," Richard reminisced.

"Thank you, love," she smiled at him. Alex rolled her eyes and James smiled indulgently.

"It was at that moment that I knew I had to get The Acreage back into our family."

"Your grandfather would be very pleased to hear that if he was still alive," Deborah assured him.

"Tell us about this girl that you met," insisted Alex.

"How did you know about that?"

"I know everything, dear brother. Now confess all, if you can," she added slyly. James made sure that his face was expressionless, for all three of them were watching him intently.

"There is nothing to confess," he lied. Oh God, lies were becoming a way of life for him now. "Jemima Andrews was an indentured servant who work at the boarding house where I stayed. God softened my heart towards her and I felt moved to pay for the remainder of her indentureship and set her free. It was the least I could do after what Mother went through."

"I am very proud of you, Son," his mother praised him.

"How much did you have to pay?" asked his practical father.

"Twenty pounds."

Alex whistled. "Wow, she must really be beautiful," she teased him, earning her a cushion thrown at her head. She ducked easily and picked it up from the floor to prop it behind her. The housekeeper came in with a tray of food for James, interrupting the story for a few minutes. As soon as the door was closed behind her, Alex picked up the topic again. "Well, tell us about this amazing Jemima."

"There is not much to tell. She is beautiful, about the same colour as Mother with vibrant red curly hair. She is very well-spoken, as her father was a teacher who came from England to help teach the children of the plantation owners. Her mother was a mulatto houseslave."

"This sounds like history repeating itself," remarked Richard.

"I don't know about that. She was barely speaking to me when I left."

"Oh, why was that? Tell us everything," Alex insisted.

She and his mother questioned him relentlessly about Jemima until his father intervened and began talking about the business of buying the mortgage over The Acreage. It was a relief to stop talking about Jemima, for every question made him long for her with a hunger that shocked him. She had found her way under his skin and he didn't know what to do about it.

"I sent the draft as soon as I got your letter. How much is the mortgage?"

"It's £6300 including the interest which is in arrears. The draft was a deposit to secure the transaction."

"Wow, that's a fortune!" exclaimed Alex. "I do not even need a fraction of that for my business and I have to give Father a plan of what I want to do," she complained.

"That is nothing compared to what the plantation is worth, so if I call in the debt I will gain."

"But James, do you have the heart to do that?" his mother asked.

"To tell the truth, it is not something that I will enjoy doing in the least, but Samuel Bailey treats his slaves terribly and they are poorly clothed. I had to stop him from hitting one of the house slaves about the head one night for spilling a drop of wine on his breeches."

"What! I would like him to try that with me!" screeched Alex angrily. "He would rue the day he was born!" James laughed and called her a termagant, only to have to shift to avoid the cushion he had thrown earlier, which she returned forcefully.

"What about his wife? Is she like him?" Deborah asked, remembering the whipping that Elizabeth Edwards had ordered for her.

"Not in that regard. She is kind to the slaves, but she is neglected by her husband and so she…" he broke off, not wanting to expose her, especially in front of Alex.

"Did she try to seduce you?" Alex asked knowingly.

"Alex! That is not an appropriate word for a young lady," her mother scolded her. Alex rolled her eyes and bit her tongue, for she had been exposed to a lot more than her mother was aware.

"So, did she?" Alex continued, earning a hard stare from her mother. Nevertheless, they all waited attentively for James to answer.

"Well, she made it clear that she would welcome a relationship with me, but of course I refused, especially when she invited me to partner with her in getting rid of her husband."

"What! You jest," Deborah exclaimed.

"Good riddance is what I would say," Alex interjected.

"You cannot be serious," his father added, entering the conversation.

"I am dead serious. No pun intended," James deadpanned.

"My goodness! You have had an adventure in Barbados. And we thought that Charles was the adventurous one," his mother teased him. "How are you now?" she asked more seriously, and he knew that she was referring to Harriett.

"I believe that I am ready to go on with my life."

"I am glad, Son. Even if it means losing you to Barbados."

"I believe I have lost my heart to Barbados, Mother, and although I will miss you all terribly, already she is calling me to return."

ꟷ

James unlocked the door of the house that he had shared with Harriett for just a year and pushed it open slowly. He paused as he stepped over the threshold and closed the door behind him, expecting to be greeted with the musty smell of a place that had been shut up for a long time. Instead, he smelled a faint lemony fragrance that he placed as furniture polish. The smell reminded him of the night with Jemima. Her skin had smelled faintly of lemon from the soap that she had bathed with before coming to his room. She had obviously planned to be intimate with him or she would have come straight from the kitchen. Even in their house, when Harriett should be the woman in his thoughts, Jemima intruded.

Everything was as he had left it, except tidier, and there was not a speck of dust in sight. His mother must have arranged to have it cleaned regularly in his absence. She was really a wonderful woman whom he respected greatly. She had done what she needed to secure her freedom, so why did he try to condemn Jemima for doing the same? She was right; he was a hypocrite.

As he looked around each room, images of Harriett came back to him. He could see her in the kitchen preparing a meal, sitting in her favourite rocking chair sewing a shirt for him and, as he pushed open the bedroom door, he pictured her looking frail and weak on her side of the bed, as he had last seen her. He dropped down on the bed and smoothed the pillow where her head had lain.

"Harriett," he started, as if she were lying there listening to him, "I regret that we did not have more time together, but God knows best and I have made my peace with him. I am going back to Barbados and …" he paused. "And I have met someone whom I may ask to be my wife. I know that you would want that for me. So, thank you for your blessing. I will see you again in the life to come and I will always love you."

Instead of the grief he expected, peace washed over him and he felt joy and a freedom to move on with his life. He could now return to The Acreage and, hopefully, to Jemima.

The Royal Inn

Jemima lay on the soft mattress of James' bed which should have given her great pleasure, considering how only a short time before she had resented the fact that there were comfortable beds upstairs while she slept on a pallet on the floor. Now she was occupying James' bed which was spacious and comfortable, but she derived little satisfaction from it. How could she when he was not in it with her?

She curled herself into a ball, as if to suppress the ache in her heart. When had she lost her heart to James? Was it when he gave her the papers to her freedom? Was it before that? When he rescued her from Samuel Bailey and was upset that he had not got to her sooner? She could not say for sure. All she knew was that she craved his presence. What she would not do to hear his voice and feel his touch. He had treated her like a precious gift, even though she had not come to him untouched. Far from it. And she had stalked out of the room angry because he had said he was sorry it had happened. She had been hurt because she was not sorry and for him to say that made her feel dirty, as if she had entrapped him. But she had to be honest with herself; she had planned to use his weakening to her advantage.

She had bathed with a precious piece of lemon-scented soap, changed her clothes and discarded her handkerchief, leaving her hair free, before she went to his room. She knew that he would not be able to resist her. She refused to feel sorry, for she was not. The only thing she was sorry about was that she had let her anger get the better of her and refused to speak to him until the very last day before he left. She had wasted time that she could have been with him, could have been in his bed, for although he said it shouldn't have happened, she knew that he would not be able to resist her again.

Now she did not even know if he would return. She could not imagine what business would have taken him back to England so suddenly. Would he come back to Barbados? Once again, she had been left by a man who had promised to return. At least she had her freedom this time and she was now earning wages. She did not care if James Fairfax came back or not. Who was she fooling? Her heart ached for him.

Chapter 22

The Fairfax Residence
Bristol, England

Alexandra lounged on the sofa in an old dress that had seen better days, but as she was not planning to go out that evening, she opted for the comfort of the soft, white muslin dress. She lazily watched her parents playing chess across the room and she smiled as she looked at her mother's face, intense with concentration. Her father had taught her chess some years ago and they often had fierce battles, with her mother taking her father's king every so often. She enjoyed the game immensely herself. Whoever said that chess was a game for men did not know what they were talking about, for women could be just as strategic as men.

They heard the front door slam and voices floated down the corridor. It sounded like James and Charles who had gone out to a club before dinner. She wished there were clubs where women could meet and converse like the men did. She abhorred those sewing circles and teas where the women only gossiped and talked about fashion. She wanted to meet women who were of the same mind as she was about issues of equality and fairness. Maybe she would have to start her own salon, one of those gatherings she had heard about in France with a focus on literature, learning and debate.

"Father and Mother, I ran into a colleague at the club and invited him around for dinner. This is Dominic Durand. Dominic, my parents Richard and Deborah and my little sister, Alexandra." James made the introductions.

"Enchanté. Pleased to meet you," Dominic replied, bowing to the occupants of the room.

"Welcome, Dominic. Please sit down." Deborah gestured to a side chair as she and Richard got up from the chess table to join them.

"I did not mean to disturb your game."

"You are not disturbing. You came at the right time to get me out of a tight spot," Richard assured him, with a smile.

Alexandra surreptitiously pulled herself into a sitting position, mortified to have been caught lounging and in one of her oldest house dresses. She would murder James later for not giving them adequate notice that he was bringing home someone who happened to be one of the most handsome men she had ever seen. And to refer to her as his little sister! Not that his friend had spared her more than a glance, for which she was quite thankful only because of the state of her attire. She tried to smooth her hair, which had been displaced from its bun by the cushions she had been lying on. It wasn't that she was interested in him, but neither did she want to be caught looking like a frump.

"Hey squirt, how are you doing today? I'm surprised you're not out shopping," Charles teased her, dropping down beside her.

"Really, Charles, how often do you see me out shopping?" she asked coldly. She could have murdered Charles quite happily. Little sister and now squirt?

"Maybe that is my way of telling you that you should be," he replied laughingly, gesturing to her dress. Alexandra's face grew hot with embarrassment and she was glad that she did not blush.

"Charles! That is rather unkind of you," scolded his mother. "We were not expecting company, so none of us is properly dressed. Please excuse us, Dominic."

"On the contrary, it is I who must ask your excuse, for I am the intruder." Alexandra felt she could listen to his voice with the slight French accent all day.

"Not at all. Guests are always welcome here. Our children have always brought friends home unannounced. It is not a problem," Deborah assured him.

"From your name I assume that you are French," Richard stated.

"Half. My mother is English and my father is French."

"Dominic was at school with me for a few years and then he moved to France. We have corresponded on occasion, but I was astonished to see him this evening when Charles and I went to the club. He recently accompanied his mother back to England so that she can stay with his grandmother for a while, as she is ailing. He was planning to call on me tomorrow. Can you imagine?"

"What a coincidence," Deborah remarked. "So sorry to hear about your grandmother."

"Thank you, madame."

"You caught James at the right time too, for he is soon to return to Barbados," Deborah added with a wistful smile.

"Yes, he told me."

"I do not believe in coincidences, so you must have met before he left for a good reason," Deborah asserted, glancing at Alexandra.

Alex wished she could sink into the sofa. Her mother did not just allude that she might be the good reason they had met, did she? Or was she being overly sensitive? No one else seemed to give her comment any thought. Dominic must think she was an empty-headed fool, for she had not uttered a single word since she answered Charles. What was wrong with her? She was never impressed by her brothers' friends and she was not impressed by Dominic Durand, no matter how thick and vibrant his black hair was or how startingly blue his eyes were in contrast. His height was impressive, maybe an inch over James', but he was slimmer and very elegantly dressed, unlike her. She cringed silently, wishing she had worn something more attractive. It was one thing not to be interested in him, but to be completely overlooked by him was quite a blow to her ego, as men were always vying for her attention.

"Alex, will you go and tell Mrs. Stratton that there will be one more for dinner? And perhaps we should both change since we have company," Deborah suggested.

"Please do not change on my account," protested Dominic.

"It is nothing. We will be right back."

Alexandra practically sprang from the sofa and hastened towards the door, with Deborah following behind her. The door had barely closed behind them when Alex hissed at her, "Mother, did you really say, 'You must have met for a good reason' while staring at me as if I was the good reason?"

"I was not staring! No one noticed. And you must admit that he is very handsome."

"He may be handsome, but I am not interested in him or any man for that matter. Besides which, he did not spare me a glance anyway. And my conversation was non-existent, so he must think I am lacking in wit and intelligence."

"Don't be ridiculous! I'll go and alert the cook. You go and change into something that will make him look at you twice."

"Mother, I am not looking for a husband, so don't get any ideas about matchmaking."

"Of course not, dear," her mother assured her with an innocent smile. Her matchmaking days were over. Getting her parents back together had almost gone terribly wrong all those years ago, so it would do her well not to get involved in trying to matchmake between Dominic and Alex. He was very handsome, though. She wondered if he was married. It wouldn't hurt to find out.

ꕥ

Dominic thought he had done remarkably well not to stare at James' little sister, as he had called her. He knew that when any man came near to his sisters he was less than happy, so he schooled his features and tried not to look in her direction. His first glance could not miss the fact that she was a beauty, with thick reddish-brown hair that was escaping from the loose chignon she had no doubt secured it in before lounging on the couch.

He almost smiled when he saw her trying to ease into a sitting position without drawing attention to herself, as if he could miss the surprisingly significant thrust of her bosom given how slim she was in her well-worn house dress. Not that he had any problem with it, for it was tight enough in the right places to delight. Her brothers would call him out if they could read his thoughts.

He hoped that she could at least carry on a decent conversation and that she was not all beauty and no brains. Not that he was looking for a relationship and especially not with an innocent like James' sister. He had just extricated himself from a rather messy relationship with his current mistress who had started to become rather clingy and was dropping hints about marriage. Why on earth would he buy the cow when he was getting the milk free? Well, not quite free, for he had been paying her rent and providing her with whatever she desired in the way of clothes and accessories. He had no problem with that, as money was not an issue for him, but it was when she began to get too possessive that he had decided to end it. Having to take his mother to England since his father was unable to leave the business just then gave him a good excuse.

"So, Dominic, what line of business are you in?" Richard asked him, breaking into his thoughts.

"My family owns a vineyard in the Bordeaux region and we produce a cabernet sauvignon that has done very well both at home and abroad."

"Is that so? James, are we importing any of this wine to send to the West Indies or America?"

"Not as yet, but we should be," he agreed. "Dom, have you got any samples with you? We should meet to discuss this further."

"Indeed, I always travel with samples. I would be happy to give you a tasting and talk business before you leave. How much longer will you be here?"

"I was planning to go back almost immediately, but it will take a while to sell my house and get my business in order."

"Surely, there is no rush," Deborah said, coming into the room. She had changed into an attractive dress and tamed her hair into a neat style. "We will have dinner as soon as Alexandra comes back."

"I may be interested in renting a property rather than staying with my mother and sisters at my grandmother's house. Would you consider renting yours or do you need to sell?"

"I don't need to sell, but I had wanted to put that part of my life behind me, and since I will be living in Barbados, I don't need the house here. But we can talk about that as well."

"That's fine." Before he could say anything else the door opened and Alexandra entered the room. If he thought that she was beautiful before, he had been wrong. Breathtaking was the word he should have used. While her mother's curly hair had been tamed, her thick slightly wavy hair had been brushed until it shone and was left loose around her shoulders and down the middle of her back. Dominic itched to run his fingers through it. She had taken her mother's advice as well and now wore a bluish green dress that complimented her colouring and revealed her shapely figure. Dominic realised he was staring and made a conscious effort to look elsewhere.

"I've been asked to let you know that dinner is ready," she announced, looking more confident and collected than she had been before.

"Thank you, darling," her mother said, rising from her chair. "Come, Dominic, let us get you fed. You must be starving. Alexandra, lead the way. After you Dominic," she instructed.

Dominic inclined his head and followed Alexandra. Her mother would not have suggested he follow her if she knew how his eyes were mesmerised by the sway of her hips and the way that her hair bounced gently against her back. Thankfully, they reached the dining room quickly and he took the seat that Deborah indicated to him next to her husband at the head of the table. Alexandra was placed next to him and James and Charles seated themselves on the other side of the table so that the numbers were even. Dominic helped Alexandra into the seat next to his before sliding into his own.

Charles, who had not said much before, now began to ask Dominic all kinds of questions about winemaking and his business, giving Alex quite a lot of insight into the business without having to appear overly interested. As Charles paused to eat the delicious sole in a white sauce that the cook had prepared, Alexandra took the opportunity to speak to

Dominic just so that he would realise that she could actually carry on a conversation.

"James said that you used to live in England, I believe. Which do you prefer, France or England?"

"They both have their advantages and disadvantages, but it benefits me to live here for now."

"Do you intend to carry on business while you are here?" she asked. "Perhaps look for new markets for your wine?"

Dominic looked at her with fresh interest. Beauty and brains; a winning combination in his books. He could see the intelligence in her eyes now that his eyes were not focused on her figure, and he was impressed with her question.

"Yes, that is correct."

"Alex is planning to start her own business," Richard told him proudly.

"Indeed? What business are you thinking to get into?"

"I do not know as yet, but it will not be a boutique or some store selling fripperies."

"You have something against boutiques? They can be very profitable if well run, for women seem to do an inordinate amount of shopping."

"I am not one of them so I do not know, nor do I have any desire to sell clothes. I prefer to do something more meaningful."

"Like what?" he asked her.

"I have not decided yet. Perhaps be the hostess of one of those salons like you have in France where people get together to review books and discuss important issues."

"How will you make money doing that?"

"I do not know. Must everything be about making money?" she asked, annoyed.

"I thought the whole purpose of business was to make money. Otherwise you only have a hobby. Are you sure it is a business you want and not a hobby?" he teased her, wanting to see her response.

Alex's eyes flashed at him "I assure you that I know exactly what I want." Her voice was cold, in contrast to the fire in her eyes. *And it is not someone like you.* Her unspoken words almost shouted at him.

"Dominic, may I pour you a glass of wine? Although it may not come near to yours in quality," James warned him, changing the subject quickly. He could tell that Alex was about to tell Dominic exactly what was on her mind. "Anyone else like one?"

"I will have one," Alex told him.

"Are you even old enough to drink?" Charles teased her.

"Are you even old enough to sit at the table with adults?" she fired back at him, making Dominic smile. They reminded him of the banter that he and his sisters often had. He enjoyed her quick wit and fast come back.

"Children, even with company you cannot be on your best behaviour?" their mother chided.

"We are hardly children," Alex corrected her. Dominic concurred, for she was definitely not a child.

"Please excuse my younger siblings," James said. "Our parents only had success with me." Everyone laughed, breaking the tension. "Now, when can we do that wine tasting? I'm eager to sample your wine."

"Are you free tomorrow?"

"Yes, as a matter of fact, I am."

"Can I come too?" Alexandra shamelessly invited herself along. "I have nothing of importance to do and it will be something different."

"I do not think it would be a good idea for an untried young lady to be tasting a great many wines," Dominic told her. James braced himself for the explosion to come. Nothing started up Alex more than to be told that a woman could not do something. He wondered if Dominic did it on purpose just to get a rise out of her, for he knew that his sisters were very much a part of their business and surely must taste the wines.

"Untried?" sputtered Alex. "You know nothing about me! Why should I not be allowed to taste your wine? Is this something that a man can do better? Or perhaps you fear that I may find the quality lacking!" she challenged him.

"Alex," her father said warningly.

"On the contrary, I was seeking to protect you, as I would one of my sisters. I would not want you to imbibe too much and find yourself in a vulnerable position."

"Since it will only be you and James present, I cannot see how I would be in a vulnerable position, as I am sure my brother will be watching out for me in the unlikely event that I become inebriated. And I am not one of your sisters."

"I stand corrected. By all means come along."

"You are too kind," she said sarcastically.

"And no, you are definitely not one of my sisters," he smiled slightly.

Deborah watched the play between them with secret amusement. Their interaction reminded her of hers and Richard's when they had first met and look how they ended up. Worse things could happen.

"I have not heard you mention a wife, Dominic, so do I take it you are not married?" Deborah enquired. Alex stared across the table at her mother in disbelief. Where had that come from?

"You are correct. My poor mother despairs of me finding a wife."

"I cannot imagine that such a handsome man like you would find any difficulty in that."

"Perhaps women have discovered that handsome is only skin deep and have given him a wide berth," Alex suggested archly. Dominic smiled at her not-so-subtle insult, for she did not deny that she found him handsome.

"On the contrary, they seem to love me," he parried jokingly. "I have just not found one that I could contemplate spending my life with as yet."

"Oh, I see that I will have to pray for you to find that special woman," Deborah told him with a smile, glancing at her daughter next to him. Alex studiously ignored her.

"You probably should not waste your prayers on me," he smiled. "Besides, I have no desire to marry any time soon."

"Prayers are never wasted. And before we call he answers, so beware," Deborah replied, undeterred.

Alex restrained herself from rolling her eyes. Her mother had better not be getting any ideas in her head. Dominic Durand may be tall, good-looking and rich, but he obviously did not have much regard for women or their abilities. The less time she spent around him the better for her peace of mind, for he annoyed her greatly. Dinner could not come to an end soon enough so that she could escape his overpowering presence next to her. He might be considered a good catch to some women, but she was not one of them. In fact, if they were the last two people on earth, they would be the last two people on earth!

Chapter 23

The Royal Inn

Jemima stepped on the first riser of the stairs and looked tiredly at the flight before her. This Friday was particularly busy as every table in the diner was full and Mrs. Perch had even had to turn away a few people, much to her annoyance. Not only did she, Jemima, have to cook for about twenty people, but she also had to help Ruth serve because Mrs. Perch had said that she needed to stay at the front in case people came in. Mrs. Perch would have to hire someone else if things stayed so busy, for the two of them could not do all the work. Maybe if they hired another person they could offer lunch two or three days a week.

Word had spread about the food at The Royal Inn, as Mrs. Perch had hoped. Jemima was amazed that so many people were coming there because of her cooking, which she had taken for granted until James told her how good it was. Lately, however, resentment had begun to creep in because, while she was earning a reasonable amount of wages, Mrs. Perch was making a great deal more money from her skills. If she had her own place, the money could have been going into her pocket.

"Jemima, you did an outstanding job today. We have never had so many people to lunch." Mrs. Pearce was much freer with her praise now that she saw how Jemima's cooking was drawing customers.

"Yes, there was quite a crowd," agreed Jemima. "I am very tired, so I am going up now."

"You know, Jemima, your room is only paid up for two more weeks. I certainly don't expect you to go back to sharing with Ruth, so you are welcome to stay in it, provided you can pay the charge."

"I don't see how I will be able to do so, unless you increase my wages." That would be a surprise, for Mrs. Perch kept a tight hold on her money. Jemima wondered if she was worried about losing the boarding house, since she did not have Mr. Perch to look after their affairs, and that made her watch each penny like a hawk.

"Maybe you should consider finding a new benefactor to pay for your room. It is unfortunate, but you don't seem to have good luck with benefactors, for Mr. Fairfax is the second one to leave and not return," she remarked, rather insensitively. Jemima felt a stab to her heart, for it was true. She could not say if James would return, although Cassandra said he would. Not that he was her benefactor, in any case.

She turned to face Mrs. Perch. "I don't see why that should be your concern. I am quite content to make my own way," she answered boldly. Mrs. Perch did not need to know that she worried about what she would do after the time was up. Would her wages be enough for her to rent a room somewhere? Could she stay with Cassandra, perhaps?

"You don't have to be so high and mighty. You know full well that you have always been able to find a man to pay your way. It is nothing to be ashamed of, child. Use what you have to get what you want." Jemima sucked in her breath at the insult and turned to trudge up the stairs. What could she say? It was true. Or at least it had been true until James told her that she no longer had to do that. But where was James? Would he ever come back?

"You better start looking if you want to keep the room here," Mrs. Perch called after her.

Jemima ignored her. Mrs. Perch clearly wanted to make sure that she would continue to get money from Jemima in the event that James did not return. She would leave after the time was up and find somewhere to stay. She did not need to continue to work for Mrs. Perch anyway. The customers were coming because of her cooking. She had to find a way to start her own diner because she knew the customers would follow her. She smiled victoriously at the thought. She would see what Mrs. Perch would do then.

She closed the door behind her and dragged herself to the bed. She was too tired to even think about stripping off her clothes, so she told herself that she would get up and change later. Before sleep overcame her, she idly wondered how much it would cost to run a diner and made up her mind to start looking for a location in town. How would she get the money to start though, for her wages were barely enough to save and she didn't even have to pay for lodgings yet?

Her mind drifted to the men who had come in since the diner opened for lunch. Several of them had made it clear that they would be happy to make her their mistress, but she had ignored them. She had been waiting for James to come back. But suppose he did not? And even if he did, he had not made any promises to her. Maybe it was time for her to consider one of those offers.

ꟾ

A week later

It was getting dark by the time Jemima left the boarding house to visit Cassandra. She wanted to get there before the students so that she could talk with her. Thankfully, she was not needed to serve dinner as there were only two guests remaining at the boarding house. The day had not been as exhausting as the week before, which was both good and bad. Good because she was not as tired, but bad because Mrs. Perch was in a foul mood, as if she was somehow responsible for the fact that fewer patrons had come in.

She patted her pocket, finding comfort in the feel of the knife hidden in it. Not that it had been much help the night that James had easily disarmed her. How she wished she could get him out of her mind. Never had she missed Tobias like this when he went away. Maybe she did love James. He had been gone seven long, unbearable weeks. She wondered if he even thought about her half as much as she thought about him.

Only yesterday Mary-Ann Bailey had come in for lunch. It was the third time she had come in since James had left. The first time she had been both angry and distraught to hear that he had returned to England, especially without informing her. The second time she had questioned her at length to try to find out why he had left, but Jemima had no information to give her, for she had no idea herself. Today she had seemed quite anxious that he had not sent any word back and had even asked Mrs. Perch for his address. Jemima was glad when Mrs. Perch told her that she was not at liberty to disclose the address of a guest.

Her husband had come on separate occasions and had been bold enough to proposition her on hearing that James had left the country. Not that she would ever consider him as a benefactor after the way he had treated her the night that James rescued her. He, too, had questioned her, but she told him the same thing she had told his wife; she knew nothing. It hurt to admit that, especially when they had both looked pityingly at her because James had left her without a word concerning his business in England and when he was coming back.

She squared her shoulders. It was time to forget James and move on. Only today a decent-looking man who looked to be about forty had discreetly asked her if he could meet her outside of the boarding house to discuss a proposition. She was fairly sure it was not a business proposition, at least not the kind she wanted. He was nowhere near as appealing as James, but his clothes were very well made and he seemed kind enough. He had treated her respectfully and did not look at her lustfully or make lewd remarks to her as some of the men did. He reminded her somewhat of

Tobias. She was torn. Should she meet him or should she continue in the hope that James would return? It was not even as if they parted on the best of terms, which was her own fault. She groaned as she remembered how she had ignored him for the last week he was here. How she wished she could take that back.

Cassandra's house appeared before her without her fully realising how she had gotten there. Thankfully, it was still early enough for quite a lot of people to be about as it was a Friday evening, so she had felt safe. In fact, she had never felt unsafe until James put thoughts in her head about someone being able to overpower her easily and take away her weapon. James again! She knocked loudly on the door, taking out her frustration on the wood. Cassandra opened and let her in.

"You are very early. Not that I am complaining," she hastened to add with a smile.

"I needed to talk to you before the students arrived."

"What's happened? Have you heard from James?" Cassandra asked her that every week.

"Why would I? We had no understanding when he left. I do wish you would stop asking me that," she snapped.

Cassandra held up her hands in surrender. "Sorry! I am just concerned about you."

"I am sorry too. It's just that I am angry with James for leaving and not telling me why he went away and if he is coming back." She sighed.

"Come to the kitchen and let's talk." Jemima followed her to the back of the small house. She realised that Cassandra probably only had one tiny bedroom, so she couldn't stay with her if she moved out anyway.

"Cassandra, how do you pay for your house?" she asked abruptly.

"When my master freed me, he gave me this little house, thank the good Lord. And some women in England send me money every now and then to help with the school. And you know that I take in some sewing too. Why are you asking this now?"

"I only have about two more weeks in the room that James paid for in the boarding house and then I have to find somewhere to live. I can't afford to keep paying for the room with my wages."

"You know that you are welcome to come here," Cassandra offered.

"I couldn't do that, Cass. This is barely big enough for you. I met a man today. He seems very nice and respectful. I think he wants me to be his mistress." She looked at Cassandra and waited for a response which was not forthcoming. "Well?" she urged her.

"What you want me to tell you? You already know what I think about you doing that."

"But with the little wages I get I will never be able to afford my own diner. This man might be willing to give me the money to start my business. He looked like he had money."

"It sounds as if you already made up your mind. What do you think James would say to that?"

"James is not here and he didn't leave me with any promises. Just because we shared a bed doesn't mean anything. Anyway, he may not come back."

"He told me that he would. Suppose he comes back and you have taken up with this other man? How do you think he would feel?"

"I will have to deal with that if the time comes. In the meantime, I have to do what is best for me. It is not as if it is something I have not done before," she added defiantly. So why did she feel so sick at the thought?

ꙮ

Six weeks later
Carlisle Bay, Barbados

The calm blue waters of Carlisle Bay welcomed James back to Barbados, along with the blistering heat that had been noticeably absent when he left the island in April. Fortunately, a good breeze made the temperature almost bearable as he waited impatiently to be taken to shore in a smaller boat. He was anxious to set foot on the island again for many reasons. His thought swung to Jemima as they had so many times over the last few weeks. As he had grown closer to Barbados, thoughts of her replaced the sadness he had felt on leaving his family.

A lot had happened in the time he had been home and he was very grateful to have spent many days with his family, particularly his grandmother Sarah, who was delighted that he was going to bring The Acreage back into the family. She was especially happy since she knew that Thomas had loved it but had given it up for her and moved to England. They had spent many hours talking about it with her reminiscing and him bringing her up to date on what was happening both at the plantation and in Barbados. She was also glad that he had found time to help at the school.

He had decided not to sell the house that he and Harriett had owned, but he had rented it to Dominic who had found it perfect for his use, saying that it was close enough to his grandmother's house in case he was needed there quickly, but far enough to maintain good space between him and his mother and sisters. For although he loved them dearly, he had said he certainly did not want to live with them. James could understand that a twenty-seven-year-old bachelor like Dominic would hardly want to live with his mother and sisters. He had only spent a month at his parents' house and that was enough for him. Any longer and his mother would have started matchmaking for him as she had threatened to do for Dominic. It did not take much discernment to know that she was already planning to get him and Alex together, for she had taken to Dominic.

He smiled as he remembered some of the heated encounters that he had witnessed between Dominic and Alex each time they met up. Alex was a strong, feisty young lady who could certainly hold her own with anyone, male or female, so he was not worried about her. She and Dominic seemed to combust every time they came near each other. He suspected that Dominic went out of his way to provoke Alex into an argument. However, he had caught Dominic on several occasions looking at her with an expression that was far from brotherly, so he had warned him to keep his distance, especially as he had said he was not ready to marry.

Unfortunately, he wouldn't be there to make good on the threats he had issued and Charles was soon going to be following him. He had been between two minds whether to say anything to his father, but he decided to trust Dominic to be a gentleman with his sister if they happened to encounter each other. He hoped that he was not misplacing his trust. After all, they had not seen each other for many years and although they were friends, one did not always know the level of integrity of someone until it was tested.

It had taken about four weeks to get his affairs in order and he was now in possession of practically all of his money in the form of banker's drafts and bank notes secured in the bottom of his trunk once again. He now had the means to purchase the mortgage over The Acreage and to set the plantation back in good order. His heart beat faster at the thought.

The trip to the shore was short but felt like an eternity to James. Finally, he and his trunks were safely delivered to the shore where he took some time to find his land legs. He hailed a carriage to take him to The Royal Inn, thirstily drinking in the familiar sights as he travelled the short distance to the boarding house. With each minute his heart sped up at the thought of seeing Jemima again.

What would she be doing now? It was a Tuesday so she would not be preparing for lunch. Did she miss him? Was she still staying in his room? He had only paid for two months and three had gone. He wondered if Mrs. Perch had put her out, for she would not be able to afford the room with her wages. Perhaps she was no longer at the boarding house. Not knowing the answers to his questions made him uncharacteristically anxious and he silently willed the driver to go faster.

Thankfully, the carriage soon was outside The Royal Inn, which he noticed had been recently painted and a new sign had been added saying that lunch was offered on Mondays, Wednesdays and Fridays. Business must be good. He was proud of Jemima, although she did not own the boarding house, for it was surely her talent that was drawing people.

He opened the door and stepped inside while the driver manhandled his trunks from the carriage. Mrs. Perch was exactly where he had left her. He found himself surprisingly glad to see her there, for it made him feel as if nothing had changed.

"Mr. Fairfax! What a wonderful surprise!" she exclaimed, rising from her seat. "We were not sure if you would really return."

"Mrs. Perch, you know that I am a man of my word and I said that I would return," he chided her with a smile. He was actually happy to be back at the inn. He looked towards the stairs. "Is my room available? I know it is more than two months."

"Jemima is still in your room, but I can move her into another one and give you back that one, as it is the best I have."

"Jemima is still in it? How –?" He almost blurted out "how could she afford it", but perhaps Mrs. Perch had allowed her to stay since she was obviously drawing business. Mrs. Perch looked rather uncomfortable and her eyes slid from his. Something was not right.

"You will have to ask her that yourself." She evaded answering his question.

The carriage driver dropped the last trunk and waited for James to pay him. He was travelling a lot heavier than he had last time. Mrs. Perch eyed the mountain of trunks and boxes with blatant curiosity.

"Are you here to stay?" she asked hopefully. A permanent tenant would do her good.

"Not here at The Royal Inn, but yes, I am here to stay in Barbados."

"My goodness, I had no idea you have planned to move here. That is wonderful news."

"Perhaps you can get Rufus to help me carry up my things. There is no need to move Jemima. Any of the other rooms will do. Is she in now?"

She looked uncomfortable again. "She is off today so she is out. She has a new gentleman friend, so she may be with him," she warned him.

James was surprised at the stab of pain he felt in his chest. He made sure that his face did not provide Mrs. Perch with any indication of how her words impacted him. Jemima had a benefactor? After he had paid for her to be free, she had turned around and sold herself to the first man that propositioned her? He felt anger begin to build in him at the thought of her selling herself to some man, for that was what she had done, he was sure. *Once a harlot, always a harlot*, he thought cruelly.

"I will take a room for about a month," he said calmly.

"Are you planning to buy a house?" Mrs. Perch asked, heading towards her desk for a key.

"You will be the first to know if I do," James said sardonically. "Which room is it?"

"It's the one across from your old room. That has a nice view as well, but it is a little smaller."

"Thank you, ma'am. I am sure I will be very comfortable. Let Rufus bring up my things please."

James headed for the stairs with a number of emotions churning in his belly – anger that Jemima had not waited for him but reverted to her old ways, jealousy at the thought of her lying with another man and, to his disgust, longing to see her again in spite of everything.

Chapter 24

Later that evening

Jemima closed the door to the boarding house quietly. She had spent the whole day out and was happy to have some time off to go to the school and help Cassandra with the children, but Henry had sent word he would be in town and wanted to see her. He owned a small but, apparently, prosperous plantation somewhere in St. George, but stayed with her when he came to town. After all, he was now paying for the room. Thankfully, he was content to see her no more than every other week, so she could endure their times together, provided she did not compare him with James.

She was glad that Mrs. Perch was not at her usual place behind the desk, for the less she interacted with her, the better she felt. Henry had promised to help her get her own business started, but so far he had only given her a few gifts and a few shillings last time he came. At least he was kind to her and not too demanding. He certainly did not stir her to passion as James did, but she was not looking for passion; she was looking for provision. She did not know if he was married or not and she did not want to know. All she wanted from him was enough money to start her business. And soon.

Ruth was in the kitchen preparing to serve dinner. She was glad that she would not be needed to help, so she climbed the stairs to prepare herself for Henry's visit. She was almost to the door of her room when the door opposite hers opened. She stopped in surprise, for she had not known that anyone was staying there. Her surprise turned to shock as James Fairfax emerged from the room. Her heart seemed to stop before it took off at such a pace that she became breathless. She noticed that he had cut his hair, but it suited him. He looked more handsome than ever.

"Hello, Jemima," he greeted her.

"James!" she exclaimed. "I-I did not know that you were back." Guilt caused her to stutter for some reason, although she had no reason to feel guilty. "I did not even know that you were planning to come back."

"So it seems," he said enigmatically, making her wonder if Mrs. Perch had already told him about Henry. "How have you been?"

"Good, thank you. And you?"

"I have been very well."

"I see that you cut your hair," she voiced her observation. "It is unusual, but I like it." His hair was now short at the back and around his ears but fell attractively over his forehead.

"Thank you. I am surprised that you have managed to keep paying for the room." He nodded in the direction of his old room as he threw down the gauntlet, challenging her to confess the means she had chosen to finance her room. He would not be diverted by comments about his hair.

"I have my ways of getting things done," she said defensively.

"I am sure that you do," he mocked her. Jemima could almost feel the anger rising in him. What did he have to be angry about? Did he leave her with any promises that he would come back? Any means to provide for herself beyond the two months?

"If you will excuse me, I have to prepare myself for company." She moved towards her door, but before she had taken two steps James grabbed her, pushed her up against the wall and began to plunder her mouth as if he could not get enough of her. Jemima wound her arms around his neck and returned his kiss with wild abandon. How she had missed him! Missed this!

"You harlot," he ground out, pushing away from her. Shock paralysed her for seconds before she slapped his face with all the anger and hurt she felt behind it.

"Then you better stay away from me before you get tainted, Saint James," she spat at him before hastily unlocking her door and slamming it behind her.

James slumped against the wall, feeling the anger drain out of him only to be replaced with shame. He could not believe he had called Jemima that word or that he had treated her with such contempt. Barbados truly seemed to bring out the worst in him. He would never think of acting that way in England. There seemed to be an atmosphere of incivility that influenced him whenever he set foot on the island. He ran a tired hand over his eyes and forcibly pushed off the wall, feeling as if all the life had gone from him. He needed to apologise to Jemima, but he knew better than to try to do it now. He would wait until she cooled off, if she ever did.

He started towards the stairs only to slow down as he saw a man half-way up. He was of average height and looks, nothing to recommend him, to be honest. He was well-dressed and looked to be prosperous, so perhaps he was a guest. He hoped so. That would be preferable to knowing he was Jemima's new benefactor, for if he was, he did not know how he would stand watching him go into Jemima's room to have what he could not.

"Good evening," the man greeted with a polite nod. James' face felt wooden and he barely managed a nod in response as he passed the man and headed towards the staircase. He hovered at the top of the stairs so that he could see which room the man went into. When he could delay no longer, he took the first step down and glanced over his shoulder in time to see the man knock at the door that Jemima had just disappeared into. He quickly turned around before hot jealousy and anger caused him to do something foolish. Jemima had made her choice and he had to respect that, but it did not prevent the jealousy and anger that raged in him.

ꕥ

"Your landlady seems to have a new guest," Henry remarked, entering the room. He pulled Jemima to him to press a kiss on the lips that James had recently ravished. She wondered if he could see the evidence of that kiss on them. Jemima turned away, not responding to his comment. She knew with utter certainty that she could not lie with him while James was in the same country, far less in the same building, or worse yet, across the hall.

She was probably the biggest fool alive, but she could not continue the relationship with Henry. She knew it would hurt James, and although he had just deeply insulted her, she did not have it in her to cruelly disregard his feelings, assuming that he did have feelings for her. He must have, which would explain why he was so angry. She should never have taken up with Henry, not when she loved James. She knew she loved James, but she had buried her feelings when he left for fear that he would not return. Now he seemed to hate her and with good reason.

The memory of the journey back from The Acreage stirred in her mind. She saw herself offering James her hand and introducing herself to him. She had decided to change her life then. How did she get back to this place where she was giving herself to another man to get what she wanted? James was right! She was a harlot. A sob caught in her throat, making Henry come up behind her and gently hold her shoulders, drawing her back against him. Jemima stiffened.

"What is the matter, Jemima?" He gently kissed her neck.

"I cannot do this anymore. I am sorry, Henry, but I cannot."

"What do you mean you cannot? What has happened? What has changed?"

"Nothing has happened," she lied. But for a short time I forgot something very important."

"You forgot something? What? I do not understand." He sounded confused and impatient.

"I forgot that I am Jemima Andrews," she smiled wistfully, turning around to see the puzzled look on his face. "Thank you for all you have done for me, Henry. I am very grateful, but I can no longer be with you. I no longer want to live this life."

"You can no longer be with me?" he laughed cynically. "You whore! Who do you think you are? I have paid for your room, bought you clothes and given you money and you think you can tell me 'thank you for all you have done for me' and just walk away?"

His face, now hard with anger, was unrecognisable to Jemima. Having always seen him as mild-mannered and lacking in passion, the transformation cast fear into her. Desperately wishing for the knife that she no longer carried, she eased towards the door, intent on getting away from him. The movement did not escape him, and he grabbed her arm, arresting her. She knew that there would be a bruise on it the next day, if she was still alive.

"I asked you a question," he snarled.

"I did not think you required an answer." She was glad that her voice did not betray the trembling that shook her knees beneath her skirt.

He released her arm, only to grab her hair painfully, pulling her head back and exposing her neck. Jemima wondered if he intended to break her neck. She tried to bring her knee up to his most vulnerable place but did not get the leverage she needed to incapacitate him. He pushed her off with such force that she fell against the bed hurting her back and knocking the wind from her. In an instant, he was on her, slapping her about the face before he grabbed her by the hair and threw her face down on the bed. Before she could recover, he straddled her while working to free himself of his pants.

She turned her head to one side and screamed James' name. Henry rolled her over and covered her mouth and nose roughly with his hand. She thrashed helplessly, panicked as she fought for air.

"James? Is that the man who I saw leaving? Well he can have what's left of you after I get what I paid for," Jemima heard him say before darkness enfolded her.

ꙮ

James could hardly taste the food that he forced down his throat. It could have been prepared by Jemima for all he knew, but he could not tell what he ate or what it tasted like. All he could see imprinted in his mind was the man going into Jemima's room. When the food threatened to return to his throat, he pushed his plate away and stomped out of the dining room, past a startled Mrs. Perch and out the door. His feet took him towards the beach where he knew the sound of the surf and the cool breeze coming off the ocean would calm him.

He did not know why he allowed Jemima to affect him like this. He wanted nothing more to do with her, no matter how much his body made him out to be a liar. When he thought of how sweet and pure Harriett was, he could not understand the overwhelming desire he had for Jemima. What would he do about it? What could he do? She was in a relationship with someone else. She had barely waited for his back to be turned before she resorted to her old ways. Could he ever trust her? Maybe he should just move on. Pay for The Acreage, call in the debt and move there, away from the temptation of Jemima. Or at least from seeing her with her new benefactor, or worse yet, hearing them behind her closed door.

He would go and see Augustus Berkshire first thing in the morning. Then he would take a trip to The Acreage. No point in wasting time. And in the mood he was in after what he had just witnessed, he would have no qualms asking Samuel Bailey to get off his property. His conscience pricked at the thought of Mary-Ann. Where would she go? Back to England?

The beach was dark as there was no moon that night, but it suited him fine. The walk along the shore with the sound of the waves gently teasing the sand before pulling back soothed him as he knew it would. He made sure that he stayed well above the wet sand, for he didn't want the discomfort of wet shoes to add to the other discomfort that his body was enduring. He had been better off before he had lain with Jemima, for then he had no knowledge of the secrets of her body. But now he groaned as he imagined her in her room with the man he had passed in the corridor. That image was not helping, so he forced his thoughts away.

When he could delay his return to the boarding house no longer, he braced himself and retraced his footsteps. He hoped that Jemima's benefactor was not spending the night, although it might be a vain hope. He slowly climbed the stairs and headed to his room while trying to avoid looking in the direction of Jemima's room. but against his will, his eyes were drawn towards her door. Should he go and apologise? Surely her benefactor was still there. Yet something was pulling him towards her door. He knocked quietly and then louder as he got no response. A feeling of urgency, like the night at The Acreage, prompted him to turn the knob. It opened under his hand.

"Jemima?" he called, pushing open the door cautiously. His heart lodged in his throat when he saw her sprawled across the bed with her skirt hitched up and her face bruised and swollen. She whimpered softly, propelling him across the room to her side. Love and compassion flooded him on seeing her devastation, washing away the anger and jealousy that had possessed him.

"Jemima!" His hand shook as he gently pushed her hair away from her battered face and smoothed down her skirt. The gentleness of his touch was at odds with the fresh rage that he was trying to contain, for he wanted nothing more than to find the man who had done this to her and rid the earth of his presence.

"James," she forced his name through lips that were cracked and covered with dry blood. "You were right. I am a harlot. And he treated me as one. I tried to stop him, but he was too strong for me. It was as if he was possessed by something that gave him strength. I never knew he could be like that," she mumbled on, obviously in shock. The tears that fell from her eyes burned their way into James's heart causing it to ache as he helplessly watched her suffering. His hands shook with the effort to appear calm for Jemima, while inside a volcano threatened to explode.

"Shh, don't try to talk." He forced himself to leave her side briefly to wet a towel with water from a jug so that he could gently wipe her face and lips.

"I need to bathe." She struggled to sit up. "I have to wash. I feel so dirty," she cried.

"I will get Ruth to help you in a minute. Stop, Jemima." She obeyed, spent by the effort to get up. "Is anywhere else injured? Your ribs?"

"I hit my back against the bed when he pushed me, but it is only hurting a little now. I didn't even have my knife. I could have stopped him if I had my knife," she continued.

James said nothing but he was glad that she did not have it, for although she had been sorely abused, at least she was still alive. If she had attacked him with her knife, he may have disarmed her as easily as he had that night and used it on her.

"I am so sorry this happened to you, Jemima. I am sorry I called you a harlot. You are not a harlot and you do not deserve anyone to treat you like one. I am so sorry," he repeated. She nodded her forgiveness, touching her hand to his cheek. He was humbled by her willingness to forgive him, even after what she had suffered.

"I want to change the way I live, but I cannot seem to help myself. Please help me." The eye that was not swollen pleaded with him.

"I cannot help you, Jemima. But I know someone who can. His name is Jesus. If you ask him and if you truly want to change your ways, he will help you. You will be a new person, not like when you introduced yourself as Jemima Andrews in the carriage, but truly new."

"Please introduce me to him," she whispered as a new tear fell from the corner of her eye.

Chapter 25

Next morning

James had been reluctant to leave the boarding house, but after finding Jemima asleep he decided to go into town and deal with the mortgage and hope to get back before she woke up. He gave Ruth a few coins to look after her and told Mrs. Perch that Jemima was not up to preparing lunch. No doubt she would make her way upstairs to find out why. Before he left for town, he sought out Rufus who was happy to tell him where he could find the plantation that was owned by the man called Henry Parkinson. He would pay him a visit afterwards.

After having waited three months, James could hardly believe that the mortgage papers and title deeds to the property were in his hands and he now was within reach of owning The Acreage. Augustus Berkshire had been happy to hand over the papers to him and be rid of the debt. Apparently, Samuel Bailey had managed to come up with a small payment in his absence, at which time Augustus had served him with a notice to foreclose on the property if the amount was not paid in full in two months.

He had pleaded with Augustus to be patient until he received payment from the current sugar crop, although James would be surprised if he had not already used it to get other credit to finance his lifestyle. The two months had passed and he had not returned to pay the mortgage, so Augustus was free to transfer the mortgage and all the other papers to James. All he needed to do was serve the foreclosure papers and the property would be his.

James wanted to rush back to the boarding house and celebrate the news with Jemima, but more than that he wanted to visit Henry Parkinson and give him a sample of what he had given Jemima.

As he climbed into a carriage and gave the driver instructions to Parkinson's plantation, he was halted by words that dropped into his head. *Vengeance is mine, I will repay.* He tried to ignore them, for his anger still raged unassuaged and he wanted blood. All he could see was Jemima's battered body on the bed with telling bruises on her face and near the top of her thighs and he wanted vengeance.

Jemima is one of mine now. I will repay.

He drove his fist into the side of the carriage in frustration, for he knew that he could not ignore the words. The driver stopped, thinking that he had hit the carriage to stop him, so James stuck his head out the window and grudgingly gave him new instructions: "Take me to The Acreage plantation instead." Henry Parkinson would get what was coming to him one of these days and he would be there to enjoy seeing it happen. Unfortunately, it wouldn't be today.

ꙮ

The carriage ride seemed to take an interminable time and it didn't help that in spite of the excitement he had had before about owning the property, he now wrestled his conscience every mile of the way. He knew in his heart that he was not doing anything illegal or immoral. Samuel Bailey had taken the risk of signing a mortgage for which he had offered the plantation as security and he had not honoured the agreement by paying back the debt. Neither had he responded to the foreclosure notice that Augustus Berkshire had sent him. Therefore, it was well within his right as the new lender to call in the debt and acquire the property as he was doing.

As the carriage rolled up the driveway, James saw Mary-Ann get up from her rocking chair and approach the edge of the patio to see who was in it. When it stopped, he let himself out and instructed the driver to wait beside the house, for he did not expect to have a long visit, especially after they learned of his business.

"James Fairfax! My eyes must be deceiving me," Mary-Ann exclaimed as he approached the patio.

"Hello, Mary-Ann."

"Don't you 'Hello, Mary-Ann' me. I don't know if to hug you as I am so glad to see you or murder you for disappearing like you did," she complained.

"Well, since I know that your threat of murder may be real..." James teased her, trailing off his words with a smile.

Needing no encouragement, she launched herself at him and gave him a long hug.

"I have missed you terribly. How dare you leave without telling me?" she scolded, drawing him to the patio. "And you cut your hair. You look good enough to eat," she flirted. James could not resist a smile.

"Mary-Ann, you have not changed your deplorable behaviour."

"But of course not. What is this? Are you not planning to stay a while?" She gestured towards the waiting carriage.

"No. And in any case, you may not wish me to stay when you hear why I have come. Is Samuel here?"

"He is out in the fields, can you imagine?"

"Please have someone fetch him. I need to speak with him."

"I am more than curious. What has happened?"

"I will tell you all, but please send a message to him."

She looked at him curiously before disappearing into the house to tell one of the girls to fetch their master. She was back in record time as if she could not wait to question him.

"There is no way I am waiting until Samuel gets here to find out what you want to speak to him about. Now tell me," she demanded.

James weighed whether he should wait for Samuel or not but decided that he wanted Mary-Ann to be prepared for the shock that was soon to come. He found himself reluctant to do the deed now that he was faced with the reality of it. Just as he opened his mouth to explain, Hetty came out bearing a tray with drinks. She smiled shyly at him and greeted him, looking him in the eye. James marvelled at even that small progress, for he remembered when he first came to The Acreage when she would not even meet his eyes.

The night that he had stopped Samuel from beating her came back to him and strengthened his resolve. He knew in his heart that he had not only come to The Acreage to restore it to their family but to bring dignity and humanity to the slaves on the plantation, something even his grandfather had not fully done. He was making restitution. He had a plan of how he could successfully operate the plantation without the oppressive system of slavery.

"Mary-Ann, while I was here, I discovered that Samuel had taken out a mortgage using the plantation as security and that he was months behind on the payments. Did you know that?"

"Why, no. He never said anything. He would make remarks about me spending money on clothes, but he never said we could not afford them." She now looked distraught. "How bad is it?"

"It is very bad. The worst, in fact. I have taken over the mortgage from Augustus Berkshire and I am sorry for your sake, but I am calling in the debt. I will give you and Samuel a month to get your affairs in order and leave the plantation." He delivered the last part regretfully, for he truly felt sorry for her.

"Leave the plantation?" she replied vaguely, obviously trying to absorb what he had said. James could see her visibly brighten after a few minutes and she looked at him with a lively smile. "I do not need to leave at all. This is perfect, James! Exactly what I told you before. You can now have the plantation and its mistress and we don't necessarily have to employ the use of foxglove," she added, as if she was talking about aloe or some other plant.

James shook his head in disbelief, not totally able to hide the smile that threatened to lighten the seriousness of what she said. "Mary-Ann, you are still married to Samuel. Besides, the papers I have give me access to the plantation, not its mistress."

"That was never an issue, James. You know that I would be yours in a minute. You only need to say the word. But then, you took up with Jemima! I cannot believe you chose a servant over me." She pouted prettily. "But I am willing to forgive you."

James tried not to wince at the mention of Jemima's name, especially since the whole thing had been a lie. And now she lay in bed battered while he was dealing with business instead of being at her side.

"Mary-Ann, you are a lovely woman, but you are still married." Before she could reply, Samuel galloped up the driveway, halting her words. James caught the secret smile that ghosted her face before she settled for a blank look as Samuel joined them and he felt a pang of unease.

"My dear boy, it is wonderful to see you. How rude of you to take off without so much as a by-your-leave," he chastened James while shaking his hand enthusiastically.

"My apologies, Samuel, but I had some urgent business to attend to in England. Actually, that is the reason I am here. Perhaps you might like to sit down while you read this document." James reached into the satchel he had brought and handed Samuel the copy of the document transferring the mortgage over The Acreage to him as well as the notice of foreclosure on the property.

James could tell exactly when Samuel understood the words he was reading, for his face turned deathly pale. He finished reading and looked up at James with horror in his eyes.

"You are calling in the debt over my plantation? You are turning us out?" he asked in disbelief.

"I am sorry, Samuel, but you have had ample warning from Berkshire and you did not heed them."

"I asked him to give me until I received payment from this crop," he insisted. "I can pay you some of the money then."

"I am sorry," James repeated, truly hating the situation. He had known it would be hard, but it pained him to see even Samuel humbled in this manner. "I will give you some time to get your affairs in order and leave the plantation. I believe a month should be sufficient time but let me know if you need more time."

He looked at Samuel, but he was staring blankly ahead, his mind grappling with the implications of what it all meant. Turning towards Mary-Ann, he gave her a sympathetic look and she nodded gravely in return. She did not look as devastated as Samuel did, but then again, she had had more time to accept the situation.

"I will take my leave now. My attorney will be around to take an inventory next week, so anything that you particularly wish to keep that is listed as security in the mortgage, Mary-Ann, please let him know." She nodded again.

James returned the papers to his bag and with a brief nod to the Baileys he walked out of the patio and to the carriage. As they drove down the driveway, he looked back and beheld the plantation house that was now his. The Acreage had been restored to the Edwards and Fairfax families, but somehow he couldn't bring himself to celebrate it at that moment.

Chapter 26

"Mistress Bailey! Wake Up! Come quick!"

Hetty's frantic cries woke Mary-Ann from her sound sleep. She had not slept well that night, worrying about the future and what she would do when James took over the plantation, unless she could convince him to somehow allow her to stay. That might be rather difficult with a husband around, but he did not have to be around forever.

She sat up groggily, rubbing her eyes. Hetty was beside her bed, the whites of her eyes wide against her dark skin and she was wringing her hands as if that would somehow hurry her mistress up.

"What has happened, Hetty? What is all the fuss about?" she demanded grumpily.

"It is Master Bailey. I just find he in the office collapse' 'pon the desk. He-he like he dead!" Her voice rose in her distress.

"That's preposterous, Hetty. He must have drunk himself into a stupor," Mary-Ann told her, grabbing a dressing gown and throwing it on. She pushed her feet into a pair of soft slippers and led the way from the room.

"Did you try to wake him up? Did you shake him?"

"No, mistress. I was too frighten. So I call Dottie and she touch he, but he didn' move and she say, 'He like he dead. Go and call the mistress'. So I run up and call you."

"Oh God!" Mary-Ann rushed into the office to find Dottie and two of the other house slaves standing to the side of the room looking shocked. Samuel was slumped over the desk on some papers. There was a glass with a little liquid in the bottom that could have been brandy near one of his hands while the other hung by his side. She approached the desk, almost tripping on some things that were strewn around the floor as if they had been knocked off the desk. She cautiously touched the back of his neck which was exposed. It was as cold as death.

"He is dead! Oh my God. What are we to do?" she asked in a panic. Tears filled her eyes as she looked around wildly at the slaves.

"We could send for Moore, the overseer. He would know what to do," Dottie suggested.

"Yes. Yes. Somebody get one of the boys to go for him. And maybe we should send for the doctor, although it is too late for him now. I will go and dress. Hetty, come and help me."

Mary-Ann moved as if in a daze. She could not believe that Samuel was dead. Could someone cause a death just by wishing the person dead? If so, she was guilty of killing him, for only last night she had thought how fortuitous it would be if he was out of the way and she could marry James. Now guilt and shame made tears fill her eyes afresh. She had never loved Samuel, but they had been together for a long time. To think that he was no longer a part of her life was a shock but, if she was honest with herself, also a relief.

She let herself into her room, went through the motions of washing and let Hetty dress her and fix her hair. Her mind was a mass of confused thoughts, jumping from one thing to the next. She wondered what had caused his death and for a brief moment considered the possibility that he might have taken his own life rather than face the disgrace of losing the plantation. She wondered what was in the glass. Could it have been poison? Oh goodness, she hoped not, for James would be convinced that she had done it. James! She should send for him. She wrote a quick note and gave it to Hetty to find someone to deliver it to him in town.

Downstairs, the house was in a state of confusion. The overseer had come in and had instructed one of the slaves to send for Mr. Bowyer who was their closest neighbour. Mary-Ann was glad to leave everything to him, for she was still numb with shock. She sat in her rocking chair on the patio, blindly staring at the driveway until the doctor and Henry and Susan Bowyer arrived within minutes of each other.

"Oh, my poor dear," wailed Susan, pulling her to her sizeable body to wrap her in a warm hug. "I'm so sorry. So sorry," she repeated, easing Mary-Ann back into her chair and pulling one close to it so that she could hold her hand.

Henry and the doctor murmured greetings and offered sympathy that she must have acknowledged before they hastened into the house where they were directed to the office by Dottie.

"I can't believe this, Susan. He was fine yesterday. He was out in the fields and everything before James came over."

"James Fairfax? The one we met here?"

"Yes. You will soon find out anyway, so I should tell you that he has acquired the plantation."

"What? Do you not know who he is?" she asked.

"What do you mean, who he is?"

"Last week one of Henry's sisters was over for dinner with her husband. She and Henry started reminiscing and she asked him if he remembered William Edwards' cousin who had come from Carolina when William was in England. William was the son of Thomas Edwards who used to own The Acreage. Remember we told you about the scandal when his cousin from America married one of the coloured slaves from the plantation?" Mary-Ann nodded, confused about where the story was going.

"Well, his name was Richard Fairfax and he caused quite a stir among the young ladies when he was here, for he was quite handsome. Henry thought he had gone back to America, but he and his coloured wife moved to England where Thomas Edwards had gone. She heard from another friend who knew the family that they had three children, two boys and a girl, and one of the boys' name is James." She paused to let that sink in. Mary-Ann tried to make sense of it in her head with all the other thoughts that were swirling around. Her head snapped up.

"James is the son of the Fairfax man and the slave? So that means he is coloured?"

"Yes, my dear! And can you imagine that we sat with him over dinner. And he acted as if he was white and all? He has fooled everyone, for no one suspected." She said that as if he had a contagious disease that he had kept secret.

"Well, coloured or not, he now owns The Acreage. Which means that it is back in their family." Mary-Ann fell silent again as she realised that it must have been James' plan to own it all along. Perhaps that was why he had come in the first place. Nothing had changed for her, coloured or not. She still wanted him and now she was free to pursue him. Once her husband was buried, of course. May he rest in peace.

ᢒᢓ

"Mr. Fairfax! Mr. Fairfax!" Mrs. Perch interrupted his breakfast. She held a note in her hand which she quickly handed to him. It was a piece of paper that looked as if it had been folded hurriedly. He had no doubt that Mrs. Perch had already read it as she hovered anxiously by his side waiting for him to do the same. He unfolded the paper with a feeling of dread.

Dear James

Please come as fast as you can. Samuel was found dead this morning. I need you.

Mary-Ann

James stared at the paper in shock! Samuel was dead? How? He had seen him just yesterday and while he had looked quite pale when he left, he was very much alive. Mary-Ann! He recoiled from that thought in horror. Mrs. Perch cleared her throat, reminding him that she was standing by watching him closely.

"Has something happened?" she asked, as if she had not already read the note. James pushed back his chair.

"Yes. I have to go to The Acreage. Lord Bailey has died." She gasped convincingly. "I'm going to hire a horse which will get me there faster than a carriage," he said, heading for the door.

"Indeed. Lady Bailey will be needing the support."

James rushed up the stairs to his room to change into riding clothes and grab his hat. He paused and knocked at Jemima's door, opening it when she answered. She was in bed still and thankfully her face was not as swollen as before, but her eye had darkened to a reddish purple.

"James, what has happened?" she asked, seeing his urgency.

"It's Samuel Bailey. I just got a note from Mary-Ann telling me that he has died." Jemima sucked in her breath in shock.

"What? What happened?"

"I don't know. Mary-Ann needs me. I have to go," James said before closing the door again and took off down the hallway running.

Jemima stared at the door where he had stood with his words echoing in her ears – 'Mary-Ann needs me'. Did Mary-Ann really need him or did she want him? She had made it plain even when her husband was alive that she wanted James. Now that he was dead, James did not have a chance. Maybe he would no longer feel the need to resist her advances. So where did that leave her? Immediately, Jemima felt guilty for thinking badly of the woman who had just lost her husband, but she couldn't help but wonder if she was already planning to replace him with James. The way he had gone running to be at her side suggested that she might not find it that difficult to convince him. He had been wonderful to her since the incident and he was happy that she had made the decision to change her ways, but never once had he said he loved her or wanted to be with her. Any hope that she had for her and James withered away. There was no way she could compete with Mary-Ann Bailey, the widow.

ꟿ

James raced along the road after the slave who had brought the note. Thankfully, he had been told to wait, for he was able to take him through some short cuts that he would not have known. He could not believe that Samuel was dead. How was that possible? Then he allowed himself to ask the question he had been avoiding asking. Did Mary-Ann kill him? Did she use the foxglove she had been threatening to use to get rid of Samuel? And if she did, was it because of him?

Yesterday she had told him he could have the plantation and its mistress and today her husband was dead. It was a bit too much of a coincidence for him. She was mad if she thought he would marry her after she killed her husband. She would be lucky if he did not send for the authorities and tell them all that she had told him. He felt ill which had little to do with the breakfast he had abandoned and all to do with the thought that Mary-Ann may have killed her husband so that she could stay at The Acreage with him. *Lord, let that not be true.*

He had not even had time to explain anything to Jemima before he rushed out. He had not seen her much yesterday since she had slept quite a bit and when she had been awake he didn't want to bring up the topic of The Acreage. Besides, he didn't feel like celebrating when she was still in distress and when he was feeling a little guilty about turning out the Baileys.

He really needed to talk to her, as soon as she was stronger. He had missed her when he was in England. He missed the conversations they used to have, her direct way of speaking, her boldness. He missed her kisses and – Lord, help him – he missed her body. Although it had only been that one time, it was etched in his memory. He loved her. He wanted her. He wanted her to be the mistress of The Acreage.

Since he hadn't said anything, she did not know that he owned it and she probably thought that he had gone running to comfort Mary-Ann. However, rather than going to comfort her, he was going to interrogate her until he got the truth, and God help her if she confessed to poisoning her husband.

ഇ ര

"It looks like it was his heart," the doctor announced, coming back to the patio.

"His heart? Are you sure?" Mary-Ann asked in disbelief. She was surprised at the relief that washed over her, for she had been convinced that Samuel had taken his own life. "He never suffered with his heart."

"Sometimes these things just happen. A shock may bring it on or it may have been something that was happening over the years and suddenly the heart just gives out. You have my deepest sympathy. If there is anything I can do for you, please don't hesitate to send a message."

"Thank you, doctor." Mary-Ann felt that she could weep with relief.

"We would be happy to stay with you and help you with Samuel," Susan Bowyer offered.

"That is very kind of you, but I will be fine. In fact, I think I will go and lie down for a while."

"We understand. I will come over tomorrow to check on you," she promised, while Henry gave her a hug before they left just behind the doctor.

"Mistress, you want me to help you prepare the body for the laying out?" Dottie asked her.

"You do it, Dottie. I have no desire to." She got up and went to her room. She wondered if James would come. She needed the strength of his arms around her.

An hour or so later, Hetty came to rouse her from the light sleep she had fallen into.

"Mr. Fairfax downstairs," she announced.

"James is here?" Mary-Ann asked, quickly getting out of bed and putting back on the black dress that Hetty had laid out for her. She grimaced. Black did not become her; it made her look pale and wan. "Fix my hair quickly, Hetty."

In minutes, she was downstairs again where she found James pacing the patio.

"James! I'm so glad you came." She rushed into his arms and he instinctively put his arms around her.

"Tell me that you did not kill him, Mary-Ann," he whispered quietly against her ear.

"Of course not, James," she huffed, pulling away. James searched her face for the truth. "How could you think such a thing?" she accused him.

"Mary-Ann, you have said as much to me on more than one occasion. And the day after I tell you that I now own the plantation, Samuel is dead. What would you have me think?"

"I will have you know that the doctor said it was probably his heart and that he may have had a shock. Can you think of anything that might have shocked him yesterday, James?" she asked reproachfully, tossing the accusation back at him. James got her meaning immediately.

"Don't you attempt to place the blame on me, Mary-Ann. When I left here he was alive and well, even if a little pale. Did you not tell me that foxglove poisoning can be mistaken for a heart attack?"

"Believe me, James, I may have spent the night wishing him dead, but I did not kill him." He stared at her and saw the truth written there. Relief made him sag, for he didn't know if he had it in him to turn her over to the authorities if she had been guilty.

"I am glad to hear that, Mary-Ann."

"Now, if we wait a few months more than Margaret Berringer we should not cause a scandal," she smiled.

"Mary-Ann, your husband's body is barely cold and you are planning a wedding? I have come to like you and I will help you to get back to England, but I am afraid that I have no intention of marrying you."

"James, do you think that any white woman will marry you? Susan Bowyer discovered who you are and told me yesterday. You are coloured, although no one can tell by looking at you. But I am willing to overlook that because you have so many other attributes. Besides, I'm not that discriminating; I have sampled your colour already and I was very satisfied," she purred at him, coming closer.

James was relieved that he no longer had to pretend to be someone he wasn't. He felt free and proud of his heritage. He laughed, startling Mary-Ann.

"I don't care if no white woman will marry me, for I have no desire to marry any, you included. If Jemima will have me, I intend to marry her and make her the mistress of The Acreage. I am still prepared to help you get to England so you can send word when you're ready to leave, but as I said yesterday, you have a month to get your affairs in order. Goodbye, Mary-Ann."

He leaned over and kissed her briefly on her cheek before striding to his horse and mounting it. He left The Acreage at a gallop, telling himself that the next time he came back he would be bringing his bride with him. He hoped.

ꟾ

James knocked at Jemima's door, hoping that she was awake, for she seemed to be sleeping all the time. The door opened and Jemima's face appeared in the opening. She looked as if she had been crying. And her already ravaged face was red and splotchy. James' heart hurt at the traces of her tears and her red-rimmed eyes.

"What are you doing out of bed?" he asked. She moved back and allowed him in, closing the door behind him.

James stopped suddenly at the sight of clothes piled on the bed and an open trunk on the floor. She had obviously been packing.

"Where are you going? You're not well enough to go anywhere."

"I'm going to stay with Cassandra for a short while until I find somewhere I can afford."

"Jemima, you do not need to leave. Let us have a talk. One that is long overdue."

She nodded and made room on the bed for them to sit down.

"I need to tell you about my ancestry. This will come as a shock to you, but my mother was a coloured slave at The Acreage. Thomas Edwards, who owned it, was her father and my grandfather." Jemima was speechless with shock. James smiled slightly and continued. "My father was his wife's nephew and when he came to Barbados to stay at The Acreage he fell in love with my mother and bought her from my grandfather –"

"He bought her?" she exclaimed, finding her voice again.

"Yes. It's a long story, but he bought her and later set her free. She paid for her freedom with her body." He let that sink in. "They eventually got married and followed my grandfather and my grandmother – my mother's mother – to England. My grandfather gave up The Acreage for her. When I came here, I was grieving for my wife, as you know, but two things changed my life: you and The Acreage. From the time I saw The Acreage I knew I had to find some way to bring it back into the family and from the time I saw you I wanted to run in the other direction," he joked.

Jemima hit him playfully on his shoulder. Hope was beginning to blossom in her. James would hardly be here instead of with Mary-Ann Bailey and telling her all this if he didn't feel something for her.

"Thankfully, you were a bold hussy and you wouldn't let me run. You challenged me to let go of my grief and guilt and live again. More importantly, because of you I now know what it means to love unconditionally and how to forgive even when someone has disappointed you."

"I am sorry I disappointed you by becoming Henry's mistress," she agonised. "I accepted him because of what he could give me, not because I felt anything for him. I am so ashamed of that now."

"I am also sorry that I dishonoured you by lying with you outside of marriage. I never want to do that again," he declared. Before she had time to protest, he continued, "Because I want to marry you, Jemima, and make you the mistress of The Acreage. I love you and I don't care what you have done in the past to survive and to provide for yourself. Forgive me for judging you. From now on, I want to provide for you and love you and honour you, for you are precious to me. Say that you will marry me."

"Oh, James. Yes! I will marry you and be the mistress of The Acreage. I love you so much! I have never had a man treat me as you have and made me feel valuable despite not being pure and untouched. You made me look at myself differently and because of that I am a new person."

"I promise to honour you and continue to treat you as my own precious jewel. Now, put all your clothes back, for you will stay here for the next month until we get married and move to The Acreage."

"Stay in this room? You mean that I cannot share yours?" she wailed.

"Absolutely not, young lady. We are going to do this the right way. I will not touch you again until we are married and I carry you across the threshold of our room at The Acreage."

"Oh, James, how am I supposed to bear it? A whole month?"

"I survived for two years before you seduced me, so you will not die. But I might," he sighed. "I think kissing would be fine, though," he compromised. "We definitely need to seal this with a kiss."

He pushed her back against the bed and followed her down, leaning over her but not daring to join anything more than their lips. Jemima wound her hands around his neck and pulled him closer. He kissed her with tenderness, showing his love with every movement of his lips, keeping a tight rein on his passion, knowing that if they waited, it would be well worth the wait when they were finally joined together as man and wife.

Epilogue

One Month Later
The Acreage

James carried Jemima over the threshold of their room at The Acreage and kicked the door to close it behind them. They were in the master bedroom, the one where his grandfather and grandmother came together secretly with his wife just two doors away. His heritage was not the most respectful, but he now had the chance to make things right. He and Jemima had waited until they were married, and a short while ago they had been married over by their favourite spot on the plantation, overlooking the east coast. There was no issue about them marrying, for it was now known that he was coloured. For some people that was an issue and for others it made no difference. Not that he cared one way or the other.

He had decided to manumit all the slaves on the plantation and those who wanted to leave were free to do so, but others who chose to indenture themselves for five years could stay and earn a piece of land at the end of their term. Most of them had chosen to stay. He had gotten rid of the overseer and found one who was more in keeping with the way he wanted to operate the plantation.

After convincing Mary-Ann Bailey that although Samuel was dead he was not available, he offered to pay her passage to return to England once she found out if her relatives would be willing to take her in. He hoped that she would find someone that she could love and who would love her in return, for she was still young and beautiful, and despite how she had schemed to seduce him in the past, he had come to like her.

Mrs. Perch had managed to hire another cook whom Jemima was happy to teach how to prepare some of her dishes before she left The Royal Inn. Of course, Mrs. Perch was sorry to see her leave, but she was somewhat mollified when Jemima assured her that she had no intention of opening a restaurant to compete with hers, as she would be busy at The Acreage.

He had written a letter telling his family about his plans to marry Jemima and he wished they could have been there with them, although he felt them there in spirit, especially his grandfather. In the letter he had invited Charles to stay for a month on his way to Carolina, so he was looking forward to seeing him and introducing him to Jemima. Maybe they would take a trip to England after Charles left so that she could meet his parents and Alex.

"Mrs. Fairfax, I survived two years of celibacy before, but this last month nearly killed me," he confessed.

"Mr. Fairfax, that is because you knew what you were denying yourself."

"Yes and having you across the hall did not help. Mrs. Perch must have thought I was mad not to have you in my room."

"I thought you were mad not to have me in your room," she teased him, "But I am glad we waited. I admire your strength and your restraint. You have no idea how much it makes me feel valued to know that you love and respect me enough to wait until we are married to lie with me."

"And now we are married, I wonder why we are talking so much and not doing what we have been denying ourselves?" he asked, unpinning her hair so that it fell gloriously down her back and around her shoulders. "I love your hair," he murmured. "But I love here as well." He pushed aside her hair to kiss the side of her neck, making her tingle all over. "And here." He lowered his head to kiss the base of her throat. "But most of all, here." He sunk his hands in her hair, angling her head to receive his kiss. She opened her lips to allow him the freedom to explore her mouth. Their clothes were quickly disposed of and James lifted Jemima and carried her to their marriage bed.

"You are beautiful and perfect to me and for me," he told her huskily. "This time I will make sure that you experience something new. The love of a husband who adores you and who intends to make you feel things that you never have before," he promised.

"I like the sound of that," she encouraged him. "Who ever knew that you could talk so much. I'm waiting for the demonstration," she teased.

He laughed in reply and began to demonstrate. Much later, when he held her trembling body in his arms, he murmured, "I trust that it met your expectations."

"It far exceeded anything I have ever experienced, because it was with you," she said tearfully. "Thank you, James."

"Thank you, Jemima. I thank God for giving me a second chance at happiness. With his help, I plan to exceed your expectations every day of our lives."

THE END

Author's Note

If you enjoyed this novel stayed tuned for the next book in the series, Alexandra's story, where your favourite characters – Richard, Deborah, James and Jemima – will make appearances.

Historical Novels by Donna Every

The Price of Freedom

He owned her and was prepared to give her freedom, but was she prepared to pay the price? An exciting, page-turning historical novel set in Barbados and Carolina in 1696.

Free in the City

Free in the City is a compelling story of forbidden love between Thomas Edwards and his mulatto slave mistress, Sarah, set in Barbados in the late 1600s. This is the prequel/sequel to The Price of Freedom.

Free at Last

William Edwards is banished to Jamaica, a land where the slavery is brutal and the maroons are fierce. He finally meets his match in this book, the third in The Acreage Series.

Vaucluse

Set in the 1800s, Vaucluse is the intriguing story of slavery, abolition, illegitimate children and loving relationships in the fictionalised account of the life of Henry Peter Simmons, owner of Vaucluse Plantation in Barbados.

Contemporary Novels by Donna Every

The Merger Mogul

Daniel Tennant, aka The Merger Mogul, is one of Manhattan's top merger consultants. His past has made him vow never to be poor again and so he lives by the philosophy: "Women are great but a profitable company and a healthy stock portfolio are better and definitely harder to come by."

The High Road

In this exciting sequel to The Merger Mogul, Daniel Tennant, formerly known as The Merger Mogul, has landed the project of a lifetime – to help transform the nation of Barbados. However, he doesn't bargain for the opposition he will receive, or the lengths to which the conspirators will go to discredit him in an attempt to bring an end to the project.

What Now?

Rock star Nick Badley has no bucket list; he's living it. He's been there and done that, yet a part of him is still unfulfilled and he's beginning to ask himself the question: What now?

CPSIA information can be obtained
at www.ICGtesting.com
Printed in the USA
LVHW111327081119
636778LV00001B/67/P

9 781074 433062